The Senator's Son

Anna Albo

Published by Anna Albo, 2019.

THE SENATOR'S SON
Second edition. May 2019.

ISBN: 978-1999102524
Written by Anna Albo.
Visit www.annaalbo.com

To Dana, Katherine and Shelley.

There is no way I could have done this without the three of you.

CHAPTER ONE

EMMA

When I was nine, Dad and Uncle Ron helped Jake and I build an igloo. Every weekend, and sometimes after school, we'd spend hours gathering snow and building our fortress. Dad and Uncle Ron did most of it, but we did what we could. They'd even built an ice top so we could have light shine through.

Grandma brought us hot chocolate while we worked and even on the most bitterly cold days, we were out there, knee-deep in snow. That year I hoped winter would never end. And when the temperature began to rise, and our igloo dripped then fell into ruin, the best winter of my life came to an end. Jake and I had never been closer, and I'd been trying to hold on to that moment ever since.

That had been ten years ago.

"How's the new job at Julian's?" he asked.

"I can now make any kind of latte."

"That's cool."

I glanced over at Jake. His blue eyes were trained on the road and when he looked over my heart blipped. For nineteen years we'd been best friends, but one look still sent me soaring.

"Do you think people will like me?" I asked.

"Why wouldn't they?"

I shrugged. "You know how it is."

Jake focused back on the road. In less than fifteen minutes I'd be flung into a situation I hated most: meeting new people. I was beyond shy. I could easily retreat to the most secluded corner of any party or family gathering and remain completely invisible.

"A bunch of my friends will be there and I want you to get to know them."

"I will." Or I'd try. People didn't exactly gravitate to me.

Jake's phone trilled. Likely Bianca. She couldn't leave him alone for more than five minutes. It was probably killing her that I was with him this weekend instead of her, but she had an acting gig—yes, Bianca was an aspiring actor. College was something her parents made her do because, like me, they were rooted firmly in reality, and while Bianca had the looks and determination, acting wasn't exactly a long-term career ... in Minnesota.

"Bianca?" I asked.

"Probably."

He met her at a frat party. She was his dream girl and he lost his mind when she paid him a little attention. He'd landed one of the hottest girls at Western University and he did everything he could to keep her. She ordered him around, made him run her errands and worst of all, he had to boost her overly inflated ego.

The first time I'd met her we clashed like two mama bears trying to protect the same cub. She'd graced us with her presence in Pine Falls at Uncle Ron's birthday dinner. I sat on one side of Jake and she sat on the other. We both fawned over him—probably the only time she'd ever done that—passing him his favorite dishes, grabbing his soda of choice and arguing over who would cut his piece of blueberry pie. The pie I'd made.

"How many people are going to be there?" I asked.

"Ten, I think."

"Who are they?"

"Guys from a frat, Bianca's friends. One of the guys is a senator's son and Brett, his family owns the cabin. His dad is some big shot lawyer. Filthy rich. Of course their girlfriends will be there too. It'll be fine."

"I'm sure it will be."

Rich kids. Bianca had sucked Jake into this life. It wasn't that Jake and I were the poor kids from the wrong side of the tracks, but we didn't come from senator and big-shot-lawyer stock. Grandpa and Dad co-owned an antique shop and Jake's parents owned Pine Falls' best burger joint. Hardly high rollers.

Jake turned off the main highway, and we drove down the tree-lined gravel road until it became more and more remote. We pulled up to a tall iron gate with an intercom. A voice came over the speaker and Jake identified us. The gate creaked open and soon the cabins came into view, one dotting the landscape every mile or so. All were on the lake and larger than any house I'd seen before. Jake had definitely met some very rich friends his first year at Western.

"These people are more loaded than I could have imagined," Jake said and whistled.

"These places are amazing."

"One day, Emma, I'm going to have a place like this."

Knowing Jake, I'd bet on it. His mission since middle school was to be a surgeon, and absolutely nothing was going to take him off course. First an undergraduate degree, followed by med school. Thankfully his shortlist had included Western.

"Make sure it has a balcony overlooking the water so I can sit out there and sun myself," I said.

"That and an awesome boat to jet around the water. Maybe do a little fishing."

"Until then, we can dream."

Jake parked his beat-up Honda behind a Mercedes, a few BMWs, and some high-end SUVs. I grabbed my backpack, and we headed up the stone walkway to the front porch steps, all twenty of them. The place was modeled after a log cabin, but had to be ten thousand square feet. The huge bay windows gave us a glimpse inside to its soaring ceilings, massive fireplace, and on-trend furniture. My first thought was of the kitchen. I had to see it.

Jake hit the buzzer and we waited. A minute later a guy with short dark hair and chocolaty brown eyes opened the door. He had a few inches on Jake and a stockier build. He looked at me, then Jake.

"Hey, Jake, come in," he said, stepping aside.

"Zach, this is my friend Emma. Emma, this is Zach Walker."

"Nice to meet you," I said, extending my hand. He was kind of cute, something I wouldn't normally notice. He had the stubbly face thing going and it was definitely working for him. But despite it all, he wasn't my type. Rich and privileged bored me.

He shook my hand and smiled warmly. "Nice to meet you too. Most of the guys went fishing and the girls are baking out on the balcony. Your room is down the hall, two doors from the end on the right-hand side. Bianca knows you guys are sharing a room? Because we don't have an extra."

"She knows," Jake said. "Nothing's going on between me and Emma."

"Just making sure. We don't want any trouble from her. We all know how she can be."

A bitch?

We clambered to our room. The first thing I saw was the huge king-sized bed. Jake and I had shared a bed before and it wasn't a big deal for him. For me, on the other hand, I usually spent a restless night wanting to reach out and nuzzle up against him. On the rare occasions we touched, it was like a lightning bolt tearing apart my veins. Honestly, the prospect of sharing a bed with him was the only reason I'd agreed to come.

"Let's check out the lake," Jake suggested.

My skin prickled. I was going to meet all these frivolous women who were probably exactly like Bianca. None would like me but they'd all pretend to, only to talk about me behind my back the first chance they got. I kept reminding myself that it was only two days as we walked through the tiled living room and past the stone fireplace to the French doors leading outside.

We stepped out onto the vast balcony that looked over the lake. All the girls, in their tiny bright-colored bikinis, stared back at me from behind designer sunglasses. All were sprawled out on pool chairs taking in the last few days of summer sun. The clones had lean, toned, and tanned figures and, a few had enormous and presumably fake breasts. I felt awkward and gangly in their presence.

"This is Emma, everyone," Jake said. One fake-waved like she was actually happy to see me while the other three muttered hellos and returned to their gossiping.

It was going to be a long two days.

Zach reappeared, the only friendly face. "I'm going to marinate the chicken and season the steaks. Does anyone want to help with some sides? A salad at least? Anything?" He sounded exasperated. Not one of the beach bunnies bothered to acknowledge him.

"I will," I volunteered. "I love to cook."

Zach's face lit. "Thank God! I don't think I can handle eating store-bought potato salad and shitty coleslaw all weekend. Follow me."

The kitchen was only place I felt safe. I surveyed my surroundings. It reminded me of the commercial kitchen at Julian's—chrome and stainless-steel appliances barely used and all brand new. I fell instantly in love. Zach gave me the rundown of where to find everything and then started on the marinade. I opened the huge fridge door and it was packed. For people who didn't cook, I couldn't figure out why they had all this food. I rummaged through the crisper and pulled out some broccoli that I could give a quick steam. I put to one corner a few red and yellow bell peppers and was delighted to find some kalamata olives. There was also some feta, strawberries, and, of course, a tub each of potato salad and coleslaw.

I thought Zach would take off to more interesting places once he was done prepping the chicken and steak, but instead he pulled a beer from the fridge and took a seat at one of the bistro chairs, setting the bottle down on the granite-topped island.

"You're hanging out with me?" I asked. Uneasiness bubbled in my stomach. I was perfectly happy alone. Didn't he have a Jet Ski or yacht to play around on?

"If I have to go out there and listen to them talk about clothes, shoes, and makeup, I'll self-combust."

I stifled a laugh. "Isn't one of them your girlfriend?"

"Becca."

The fuchsia bikini? The fake waver? The one with real breasts? I'd find out later.

"Why didn't you go fishing?"

"I slept in and none of the guys bothered to wake me up."

I peeked into the pantry. "Any regular potatoes? We can barbecue them, or I can pass if you're potatoed out."

"There's a bag of them in the far corner. I'm good with them as long as they don't resemble a potato salad in any way."

I laughed. "I promise."

I scrubbed the potatoes clean and he continued to watch. Typical rich kid, but I didn't care. I actually found myself enjoying his company. "Why do you guys have all this food if no one likes to cook?"

"Wishful thinking? I thought at least one of the ladies would make an attempt but this weekend seems to be all about tans. That sounds sexist, doesn't it? But I know all these guys, and they're useless in the kitchen."

"Honestly, I'd be happy spending all my time in here."

"If you can cook, I can eat."

I smiled. He was pretty cool so far. "I could make a dessert too, but will the girls eat it?"

Zach's huge eyes opened wider. "Who cares! I'll eat their dessert. What are you making?"

"Jake's a sucker for chocolate cake and I see all the ingredients here. I could add a layer of strawberries. We have tons of strawberries."

"I think it's a great plan. I'll even help you."

"That would be nice." And totally weird.

I combined the ingredients and Zach mixed it all together while I tackled the strawberry filling followed by some chocolate icing. The entire hour we worked on my cake, the girls wandered in and out to grab more drinks, but nothing else. Becca, who I confirmed as the fuchsia bikini girl, did give me a glare, but didn't bother to find out what her boyfriend was doing with me. Guess she didn't feel too threatened. I kept hoping Jake would stop in to check on me, but I knew he was busy catching up with his friends.

"My mom doesn't cook or bake," Zach said, licking the spatula. "Louisa does it all."

"Is she the housekeeper?" I took the cake batter from him before he put the spatula back in and poured the contents into two greased cake pans.

"Yes. She's been with us since I was a kid. Mom and Dad are in Washington most of the year, so Louisa is like a second mom."

I tilted my head. "You're the senator's son?"

"That would be me," he said, taking the bowl back, tilting it, ringing a finger around the sides and licking up what remained. I had the cake in the oven and now worked on the main meal. First chopping onions, then steaming broccoli.

"Does everyone kiss your ass?"

"I don't think so."

"But you've probably always been one of the cool kids."

"Mostly because I'm cool," he said with a wink.

"You seem pretty normal. How come?"

He laughed, flashing his perfect white teeth. "What does that mean?"

"You aren't stuck up."

"I think I'm pretty easy going. I don't judge. My parents taught me that much."

"It's a good quality to have."

He went to the fridge and grabbed another beer. "Want one?" he asked.

"Sure, why not."

We took a break for a few minutes and enjoyed our beers. Even though I was underage, Dad and I often sat outside on the front porch on hot afternoons drinking a cold one. We'd talk sports—hockey, mostly, since Dad was a star forward in high school. Then we'd move on to football and tennis. Sometimes Uncle Ron and Jake would join in and the four of us would debate everything from player salaries to stats.

"So you and Jake are childhood friends?"

"Since birth."

"That's awesome."

"Have you and Bianca been friends for a long time?"

He took a gulp of beer and grunted. "I wouldn't call her a friend. We hang out with the same people, but that's about it."

"Oh," I said casually. I had to play it safe, not knowing exactly where he stood with her.

He smirked. "Come on, she's a bitch. We can both admit it. Not sure what Jake sees in her other than the body."

His placid expression appeared sincere. Either he was an excellent actor, or he hated the wench as much as I did. "I think that's all he sees."

"And you two never hooked up?"

"No. He's like my brother."

Zach scrutinized me, his eyes fixing on mine. "How long have you liked him?"

My cheeks burned. How could he tell? "What are you talking about?" I set down my beer and started chopping peppers with my back to Zach.

"It's obvious to me, but I'm not sure it's obvious to an asswipe like Jake."

"You're wrong."

"Whatever you say. I'm on barbecue duty," he said, changing the subject. "When should I fire up the grill?"

"The potatoes will take about a half hour."

He looked outside one of the huge windows. "The guys are back. I'm sure they're starved."

A crowd had formed on the balcony but neither of us went to greet them. Zach barely acknowledged them. Instead, he focused on me.

"What are we going to do with the broccoli?" he asked.

"We?"

"Other than manning a barbecue, I can't cook a thing. Maybe if I learn some tips from a seasoned chef like yourself, I'll be able to feed myself a little better. Add a few real vegetables into my diet instead of the usual munching on carrots thing that I do."

"I was thinking something simple for the broccoli. I like to keep it healthy for my dad and my grandpa."

"Your mom not in the picture?"

I grimaced. The thought of her ... I was not going there. "Nope, and my grandma died a few years ago. Back to the broccoli," I said before he could get onto the subject of where my mother was. "I usually make a simple vinaigrette of olive oil, lemon juice, salt, pepper and fresh garlic cloves. Do you think everyone here will like garlic? Jake loves it."

"You mean the princesses? Who cares. Go for it."

"We can make the vinaigrette now, but we should only dress the broccoli right before serving, otherwise it will get discolored," I added, like I was on a cooking show and needed to give Zach a tutorial.

"Sounds delicious, for broccoli anyway. Where's your mom?"

He stood next to me, leaning against the counter, and his playful brown eyes were waiting for an answer. So much for diverting his attention. I considered lying and saying she was dead. That would put an end to the interrogation.

"She had me and took off. Should we bake the potatoes? Add some cheese and onions?"

"Let's barbecue them. Do you keep in touch with her?"

"No. Should I make my own salad dressing or do you think people will want the premade stuff?"

"Premade stuff for the princesses, but I'll try yours if you make it. When's the last time you talked to her?"

"Long time ago. Should you fire up the barbecue?"

"Soon. Why'd she leave?"

I bit on my lower lip. He seemed nice and all, but this conversation had to stop. Now. "I don't like talking about her."

"I know. Why?"

"Because. And if you can see that I don't want to talk about her, why do you keep asking?"

"I'm curious, I guess. I think it's strange she took off."

"Well, she did."

"Okay," he said, throwing his hands up in surrender. "I'll respect your wish and go start the barbecue."

I watched him as he went outside. A few of the others converged on him and Becca, his princess, leapt to her feet, a look of annoyance on her face. Was she jealous of me? Seriously? They spoke a few words and the light expression he'd been wearing moments ago vanished in an instant.

Two more days with these people. Two long days of pretending to like them. Had it not been for Zach, I would have already written it off. And while I still had a lingering feeling he had some hidden agenda, he did seem like someone I could let my guard down with, at least.

I set the table and kept to myself. Zach came in to grab the potatoes and steaks.

"Come out and talk to us," he said.

"In a minute," I lied.

I managed to stall until all the food was ready. I excessively cleaned the kitchen, checked on the cake, and sorted through the fridge and pantry. When the group filed in and took their seats, Becca sat across from me at the huge round table and glared at me some more. The other princesses begrudgingly admitted my food was great while the princes openly complimented it. Their admiration didn't change my feelings for any of them.

I didn't say much through dinner, which no doubt annoyed Jake, but I wasn't as open and outgoing as he was. Except for Zach, these people weren't exactly warm and fuzzy. Most of the conversation centered on someone named Lori and her exploits, which apparently included sex in public washrooms, a nasty case of genital warts, and a rampant alcohol problem. Hardly a conversation I wanted to insert myself into.

"I'll clean up," I offered.

"Why don't you hang out with us instead," Zach suggested. The hint of a welcoming smile on his face made me consider the offer.

"If she wants to clean up, let her," Becca said. She whined like a five-year-old.

"Why don't you clean up? She was kind enough to make this great dinner. Could you at least appreciate it?"

"It's okay," I said, getting up and taking away plates. "I really don't mind."

"See," Becca said, satisfied.

"Then I'll help," he said, standing up.

That wiped away her smile.

Everyone else wandered back outside with their drinks, cigars, and joints. I groaned inwardly. Since when did Jake smoke pot?

"Great dinner," Zach said. "The broccoli was delicious and I don't even like broccoli."

"Why didn't you say something? I could have made something else."

"You had the meal planned out. I didn't want to ruin it."

He loaded up the dishwasher while I tackled the pots and pans. I watched over my shoulder as he haphazardly found places to put the plates. I'd fix it once he was out of eyesight. Rich kids.

"You know, you don't have to help me. Hang out with your friends. I do enjoy cleaning up. I find it relaxing."

"I think talking to you is relaxing."

This guy was good. "I think you're feeling sorry for me."

"Not at all. If I didn't want to talk to you, I'd be outside with the other losers getting wasted."

I rolled my eyes and he laughed.

"Tell me about Emma. This is your first year at Western?"

"Yes. I took last year off."

"Why?"

"I guess I wasn't ready. I wasn't sure what I wanted to do. I still have no idea."

"That's normal," he said.

"What are your plans?"

"Law school. That's what's expected of me."

"Your parents have it all mapped out for you?"

He scratched his head and sighed. "Yes and no. Do they want me to be a lawyer? Absolutely. But if I decided to pursue another dream, I think they'd be fine with that too."

"What's your other dream?"

"That's the problem. I don't have one."

I giggled. He was funny. "I wanted to go to culinary school but Grandpa didn't want me to. He didn't think it was the right career. My dad was fine with it." I handed Zach a pot to dry and lamented, "*My* dream is to have my own bakery. I got a job at Julian's and they have me making pastries and other baked goods."

A rush of adrenaline raced through me. I was giddy telling someone about my job. Other than Jake, Dad, and Grandpa, I hadn't told anyone else because there really wasn't anyone to tell. But Zach actually seemed interested.

"That's cool. Good for you."

"I'm baking a couple of times a week and working the odd shift here and there. It'll help pay for rent and other stuff."

"Do you make éclairs? I love them," he said.

"I've only made them a few times. I should try making them for Julian's."

"Text me when you do. I'd love to get a few."

"Let me get my phone and I'll add your number."

I rummaged through my purse and discovered I'd forgotten it. Crap! I usually texted or called Dad every night. I'd have to get a hold of Jake's later. "Forgot it," I said.

"No problem. Give me your number and I'll text you with mine." He slid his phone from his pocket. He punched in my number and we finished cleaning up.

"Let's eat cake in here," Zach suggested. "If they want cake, they can drag their asses inside and get it themselves."

"Okay. And I know it's not a good pairing, but how about some beers with that cake?"

He grinned. "I like the way you think."

He cut two huge slabs of cake and spooned out enormous heaps of vanilla ice cream. We sat back down at the huge table and my heart thawed a bit. Zach was normal. This weekend wasn't going to be a complete horror show.

"What high school sport did you excel at? Because you're the type of guy who starred in something."

"Busted. I played high school football but I was an amazing hockey player. I could have played college hockey, but I knew I wasn't going to get anywhere with it."

"Are all those teeth yours?"

He gave me a toothy grin. "All mine," he said, tapping on them.

"And you were probably a straight A student?"

"Guilty."

"A million girlfriends? Never single?"

"Am I a cliché?"

"Yes, I'm afraid so."

He speared a huge chunk of cake and devoured it. "My turn," he said. "Let me use my crystal ball to figure you out. Bookworm, great student, and you played some sports or you work out like crazy because you're in sick shape."

My cheeks burned again. "Tennis."

"Still play?"

"Recreationally only."

"You must have been good."

"Ranked second in the state."

His jaw dropped. "Second in the state?"

"Yeah, but I quit when I was sixteen. My grandma died and I didn't want to compete anymore."

His face took on a more thoughtful expression. "Wow. You must have been really good. Don't you miss it?"

"Not really. It was something Grandma and I did together. She was my biggest cheerleader. With her gone, it didn't feel right anymore."

"But you still play?"

"When I can. I belong to a club and teach kids in the summer."

"Let's play sometime."

"Sure, but be prepared to get your ass kicked."

Becca came into the cabin reeking of pot. She stared at both of us and despite her elevated state, she clearly wasn't happy to see us laughing and sharing cake.

"Are you coming outside now?" she asked Zach.

"Right away. Got the munchies yet?"

"Fuck off." She turned back around and went outside.

I glanced over at Zach but he didn't appear to care about her slight. "Well, I guess I better get out there. Are you going to join me?"

"Nah. It's been a long day and I'm kind of tired."

"How did I know you were going to blow us off?"

"You're clairvoyant?"

"I wish. See you in the morning."

I went to the room I shared with Jake, changed, and crawled into bed with my book unable to wipe the smile from my face.

CHAPTER TWO

ZACH

"What's up with the broad?" Brett asked. We'd finished our last joint, and I was taking in the effects. Everyone else had hit the sack.

"Becca?"

Brett blinked a few times. "No, the chick Jake brought."

"Emma? What would be up with her?" I grabbed the bag of Doritos and polished off the last few chips.

"You were talking to her a lot. It was pissing off Becca. You know, the chick you came here with."

"I don't give a shit what pisses Becca off. I was being nice to someone who cooked and cleaned for us. Is that horrible?"

Brett's eyes narrowed. "You've got to be kidding. While you were inside being nice to her, we got the low-down from Jake. Poor guy is stuck with her the entire year. He didn't sound too happy about it."

"Because Bianca isn't happy about it?"

"I guess so."

"I think Emma's all right."

"You don't have to live with her," Brett said with a snort.

"She's a great girl. I don't get what Jake or Bianca have a problem with."

Brett leaned back in his chair and crossed his arms over his chest. "I'm thinking you've got a thing for this weirdo."

"First of all, you can stop calling her names. As for Emma, I was being kind to a girl that everyone else was ignoring."

"You'd fuck her given the chance."

"Okay, we're done here." Arguing with him was a waste of time. "I'm going to crash. You guys want to wake me up this time? Before taking off?"

Brett gave me a thumbs up. I headed to my room and got into bed. The buzz of a few beers, chocolate cake, and a joint had a way of making me forget I had to spend the weekend with Becca. She didn't know it yet, but it was going to be our last. I'd already committed to this getaway and didn't feel right breaking things off just before the last weekend of summer.

We'd nearly made it six months, but only the first few had been good. Then the veneer stripped away and what was underneath hadn't been pretty. I toughed it out all summer but I couldn't go through a school year with her hanging off me all the time. Sure, she was hot. Fucking hot. But the jealousy and the constant bickering were too much. I'd stuck this one out way too long.

"You were talking to that loser all night," she said, putting an array of creams and potions on her face. The room reeked like a cosmetic counter.

"If you're referring to Emma, she isn't a loser."

"All she wants is to get into Jake's pants. He's her only friend. That makes her a loser. You should stay away from her."

She talked to me like she expected me to obey. When had she gotten comfortable enough to think that? I didn't mind when a girl called the shots. I even liked it, but not when she was spewing this kind of crap. Becca had made her mind up about Emma before the girl walked through the door. Man, what did I ever see in this chick? Other than the body she was an empty, bottomless pit. Yes, she came from a good family, but I was long past getting involved with girls for their pedigree.

"I'm going to consider myself her friend. So now she has two."

Becca rolled her eyes. "Whatever," she said and put on what must have been her tenth face cream. "I'm sure she's trying to give him a hand job while we speak."

"When you're finished doing whatever it is that you're doing, turn off the light because I'm tired." I put my pillow over my head and tried to block out the light. A few minutes later she got into bed and seconds after that her perfume-laden hands were slithering down my chest. I grasped onto her hand before it reached her desired location. She'd be disappointed with the results.

"I'm wiped. Goodnight."

She abandoned her attempts and grunted a goodnight.

I COULDN'T SLEEP. I grabbed my phone and checked the time. A little before three in the morning. I rubbed my eyes and yawned. Sleep wasn't coming. I got out of bed and looked over my shoulder at Becca. Her face was pressed into the pillow and she emitted a drone-like snore. If I told her she snored, she'd get pissed off. Maybe she'd dump me. Something to consider.

I eased out of our room. Waking her would create all kinds of problems I didn't want to deal with. I shut the door with a dull click. Then I set down the silent hallway and into the kitchen, my feet padding on cold tiles. I pulled out a plate and cut a huge slice of chocolate cake. I took it outside and sat on one of the deck chairs, taking in the serenity of night. Other than a few crickets, I was alone.

And being alone wasn't such a bad thing. Moving out of the frat, cleaning up my act, all good things. Sure, there were times I missed the old days, but what I didn't miss was waking up in the morning next to some random girl, then trying to explain to her that it was a one-off, we didn't have a future and I wasn't going to see her again. Those days were behind me.

I took another bite of cake. Emma had whipped it up like she was making an omelet. The girl could cook like no one I knew, but on the flip side, she didn't strike me as a girl who was domesticated, or planned on living her life pleasing her husband, unless that husband happened to be Jake. What made him special? A quintessential social climber who'd been sucked in by Bianca Smythe, a girl whose goal in life was to marry rich. Jake didn't fit the bill and likely wouldn't be around long. I wasn't even sure what she was doing with him at all.

And Emma. I couldn't figure her out. She seemed grounded and flailing all at the same time. Her devotion to Jake was going to play out like a bad romantic triangle. Jake had zero interest in her and yet she pined for him. She had a lot going for her except that lack of confidence holding her back.

I finished the cake and pondered another slice. I had to get a few hours' sleep or the guys would leave without me again and the thought of another morning with the ladies made my head hurt. If they did take off, I could spend time with Emma, but then the gossip would start. I couldn't win no matter what I did.

I passed on the cake and decided to go back to bed. Sleep would come eventually.

THE ALARM ON MY PHONE buzzed on the nightstand. I grabbed it before it woke up Becca. I managed to sleep a few hours. I took a quick shower and met the guys in the kitchen. Emma was already preparing breakfast and smiled at me. I smiled back and couldn't help but notice the white t-shirt she had on that hugged her figure and showcased her perky breasts, or the shorts that fit her just right. How did Jake keep his hands off her? Did Bianca have his balls in a jar somewhere?

"Got to go," Brett said the second I finished my eggs. I grabbed two slices of toast for the road and waved goodbye to Emma.

"Breakfast was a pleasant surprise," I said.

"It put us behind," Brett complained.

I gave him a look. "Are we on some schedule? The fish have other plans?"

"You know I like being out early."

For the zero fish he was going to catch?

Matt and Jake loaded up the beer-laden cooler while Brett and Troy prepped the boat. I stood on the deck, finishing off my toast.

"Care to join us?" Brett asked.

"I'm coming."

With the cabin still in sight, Jake was already passing out beers. I declined. It was too early for me.

"Thanks for keeping Emma company," Jake said, snapping back the tab. "The break was nice."

He put his feet up on the edge of the boat and gulped his beer. I scratched my head. "Sorry, what?"

"It was nice that you talked to her. You don't have to, though."

What an ass. "Am I missing something? You brought her here. If you needed a break, you could have left her back in the city."

"I'm trying to get her to meet new people."

Matt chuckled. "Those girls are not going to make it easy for her. All last night I had to hear about her from Brandi. It's like they've already decided to hate her."

"What the hell? She didn't do anything," I said. Maybe I should have said something to Becca, to make sure she gave Emma a chance today, although that would have been a waste of my breath.

"She's not exactly like us," Brett said.

"I can't believe this. She made dinner and breakfast, and you guys are crapping all over her."

"No, just pointing out the obvious," Brett said.

"I guess I don't understand," I said to Jake. "Are you trying to make her feel left out?"

"I'm not sure what the big deal is," Jake said, an edge rising in his voice. "I figured that she'd try to get to know some people. You don't know what it's like. I had no choice but to let her move in with me. It's not an ideal situation because she doesn't make friends easy and Bianca isn't a huge fan of hers."

"You could have done a better job of helping her out instead of leaving her behind."

"I can't look after her all the time. I have a life."

I looked at the other guys. "What about you? None of you have had a conversation with her. I'm the only one who made an effort."

"I think I know why you made an effort," Brett said with a sly grin. "Remember, you came here with Becca. You should probably leave with her."

Fucking Brett. Jake glared at me. "Emma's a nice girl. If your intention is to screw around with her, back off."

If I could, I would have thrown Jake and Brett off the boat. "Look, I've got no interest in Emma, but I find it hilarious that you're suddenly concerned about her welfare."

"You're not going to sully her reputation."

"To be honest," Brett said, "I'd tap her too. She looked hot in that little T-shirt this morning."

"Okay, enough talk about Emma," I said.

The subject was dropped. The guys drank while I fished. By early afternoon, we called it a day. As usual, the fish weren't biting. We got back to the cabin and the other guys lied about all the fish they almost caught. That's when I saw Emma. Something wasn't right. Her hands were shaking and her face was flushed. She was clutching her backpack and trying in vain to get Jake's attention. I had a feeling the room was about to erupt.

CHAPTER THREE

EMMA

I was the first awake, but I lay in bed for a few extra minutes, staring at Jake as he slept. His soft breathing and contented face were peaceful. I wanted to slip my arms around him, but of course I didn't dare. How many times had we slept together since we were kids? Too many to count, and not once had he ever made an advance no matter how much I wished for it.

I eased myself up and out of the room so I wouldn't wake him and decided to extend the olive branch to my cabin mates by putting on a pot of coffee. The smell lulled some from their slumber, mostly the princes who intended to get in some early morning fishing. Jake was one of them. I watched as he walked to the kitchen, bleary-eyed and mumbling a good morning. Zach was the last to make an appearance, and I smiled at him and he smiled back and winked. Then a thought occurred to me. What if he thought I was flirting? He was nice and all, and easy on the eyes, but I wasn't interested. Besides, he had a girlfriend.

"We got to hurry up if we want to get an early start. Fifteen minutes and I want us out of here," Brett barked.

"I could whip up a quick breakfast," I suggested.

Four pairs of eyes stared at me. Slowly they all nodded in agreement. I went to work cracking eggs and frying bacon. I threw in some toast since there wasn't time for hash browns. No one said a word as they wolfed down food and twenty minutes later, they were gone. In that time not one of the princesses had stirred. I cleaned up without making a peep. I had no intention of making any of them breakfast.

I took some peanut butter-covered toast, a book, and a lawn chair and sat by the lake. A couple of hours passed and I didn't see the princesses. I knew they were all awake by this point and fending for themselves. I didn't even leave them a drop of coffee. By mid-morning a few had ventured outside to sunbathe. None said hello.

Knowing the guys would be back soon, and wanting to get in a quick call to Dad since I'd forgotten to the night before, I returned to the cabin. By now all four were outside, all sunbathing in their designer bikinis and perfect, taut bodies. Still no hello. Not to be deterred, I decided to speak.

"Hi, everyone."

One head rose and looked at me from behind her sunglasses. She sort of nodded. The rest were silent. I went inside and decided at that moment not to make another attempt to befriend them. What for?

I poured myself a glass of water and looked for Jake's phone. Knowing him like I did, he wouldn't dare take it out on the boat and risk losing it. How would he communicate with Bianca? As expected, it was resting next to the bed and I grabbed it. What did he say his password was? I tried a few but to no avail. There wasn't a landline, and I wasn't about to ask one of the princesses to borrow a phone. I made a few more attempts and when I was about to give up, it hit me. The last four digits of his grandparents' phone number. I punched it in and mercifully unlocked the phone.

He had several text messages and I assumed most, if not all, were from Bianca. He'd been texting her before he'd fallen asleep. The incessant tapping annoyed the hell out of me.

I dialed the first few numbers to my house when another of her texts popped up.

Bianca: Fishing? I'm soooo bored. That mutt following you around everywhere?

Mutt? I'd never snooped through Jake's phone before, but this text caught my attention. Was she referring to me? Obviously. My heart picked up a few beats and blood pulsed through my veins. I opened up his text messages and scrolled back through at least a couple dozen. What else did she have to say about me?

Bianca: OMG! I am so sick of her. How can you stand that bitch?

Jake: I don't!

Bianca: She stares at you like a fucking creepazoid. So weird like she's going to lock you up in her basement and never let you out.

I scrolled ahead. Nothing I'd seen so far had surprised me.

Bianca: How's your filthy mutt? Still sniffing around your ass?

Jake: She spent lots of time with Zach. What a relief! Poor bastard.

Bianca: Zach is too nice. He's always feeling sorry for disgusting strays.

Jake: Lol.

Bianca: Make sure she doesn't give you fleas.

Jake: Lol. I'll get her a flea collar.

Bianca: Brett's going to have to call in exterminators.

Jake: Or we'll all have to get vaccinated.

Bianca: LOL. I wish she'd get the hint and leave you alone. Get some friends like a normal human being.

Jake: Even tonight she didn't try to talk to anyone. At least Zach got her off my back for a while.

Bianca: I would die if I had to spend the weekend with her.

Jake: Worst day of my life was when she got into Western. Just when I thought I got rid of her for good.

Bianca: At least you had one year without the freak.

Jake: But now I'm stuck with her for at least 2 more. I'm going to lose my mind! She drives me crazy!

Bianca: OMG I hate her so much. I wish she'd go away and die somewhere. Kill herself or something. Do us all a favor.

Jake: Lol. Me too.

I stopped reading. Tears were blurring my vision and my body was shaking. Me too? That's all I kept seeing. 'Lol' and 'me too.' He agreed with everything. I was nothing more than a flea-ridden dog, a friendless weirdo. A pariah. I put down the phone and although I was sobbing not a single sound came from me. The ultimate betrayal. My best friend since birth, the person who always looked out for me, thought I was a pathetic hanger-on. An albatross. Someone he wished was dead.

I stood up and methodically packed what little I had. My book? Where was my book? I bolted for the kitchen to retrieve it, happy no one was there. I then ran to the bathroom and threw up. I sat on the cold marble floor for minutes, trying to calm myself. Jake, the person I loved most in the world besides Dad and Grandpa, was complicit in all this. I stood up, splashed cold water on my face and refused to look in the mirror. I couldn't face myself.

Then I heard the voices. They were back. I slipped out of the bathroom and grabbed my backpack and went into the main room. Everyone was there, the guys recounting their tales of fishing for the girls. Some sprawled out on the two brown leather sofas, others were milling around in the kitchen with beers.

"Jake," I said.

He didn't hear me above the chatter.

"Jake!"

He turned to look at me, clearly irritated that the mutt had interrupted his tales from the high seas. "Yeah?"

"I'm going. Give me the keys."

He saw my backpack and his phone in my hand, but the two weren't adding up. I didn't care. I just wanted to go home, even though my head was pounding and my hands were shaking uncontrollably.

"Why? Something happen? Is everyone okay?"

My Jake. All six feet of him was staring at me, perplexed but still aggravated that I wanted to leave. My once beautiful Jake. The only man in the world I trusted. The only friend I ever needed.

"Can you please give me the keys?"

"Are you all right?" he asked, walking toward me. I took several steps back. Even though I wasn't looking at anyone else, I knew their eyes were on me. They'd all stopped talking and were no doubt wondering what was wrong with the weirdo now.

"The keys?"

"If you don't tell me what's going on, I'm not giving them to you."

"Give me the keys!" I shrieked.

Zach came and stood beside Jake. He was looking at me like I'd just been released from a mental institution. "Hey Emma, what's going on?" he asked, his voice soft with concern.

"I want to go. I want the keys!"

Jake's face hardened. "I don't know what your problem is and I don't really care. Why do you have to ruin everything for me?"

Something came over me, like the Emma I knew had been replaced by someone else and I was nothing more than a spectator. This Emma was tough, a goddess warrior. "I'm sorry, Jake, that I ruin everything for you. But just so you know, I don't have fleas, and you don't need a rabies shot either. And this filthy mutt you and Bianca think I am, well, if you give me the fucking keys I'll run away and you'll never have to worry about me again! Lol!"

"Oh, shit," Zach said, cringing. He could see Jake's phone in my hand. He wasn't an idiot. "Jake, what did you say?"

"Say? No, Jake didn't say anything. They texted it to each other. Let me read it for you," I said, tears blinding my attempts to enter in his password. But I was determined and not even a few tears would stop me. "Let me quote my best friend of nineteen years and his stupid girlfriend. Bianca says, make sure she doesn't give you fleas, and my best friend Jake replies, lol, I'll get her a flea collar. Isn't that hilarious? There's more. Bianca says, OMG I hate her so much. I wish she'd go away and die somewhere. Kill herself, or something. Do us all a favor. And Jake says, lol! Me too."

The room fell silent. Not even a snicker from the princesses.

Jake snatched his phone. "You shouldn't have gone through my stuff," he said, shame dripping from his voice.

"I wanted to call my dad," I said between sobs.

Zach came and stood between us. He faced me but I couldn't look up at him. "Emma, I'll take you home. Do you have everything?"

"Yes," I whispered.

"What about me?" Becca protested from the other end of the room.

"I'm sure someone else can drop you off," he told her over his shoulder. To me, he said, "I'll meet you at my car, it's a black SUV. I'll grab my stuff and we'll be gone in a few minutes." He turned to Jake. "You're a piece of shit."

I don't remember getting in the car, only sitting on the soft black leather, wiping my eyes with a sweater from my backpack and feeling like my entire life was over. I wanted to go home. I wanted to go back to Pine Falls and if I never saw Jake again, it would be too soon. The humiliation ... it was too much.

Zach climbed into the car, started the engine and drove. For minutes we didn't exchange a word. I was beyond embarrassed and ashamed. What did he think of me now? I'm sure he totally pitied me, which I hated more than anything. I didn't want anyone feeling sorry for me.

"That was really shitty," Zach said, breaking the heavy silence.

"Yup. And I wasn't snooping. I forgot my phone, and I didn't think Jake would mind if I used his." My voice sounded small and defeated. I hated showing weakness.

"I know. You don't have to justify it to me."

"Were they all making fun of me?"

"No one was saying much of anything. I grabbed my gear and took off."

I wanted to be sick. My stomach churned, and I closed my eyes trying to catch my erratic breath. What would I tell Dad and Grandpa? They'd want to know why I was home. If I didn't tell Dad the truth, he'd see right through me, but I didn't want what Jake did to affect Dad's friendship with Uncle Ron. I crossed my arms over my chest and leaned my cheek against the cold passenger side window. What if I threw up in Zach's car?

"Are you going to be okay?" Zach asked, glancing over.

"I'm fine," I managed.

"You say that, but you can't stop tapping your foot on the floor and you're kind of bouncing in the seat like a bomb that's about to go off."

I gulped in another deep breath. "I don't know what I'm going to tell my dad."

"I'd go with the truth. Your dad should know what an asshole Jake is."

I stole a peek at Zach. He had the beginnings of a scruffy face and it looked good on him. His dark eyes were warm and trustworthy and I hated that. I hated trusting him.

"The thing is that Jake's brother, my Uncle Ron, is Dad's best friend."

Zach's eyebrows furrowed and by his bewildered expression I knew he was computing and calculating my statement. "Are you Jake's cousin?"

"No, I just call him Uncle Ron. He and Dad are best friends from high school."

He nodded but the befuddled expression remained. "If your dad and your uncle are best friends, how does that work? How is everyone related?"

Here it came, the explanation I hated. Zach would then view me like a lab experiment gone wrong and his demeanor would change because he'd know the reason for my weirdness. "Here's my deal. My birth mother and Dad weren't careful, and she got pregnant when they were fourteen. She and her family wanted her to have an abortion, but my grandparents refused to allow it. She had me and basically handed me off to them and went on with the rest of her life. My dad and my grandparents raised me. Uncle Ron is Jake's oldest brother."

I waited for a reaction, but didn't get one.

"That's kind of cool. So your dad is what? Thirty-four? It must be awesome having a young dad."

I scratched my head. Why didn't he think it was strange? How come he didn't pass judgment on us like most people did? "I guess so. My dad's pretty great."

"That explains why your mom isn't around."

"Yup."

"That also explains why you don't want to tell your dad. I still say tell the truth."

I bit on my fingernails. I couldn't do it. Dad and Uncle Ron were like me and Jake, well, what I thought Jake and I were. "I need to think about this."

"What's your gut telling you?"

"To go home for a week or so. I'll come up with something to tell my dad."

"Bad idea. You go home, I bet you won't come back. Take a few days to think it through. If you need to, you can crash at my place."

What I really wanted to do was go home. "Thanks for the offer. I'll keep it in mind."

"What Bianca said in those texts was out of jealousy. I'm sure it eats her up that you and Jake are so close. As an outsider looking in, I can see how much you care for the guy, but I also see how devoted he is to her. He already threw you under the bus. If he was any kind of man, he would have come after you and apologized."

"I know."

We didn't say much else for the rest of the ride. I gave him the directions to my apartment, and he walked me to the front door.

"Look, Emma, if you need anything, call me. My offer still stands for a place to stay. I've got an empty bedroom and everything. You have my number from that text I sent last night. Text or call later so I know you're okay, okay?"

"I will. And thanks."

I went inside to the elevator. The moment I stepped into the apartment and shut the door behind me the tears flowed. I had no friends, no Jake and I couldn't turn to Dad. I had nothing.

CHAPTER FOUR

EMMA

I sent Zach a text and he sent a few back. I didn't want to chat and told him to have a good night, thanking him one more time for all his help. I stared at my phone and not once did Jake even make an attempt to contact me. Not even a text to see if I was alive.

I sent Dad a checking-in text. I was too afraid to call him, fearing he would hear something in my voice. After a few days passed I'd be able to hide it better. In the meantime, I still didn't know what to do. Did I go home, stay in the apartment, or find a place of my own?

Since I didn't know when Jake was coming home, I holed myself up in my room with textbooks. In a few hours I was all caught up and reading ahead. I was going back through my anatomy notes when I heard the key slip into the front door. I didn't move and listened as he came in and set his overnight bag on the ground. Silence. Was he listening for me? I waited, hearing nothing until the light rapping on my door.

"Emma, are you in there? Can I come in?"

My heart pounded and a wave of nausea and panic set in. "Yes."

He sheepishly stepped inside, a look of shame marring his handsome face. He stared at me, sitting on my bed, my school books all around me and tried to smile.

"I'm sorry," he said.

My bottom lip quivered but I told myself not to cry. "You were so mean," was all I could say.

"I know. I don't know why I texted those things. Maybe because it was easier than fighting her."

"I have never done anything to her," I said, my eyes stinging with tears.

"I know."

"All those things you both said. They hurt me so much."

"You don't know how terrible I feel."

"Then dump her."

His jaw tightened. "Emma, I love her. Sure, she said some horrible things, but it's not like you two have to be friends."

I couldn't believe what I was hearing. "After all she said about me, don't you see the person that she truly is?"

"She's threatened by you. That's all."

I massaged my temples, trying to collect my thoughts. What was he talking about? "Jake, we've been friends our entire lives and you would let her say those things about me and still defend her? And you agreed with her!"

His face hardened. "Emma, here's the thing. You've been here a few weeks and haven't made any friends. Do you know how hard it is for me to be your only friend? I feel like I can't have a life unless you're included in it. It's not fair. I have a girlfriend and I love her. She happens to not like you. What do you want me to do? I need you to give me space, to not do everything I do. I need you to get a life!"

Another tear slipped down my face. When had I become such a weepy wreck? I usually had it all under control. "Zach is my friend."

He shook his head and rolled his eyes. "Zach feels sorry for you. In a week he won't remember your name."

"Why are you acting like this?"

"Because I'm frustrated. I can't babysit you all the time. When you said you were enrolling at Western, I knew immediately that you'd latch on to me and never let go. I've made a life for myself and it can't always include you. I have Bianca, and I can't even bring her here because of you. Do you know what that feels like? I'm sorry that

I'm being a jerk, but I've been feeling this way for a long time and now I've said it. I think you need to hear it."

Something passed over me, like a moment of clarity when all the clouds seemed to float away leaving only the sun and bright blue sky. "You're free," I said, my voice taking on a stronger tone. "Consider yourself unburdened."

"What does that mean?"

"It means you and I are no longer friends. Isn't that what you want?"

His eyes opened wide. "Wait, that's not what I want."

"You can tell Bianca that your little dog is running away. And that starts with me finding my own place."

He looked completely dismayed now, but I didn't care. He came over to my bed, but I got up and walked out of my bedroom and into the kitchen. He followed me. "Emma, I wasn't saying I didn't want to be friends. I just want you to have some other friends, too."

"Friends don't do and say what you did to me."

"I know you're upset, but we can get past this. I'll talk to Bianca and we can work it all out."

"I don't want anything to do with Bianca!"

"Fine, I understand that, but you can't throw away our friendship because I made a mistake. I know I screwed up royally. But let me find a way to fix this."

His pleading didn't make sense to me. Something wasn't adding up. "If you mean it, then dump Bianca."

"That's not fair and you know it."

"It's totally fair. I would defend you to the death if someone called you a filthy mutt or wished you'd go die somewhere. But you didn't. You went along with it. Who's the dog?"

He sank his head in shame. "I know, but if you met a guy and fell in love with him, you'd understand where I'm coming from."

Silence. I couldn't get through his thick skull. "I'm going home. I'll be leaving in the next day or two. I don't want anything more to do with you. Jake, you broke my heart. What you did was the ultimate betrayal and I can't forgive you."

"You can't go home! Everyone will flip out."

Eureka! The moment I'd been waiting for. I nodded my head in disgust. "I knew it. That's really what you're worried about. What I'm going to tell Dad."

He reached out to grasp onto my arms, but I stepped out of his reach. His hands fell to his sides and his body went slack. I knew he was attempting to calm himself. "If you tell your dad, he'll tell Ron. You may think you're only hurting me, but you're hurting them too. They are going to take sides and don't you think that will ruin their friendship?"

"Not once they hear what you did."

"Emma, you know I'm sorry. Why would you do this to them?"

"I'm not going to lie to my dad. And as for Uncle Ron, I think he'll see things my way."

"You do this, and we won't have a friendship anymore. I won't forgive you, Emma. So promise me you'll take a couple more days to think about this. And know that deep down in your heart I am sorry. I was stupid. And I don't want you to go."

Playing to my sympathies was a good strategy only because I already didn't want to tell Dad. I didn't want to have to explain it all and relive my humiliation. It was bad enough all the people from the cabin knew. Who knows how many people they'd tell.

"I don't know what I'm going to do yet."

"All right, good. Take some time to think. I promise you that the whole Bianca thing will be resolved. I'll talk to her. She'll never do anything like that again."

CHAPTER FIVE

ZACH

I met the guys after hockey for some beers. We sat around drinking and replaying the events of the game. I'd scored twice and one goal was a real beauty, but we still lost 5-3. We had a decent offense and great defense, but our goaltending was killing us. How did you get your best friend to admit he was the worst goaltender in the history of our rec league?

I pulled out my phone and scrolled through texts. Two from Becca. I groaned. I still hadn't broken up with her and I'd been avoiding her since the cabin incident. She was still pissed at me for not driving back to pick her up. Why would I have done that? It didn't make any sense, especially when everyone else offered her a ride home.

I scrolled past her texts and was surprised to see one from Emma. It was a few hours old.

Emma: Hey, how are you? Decided not to go home. Thought I'd tell you. Have a good night.

I wrote back: That's good news. You did the right thing. Still gonna stay with asswipe or are you looking for a new place?

A few minutes passed before she replied. In the meantime, we'd ordered pizzas and the discussion had moved to football. My phone buzzed.

Emma: Not sure yet. Might stay here until the end of semester. Finding housing midyear is going to be next to impossible.

Should I offer my place again? She didn't seem keen the first time. But it wasn't like Genie used her room.

Me: Let me know if I can help. Did you make those éclairs yet? I'm dying to have one.

Emma: I'm going to do a test batch this weekend. If they work out, I'll text you.

I put down my phone and Brett was staring at me.

"Are you going to talk to us or text?" he asked.

Brett was one of the few guys on the planet who hated his phone. The guy never texted and his idea of an "app" was some spicy wings or a heaping plate of nachos. He hardly ever had his phone with him, and even when he did, it was almost never on. And if you had your cell out in his presence, watch out.

"I'm done now."

"And who is more important than us?"

"I was texting Emma to make sure she was okay."

"Who's Emma?"

"From the cabin four days ago? Remember? Jake's friend?"

Recollection washed over him. "How could I forget?" He turned to the rest of the guys and recounted the events of that day. "She was a fucking loon!" he told them. "She starts reading off these texts that make her look like a cracker jack! Poor Jake. I felt sorry for that bastard."

"Wait a second," I said, holding up my hands. "You felt sorry for *Jake*? The guy humiliated her."

Brett laughed. "Man, are you serious?" He turned back to the guys. "This is a chick who spent the whole day either in her room or sitting around reading a book. She didn't say a word to anyone. She's a loon all right."

My back was up. "Actually, she spent most of the time she was there cooking and cleaning up for you and your lazy date."

Brett's cheery asshole demeanor disappeared. "Excuse me?"

"If you or your flavor of the week had bothered to get to know her, you may have noticed that she was normal and interesting."

A smugness came over Brett. "Oh, I see now. You want to tap her. No accounting for taste."

"The girl was freaking out and I was the only one who offered her a ride home. She's a nice girl, so cut it out."

"Whatever."

The conversation returned to football. Our pizzas arrived, I wolfed down a few slices and made my escape. I texted Becca that I'd be stopping by. It was nearing ten on a Wednesday night, but dealing with her wouldn't take long. She was in her dorm room, leafing through a fashion magazine when her roommate let me in. Becca vaulted off her bed and kissed me.

"I'll be back in twenty," her roommate said. For the life of me I couldn't remember her name.

She left and Becca snaked her arms around my waist. "We've got some time," she said, her voice deepening.

"I can't stay long. I thought we should talk."

She took a step back, her blue eyes inspecting me. "Talk about what?"

"Us."

"Why?"

No need to beat around the bush. I wanted to get this over with. "Do you think this is working?"

Her face frosted over. "You're not dumping me, are you?" Her voice had lost all its seduction replaced by snark.

"Becca, I like you and you're a great girl, but I'm just not feeling a connection. Someday you'll meet a guy who's right for you, but that's not me."

"You are such a son of a bitch," she said, her nostrils flaring. "Is it someone else?"

Strangely, she didn't seem sad, just angry. Like I'd forgotten her birthday. I knew she'd forget about it, and me, in a few days.

"There's no one else."

"It's that girl in your Poly Sci class, isn't it?"

"There isn't anyone else. I want to be single for a while and focus on school. We can still hang out and be friends."

Her eyes narrowed, ready to shoot laser beams. This side of Becca was ugly. "Bianca warned me about you. She said you'd date me for a while and dump me. You think you're some god because your dad's a senator. My dad could buy your dad any day of the week."

I let out a sigh. Her attempts to rattle me weren't going to work. "Well, I should go. I know you're pissed, but if you want to talk about it later, we can."

"Go fuck yourself."

"I guess not, then."

I left and she slammed the door behind me. That was taken care of and not nearly as difficult as I'd expected.

CHAPTER SIX

EMMA

I lied to Dad and told him everything was fine. It wasn't. My relationship with Jake was definitely something akin to being on life support. We didn't talk much, and I made a point of staying late at school to study, or would leave the apartment before he was even up in the morning. I didn't want to talk to him and the feeling seemed to be mutual.

The next few weeks I immersed myself in school and my job. I was up to date with all my assignments. At work I was baking up a storm, so much so that Billie, my boss, hinted that I was making more than we could sell. So on a quiet Friday night when all my classmates were out having fun, I stood behind the coffee counter casually reading a few pages in the mystery novel I'd tucked on the shelf with the napkins and stir sticks.

I was working with Jessica tonight, and I knew she didn't care; she often had a book out too. Jessica was nice enough, but we didn't interact a lot. She was a graduate student who worked for extra cash and took any shift available. She'd trained me, but other than normal chitchat, I knew little about her.

I felt a little guilty reading at work, but it really was quiet, and I could only wipe down the same empty tables so many times. Besides, reading for fun was getting harder and harder to do with all my school work mounting, and since I was lacking in the friends department, I enjoyed a fictional escape when I could.

"Any éclairs?"

I jumped and smiled when I saw Zach standing at the counter. "Sorry, I'm still perfecting those."

He leaned back and perused the glass display counter. "What's good?"

"Everything, but I recommend the coffee cake. It's a secret recipe."

"Then I'll have that. Large black coffee too. And whatever you're having."

"I've already had three today, but thanks for offering."

"Do they give you a break?"

"Go ahead, take fifteen," Jessica said, overhearing us. She had her tablet out and was tapping away. That's how busy we were on a Friday night.

"Thanks."

We sat at one of the many empty tables and I watched him devour my coffee cake.

"Shit, this is good," he said, licking his lips.

"Told you. So what brings you out here on a Friday night? No frat parties?"

"No, I'm done with those. I just came back from a study session with some people from class. We have a project coming up. I was driving by and thought I'd see if you were working. How have you been?"

"I'm good."

"And how are things with Jake?"

"We're co-existing right now. I decided not to tell Dad and see how things go with Jake. I've managed to avoid everyone from the cabin. Thankfully I don't have classes with any of them."

"I think you already know this, but Jake is an asswipe."

"But he's still my friend."

Zach cringed. "He's not your friend. A friend wouldn't do what he did."

"I know you don't understand. Bianca has this strange hold over him, but eventually he'll see the kind of person she is."

"And come back to you?" he finished.

I looked away from Zach's suffocating stare. "I didn't say that."

"I know you like him and I wish I could say that he feels the same way about you. I'm not telling you this to hurt your feelings, but he isn't going to wake up one morning and realize he's loved you his entire life. This isn't a fairy tale."

"I don't feel that way about him."

He smirked. "I'm going to call bullshit on that."

"You can call it whatever you want. I don't care."

His eyes scanned me, looking for a crack, wondering if I'd crumble. Little did he know that I'd spent my entire life with the façade of apathy. My survival and sanity depended on me not being broken. I'd put up an Iron Curtain and Zach Walker wasn't getting through.

"Well, when you finally realize what an ass he is, I can help you find a place to live. But the longer you stay in that apartment, the harder it will be to leave."

"I appreciate the offer."

He stood to leave. "Let me know when you get those éclairs in."

"I will."

He waved and left. I resumed my position behind the counter with Jessica staring at me. Did I spill something? I checked my black Julian's apron and saw nothing out of the ordinary.

"What's wrong? Is there something on my face? Did I get something on me?" I asked.

"No." She paused as if to ponder something. "How do you know Zach Walker?"

"Long story. Why?"

"He's the senator's son. You know that, right?"

"Yes, so?"

"Are you dating him?"

"No!" I said it like it was the most disgusting idea in the world. "He's a friend."

"He's a good friend to have."

I smiled. "Yeah, he's pretty nice."

"If you like him, be careful. He leaves a trail of tears."

"How do you know that?"

"Everyone knows that. He dates girls for a few months then gets bored. You're better off keeping him a friend than getting mixed up with him."

"I'll keep that in mind."

She tapped her nearly empty cup on the counter. "Walker sure has changed."

"Changed?"

"He has a lost year. Come to think of it, he's probably pissed away two years. I don't know him, but I've been to parties he's thrown, a few at the frat he belonged to. The guy partied hard. I mean really, really hard. He was a party boy legend, you know, the kind people talk about for years, but then something happened. My guess is that his parents put the fear of God into him because he stopped everything. He pretty much disappeared last spring. No epic parties, nothing. I heard he left his frat house, finally took a full course load and actually attends classes. Phi Alpha Delta has never been the same."

I laughed. "No way. Not Zach."

Jessica snorted. "Oh, it's true. Ask him. He had some really good times if he remembers any of them."

I was having a hard time envisioning this. And smoking a joint once in a while didn't make you legendary. He didn't scream party animal. He didn't even mention parties. "Are you sure? Could you have him mixed up?"

"Emma, everyone knows who Zach Walker is. I don't have him mixed up with anyone else. Look, he's turned his life around. That's commendable. But here's the thing: you're a nice girl from a small town. Don't let a guy like him take advantage."

"He wouldn't do that," I said. An edge found its way into my voice.

"The party Walker would, and who knows if he's really changed? You're sweet, a little innocent too. I hope that doesn't offend you, but it's the truth. If you ever decide to date the guy, just be careful. Guys with his reputation don't deserve to have a chance with girls like you."

"Thanks ... I think."

Little did she know that Zach wasn't even on my radar.

SATURDAY MORNING JAKE was waiting for me in the kitchen. He had a newspaper and a mug of coffee sitting in front of him. He set the paper aside when I entered the room.

"Hey," he said.

"Hi."

In the past two weeks we hadn't exchanged more than a dozen words. It was hard not talking to him and I desperately missed our conversations. Some nights I would sit in my bedroom as quietly as possible and listen to him go about the apartment. So many times I wanted to go out and chat with him, like old times, but then I'd remember. How could I ever forget?

"Do you have a few minutes?"

My heart skipped a beat. At one time I knew Jake so well, I always knew what he was going to say or do, but Bianca changed everything.

"Sure."

I sat across from him and we stared at each other.

"I know we haven't talked much, since that day. How are you doing?"

"I'm fine."

"You've been keeping busy?" He was asking but it sounded more like a statement.

"Yes. Working and school."

"Good."

Time to get to the point. "What do you want to talk about?" I could only dream that he was going to tell me he'd seen the light and dumped Bianca's skinny ass.

"I had a really long heart to heart with Bianca and she agreed to be nicer to you. I'm hoping that I can invite her over once in a while and that the two of you can get to know each other. I think if you spend time together, you might like her and vice versa."

He was serious. I did everything humanly possible from keeping my jaw from dropping. The same person who called me a dog with fleas and wished for my death. I sucked back a mouthful of air and took my time crafting an answer. How did I approach this? I wanted nothing to do with Bianca. Ever.

"Let's wait and see. I'm not sure I'm ready to spend any time with her."

"That's fair, but I'd like to be able to have her around. Maybe stay the night."

"She can stay here when I'm not here." My words were diplomatic, but my tone wasn't. If he couldn't hear the sarcasm, then something was wrong with him.

Jake huffed. I could see the irritation setting in. "I don't expect the two of you to patch things up instantly, but it has to happen eventually."

"And if it doesn't, then what? Have you forgotten what she said about me?"

"No, but she promised me she would stop this. I'm asking you to do the same."

"I didn't do anything. I'm telling you that I'm not ready to see her, let alone have her hanging around here."

He tapped his fingers on the table. "Then one of us has to think about moving out."

I raised my eyebrows. These were Bianca's words. She'd planted the idea in his head because this wasn't something Jake would come up with. Only a few weeks ago he'd begged me to stay. "You know, I've put up with a lot. I'm the injured party and you can't wait to get rid of me. So I will take your suggestion under advisement and I'll look for another place to live because I think that's what you're implying."

"I'm trying to find a solution. I don't want you to leave."

"You are picking her over me."

"I'm not, but I don't think you're being reasonable."

I got up unable to stomach this conversation any longer. "We can talk about this again later."

"Think about everything I've said. Moving on is best. That's the win-win solution for all of us."

I MADE ÉCLAIRS. IT took three batches until I had the custard filling just right. I then texted Zach to tell him the good news. A couple of hours later he replied. I'd cleaned the kitchen and bathroom and finished the last few pages of my English paper by then.

Zach: How do I get my hands on said éclairs?

Me: You could come get them or I could bring them to work tomorrow.

Zach: I can come get them. You busy now?

Other than me being dressed in sweat pants and an old T-shirt that had more holes than Swiss cheese, why couldn't he come over? Jake wasn't around and I'd spent much of the day in the apartment. Having a guest, my friend, was a great idea.

Me: Nope. Come now if you want.

I changed into jeans and a sweater and fixed up my hair. When I played tennis, I used to keep it long so that I could easily tame it, but the moment I quit playing competitively, the first thing I did was lop it off. I regretted the pixie cut and now compromised by keeping it shoulder length. I could put it up in a pinch or let it go into its gentle wave. My hair was a rich auburn, drastically different from Dad's dirty blond hair that turned into a light blond in the summer. I also had Meredith's hazel eyes, but I would have killed to have Dad's big blue ones. Other than the general shape of our faces and noses and Dad's height, you wouldn't think we were related. I looked like her ... Meredith. That had prompted my grandparents to seek a paternity test. Dad told me about it when I was old enough to understand. He didn't want me to hear it from anyone else. He insisted he knew I was his girl the second I was born. As for Grandma and Grandpa, they never spoke of it. My best guess was that they were embarrassed about it.

I put on coffee and as it finished brewing, Zach arrived. I buzzed him into the building and left the apartment door open. I heard him call my name from the doorway.

"I'm in the kitchen pouring coffee," I called out.

"It smells amazing in here," he said, walking in to find me. "Coffee and éclairs. I could marry you."

I laughed and thought of what Jessica had said. "I'm too young to get hitched. Besides, I hear you're not the marrying kind." I handed him a steaming mug.

"Ah, gossip. What have you heard?"

"Not much," I said, plating the éclairs. "When you came into Julian's, my co-worker was fascinated that I knew you. She warned me not to date you because you get bored easily and used to throw crazy parties, or something like that. Where should we eat the éclairs? Kitchen or living room?"

His brown eyes gave off a spark. "You're so casual about all that. I get bored easily to where should we eat."

I shrugged. "If you get bored what's the big deal? And haven't you been dating Becca for a long time?"

He frowned. "I actually broke up with her a few weeks ago."

"Oh. Well, that doesn't matter anyway. You can date whoever you want for as long as you want."

"Can you tell all my exes that?"

"How many exes do you have?" I said, leading him into the living room.

"Not that many."

"And how long was the longest relationship?"

"I don't know. Six months?"

"When you meet the right girl, you'll stay with her. Here, have an éclair." I thrust the plate in front of him.

He sat on our sofa and started in. He let out a moan of contentment as he finished it off in a few bites. "This is amazing. Are you serving them at Julian's?"

"I'm going to let Billie sample them first. They don't have a long shelf life so we'd have to sell them pretty fast."

"I'd buy them all. Em, you're going to make me fat."

I was well aware that he was the only person other than Dad to call me Em. Not even Jake called me that. "Despite all the desserts I make, I also make very healthy meals. Just ask Jake."

"Where is he, by the way?"

"Probably with Bianca."

"How's all that going?"

I sighed. "He thinks we can sweep this all under the rug. He suggested that if I can't work it out with her, one of us should move out. That means me."

Zach finished off the last éclair and leaned back on the sofa. "I think you should move out. I don't think this is a good situation for you. And I've known Bianca a lot longer than Jake has, and she is never going to want to 'work things out.' As long as that idiot stays with her, this is going to be toxic for you."

"Why is she such a bitch?"

"Because she's used to getting her way. Her parents give her anything she wants. I'm sure it's the same with Jake. He's a good-looking guy with a small-town attitude. She knows she can control him."

"He'll come around."

"Em, mark my words. While Bianca is in the picture, you will always take second place."

I sipped some coffee and tapped a finger against the mug. "The thing is, I can't afford to live on my own, so I have to stick it out with Jake the rest of the year. I might have to put up with Bianca. I can try to get into a dorm next year."

"I don't know how solid those two are, but keep all your options open."

"I will."

"I should go," he said, rising. "I really don't want to run into Jake. Make sure you get those éclairs into Julian's."

"I'll certainly try."

"And don't be a stranger."

"I won't."

He left and I slumped down onto the sofa. He was a good guy. I reminded myself that I had officially placed him into the friend category. But . . . No, I wasn't going there, I couldn't go there. Zach Walker was a friend and I wasn't going to let it be any other way, despite that little tickle in my heart. Besides, what did my heart know anyway?

CHAPTER SEVEN

EMMA

Working at Julian's was an escape from Jake and the tension that hung between us. I knew eventually he would come around and dump her, or she'd dump him. I didn't care who did the deed, as long as it was done so I could have my Jake back. Until then I spent a lot of time alone, which was nothing new for me, but college was supposed to be different. No one knew me here. I could start fresh, make friends, go to parties and have fun...except that history repeats itself. Even at Western I was an outcast, an oddity or simply invisible. Why could no one see me for who I was?

"The éclairs are a hit," Jessica said. I liked Jessica; if she hadn't been four years older than me, we might have even hung out. I obsessed a lot about my lack of friends. Jake's revelation had me thinking. I intended to join more school groups and even researched them, but nothing stood out yet. Why couldn't there be a culinary club?

"I was thinking of making them once a week."

"Billie told me we were sold out right after lunch."

My body warmed with the compliment. "I'll make more next time."

Jessica arranged the stir sticks and refilled the creamers while I made another pot of decaf. Of all my co-workers, she was the only one who bothered to make conversation. I knew I wasn't the most outgoing person in the world, but once I felt comfortable enough to come out of my shell, I think people tended to really like me. It was just that most people didn't give me a chance.

My first summer teaching at the tennis academy was a perfect example. At first I was shy and awkward with the students, but when I realized that their seven- and eight-year-old faces watched me intently and hung on every word I said, I felt like a flower blooming for the first time. And the minute I had a racket in my hand and bounced a ball a few times, I had all my confidence. By the end of summer, the kids were inviting me to their birthday parties. But it's not like I could really call them friends.

"What classes are you taking?" Jessica asked.

"A bunch of intro courses. I'm feeling them out."

"Why didn't you go to pastry school or something?"

"Long story. Let's just say my grandpa wants me to have a college education."

"I see a bakery in your future, and since there are no good ones around here, you'd make a killing."

"Thanks."

Billie had asked me to take on more baking hours, and I was considering it. It's not like I had much else to do.

"How's Walker?"

"Zach? Good, I guess. I don't talk to him a lot." Why did she keep bringing up Zach? "We're just friends."

"Sure, that's what they all say," she said and laughed.

We had a bit of an evening rush. We were a hotspot for hanging out and studying. The free Wi-Fi didn't hurt, but Billie had instituted a one-hour maximum laptop policy. She did have a business to run and having starving students taking up a table for hours with a two-dollar cup of coffee wasn't good for her bottom line. Mercifully, Jessica usually played the role of bad cop, mostly because she liked it. The rare times the task fell on me to throw out my fellow students, my heart raced, my cheeks flushed and my hands got all clammy. I hated doing it, but it was part of the job. People were mostly good about it, but there was always the rare jackass.

An hour before close, while I started some evening cleanup, Bianca and Becca came in. I wanted to hide behind the showcase and let Jessica handle it, but she was busy asking two freshmen to leave for the third time. The three of them were in a heated discussion that wasn't about to end anytime soon.

I slunk to the counter, maintaining a neutral expression on my face. She was not going to get under my skin. My Iron Curtain was solid.

"Oh great, you," she muttered.

Likewise, I thought. "Can I help you?"

"Yeah, you can vaporize."

I fought the urge to stick out of my tongue and give her the finger. Beyond being the stereotypical bottled blonde with blue eyes, perfect teeth, and enormous boobs, what did she have to offer? Every word out of her mouth was vile, and while the outside of her was flawless, the inside was a black, maggot-filled sack of rotting organs.

"Did you want to order something?" I could have used an over-the-top fake voice, but what would be the point? To piss her off? Not worth it.

"A large skinny latte with almond milk. Try not to screw it up."

I turned to Becca. In many ways she looked similar to Bianca except for the bone structure of her face. Same fake blonde hair, tiny waist, and crappy attitude. "I'll have the same thing."

Of course. Would it have been any other way? I punched in their orders and took a quick look for Jessica. She was still arguing with the two guys. At least by this point she'd evicted them from the booth and was attempting to lead them to the front door. I tried to make eye contact with her, to get her help, but she was too engrossed with the guys.

I started the drinks. I could feel Bianca's eyes searing into me and I wasn't about to give her the satisfaction of a passing look. I wanted to make the drinks as quickly as possible and get them away from me.

"Oh my God what is taking you so long?" Bianca chirped.

"I'll have them ready right away."

Becca whispered something to Bianca and they laughed. I fought hard not to roll my eyes. So childish. Bianca whispered something back and they erupted into more laughter. Could this almond milk steam any faster? I knew my cheeks were flaming red, more out of rage than anything else. Would Jake condone this behavior if he was here? I didn't even know anymore.

I finished up their drinks as Jessica returned, having successfully thrown out the loiterers. I handed Becca and Bianca their drinks. Bianca leaned in closer to me.

"Don't get home too late. Jake still needs to walk you. Woof, woof."

Our eyes met and I could feel my body slowly turn to stone. At that moment I had never hated a person as much as I hated Bianca. She grabbed her drink and the two of them giggled as they took a table in a far-off corner. I must have been staring at them, rage boiling up inside of me, because when Jessica called my name it took me a second to snap back to reality.

"Hey, you all right? What did she say to you?"

"Nothing," I said, trying to busy myself by cleaning the espresso machine.

"Did she bark or something?"

"No."

I was embarrassed that Jessica had heard that and my worst fear was that these two evil wenches would stay until close and taunt me some more.

"Are you sure?" Concern masked Jessica's face and I could see pity.

"Really, it was nothing."

Jessica gave up and fortunately Bianca and Becca left minutes later.

I TOOK THE BUS HOME, the first indication Dad had that something was amiss. He picked me up from the depot and I had to fight back tears when I saw him. With Dad I was safe.

"How was your first six weeks at school?" he asked, examining my face for any signs of trouble.

"Pretty good. I'm meeting people and even though I have a lot of school work, I'm enjoying it. I've been getting extra hours at Julian's. They have me baking a ton of stuff."

"See, I told you they'd love your desserts. Making new friends?"

"A few." I was counting Zach and Jessica, even though she was a bit of a stretch.

We got into the car and I could tell Dad wasn't buying much of what I was selling. He kept looking at me, trying to figure out how to catch me in a lie.

"Tell me about your new friends."

I fumbled with the zipper on my jacket. Damn, a tell. If I didn't put on the performance of a lifetime, Dad would be all over me. "Well, there's Zach. I met him at the cabin Jake took me to my first week at school. He's really nice and we hang out once in a while." I was counting the few times he stopped by Julian's. "And I work with Jessica. She's really cool. She's kind of showing me the ropes around campus." Ugh. That was an outright lie.

"And Jake?"

"He has Bianca, so I don't see him all the time."

Dad looked at me strange. Crap, wrong answer. He wanted to know how Jake was, not if he and I were hanging out.

"How's Jake doing?" he asked.

"Good. We don't have classes together, but he says all is well."

"Ron says he hasn't heard much from him. Come to think of it, I haven't heard a lot from you either."

"What do you mean? I text or call every night."

"But you aren't saying much. He and I think something is going on."

Dad's tone dropped and I didn't know what to do. Did he know? Had Jake told Uncle Ron something to make me look bad? My head throbbed and panic set in. First the racing heart, soon the hyperventilating. I had to get this in check. "What do you mean? What do you think is going on?"

Dad tapped his finger on the steering wheel at a million beats a second. "I know you're an adult now, so I can't keep playing the dad card, but I want you to be careful. I worried that the two of you moving in together would lead to something like this and maybe it was inevitable. You and Jake have been friends your entire lives so don't rush into anything that could ruin that friendship."

My jaw dropped. Dad couldn't have been more wrong and if I wasn't so shocked, I might have laughed. "Jake and I are not dating. He is obsessed with Bianca."

Dad's narrowed his eyes in confusion. "You aren't together?"

"Not even close. You and Uncle Ron thought that?"

"It was more your Uncle Ron," Dad said, deflecting.

I giggled. "You're so busted."

"We kind of put two and two together. Problem is that we came up with five."

"The two of you shouldn't do anymore math problems."

"Well, if that's not the issue, what is going on?"

"Nothing. We've both been busy with school."

Dad appeared satisfied and relieved. "If something is wrong, I want you to tell me."

"You know I would."

I hated lying to Dad, but in this case the alternative was worse.

I HADN'T EVEN SETTLED into my room when I got a text from Jake.

Jake: Did Paul ask you anything?

Me: Yes. He thinks we're screwing around. So does Uncle Ron. I set him straight.

Jake: That's what they think? Thank God! Say hi to your dad.

With that I was dismissed. Resentment set in. He didn't care about me, he only cared what Dad and Uncle Ron thought. Jake was an asswipe.

I put my phone away and trudged downstairs. If a cloud hung around me, Dad and Grandpa didn't notice. I made dinner which Dad objected to, but I didn't really care. I could only imagine how much takeout and TV dinners he and Grandpa had eaten the last few weeks. I scrounged through the fridge and found some sad-looking mushrooms I could salvage and put on a pot for pasta. We'd be eating spaghetti in sautéed garlic, mushrooms, and olive oil. Unfortunately, I couldn't find a protein in the house other than a carton of eggs. Then it hit me. There had been some cooked ham in the fridge. While not ideal, I could work with it. I sautéed it too, along with a few eggs and threw the concoction together. I sprinkled it with parmesan they hadn't touched since I left.

"This is heavenly," Grandpa said. He sighed and savored a bite.

"It's very simple. You or Dad could make it."

"Leave me the recipe. It can replace one of our pizza nights," Dad said.

"How many pizza nights do you have?"

"I don't know. One or two a week."

Grandpa cackled. "Try three or four."

"Dad! You promised to eat better."

"I get home from work and I'm tired. If it wasn't for my metabolism, I'd be three hundred pounds."

Dad also worked out and ran five miles every day. If he actually ate well, he'd be a fitness superstar.

"You also promised me you'd go out and meet people, go on a few dates."

"He hasn't done that either," Grandpa threw in. "Even I've been on dates."

I turned to Grandpa. "You have?"

"I met a nice lady at the shop. She's retired, divorced, and moved here not too long ago. She's got a beautiful place on Lake Simkin."

"So you've been to her place?"

Dad and I oohh and ahhed.

"She wanted to show me a few antiques," Grandpa said, blushing a little.

"What else did she show you?" Dad asked.

Grandpa pursed his lips. "I've only been out with her a few times."

"When do we get to meet her?" I asked. "What if we don't approve?"

"We'll see when you come back for Thanksgiving."

"What's her name?"

"Wendy."

"What did she do before she retired?"

"She was a lawyer."

More oohing and ahhing from the peanut gallery.

"And now we are changing the subject," Grandpa declared. "How about you, little lady? Any boys from the big city sweep you off your feet?"

"I don't have time for boys."

Grandpa let out a snort. "Your dad here and Ron thought you and Jake were shacking up in more ways than one."

"I heard."

"You can do better than Jake."

"Dad! Jake's a good kid."

Grandpa shook his head. "Don't like him all that much. The boy's always chasing big dreams."

And Grandpa didn't even know Bianca.

"Don't say that stuff around Ron."

"You think Ron doesn't already know?"

I looked at Dad and then Grandpa. I was lucky to have two of the coolest guys in the world in my life. Who needed a boyfriend?

"Well, I hate to end this fun early, but I'm beat," I said, taking plates and loading them into the dishwasher. Dad shooed me away when I tried to take away the rest.

"Goodnight, Kiddo," Dad said, giving me a kiss on the cheek.

I went up to my room and climbed into bed. Sure, it wasn't even eight-thirty, but the day had been a long one. I drifted off to sleep while reading my psych textbook. It felt like only minutes passed when my phone trilled and woke me. I pawed for it on the nightstand. I glanced at my alarm clock and was surprised to see it was after midnight. I couldn't imagine Jake had anything else to say to me, except that it wasn't Jake.

Zach: How you doing? Went by Julian's tonight and you weren't there. No éclairs either.

Me: Sorry. Back home this weekend. Making éclairs Monday.

Zach: Did you tell your Dad what happened?

Me: No. Don't want to upset him.

Zach: Wimp. Lol! Have a nice weekend. See you Monday. Save me an éclair.

Me: Will do.

I turned my phone off and smiled.

CHAPTER EIGHT

ZACH

I met some of the guys at Fixx, a new club that had opened near campus. The place was packed, but we knew the bouncer and he let us skip the line. I grabbed a beer, fully intending it to be my only one. I had to be home early in the morning for our annual Christmas card photo session, complete with fake snow and Christmas decorations galore. If I looked remotely hungover, Mom would kill me.

"This place is nuts," Brett said.

"Yup," I said, glancing at my phone. Three texts from Becca wanting to talk, then changing her mind, then wanting to talk again and another from a girl in my Terror and Espionage class. I deleted Becca's texts and replied to the girl from class. What was her name again? Jennifer? Carla? I couldn't remember and her text came up as only a number. I only knew it was the girl from T&E because of some of the earlier messages in the chain.

"You here with me, or with your phone?" Brett asked, staring at my cell with contempt.

"You're just jealous cuz all the girls love me," I said, punching him in the arm.

"Fuck off."

We got our beers and then Brett and I headed for a less crowded corner while the other guys stayed near the bar. Brett chatted up a cute brunette, but by the disinterested look on her face, I knew he was wasting his time. I took the opportunity to sneak another glance at my phone. Terror-and-Espionage girl had texted again. Wanted to know if I'd study with her and go for coffee after that. She was cute, but not my type. I texted back that I'd let her know.

"Well, look who it is."

I looked up from my phone. Bianca. I'd managed to avoid her for the weeks since the incident at Brett's cabin. A huge smile spread across her face as she batted her eyelashes a few times. I was easily six inches taller than her and she had to crane her neck to stare up at me.

"Hey," I muttered.

"I haven't seen you around campus. Hiding or something?"

"I guess we don't cross paths."

She smirked. "So I hear you were the one who gave Emma a ride home from Brett's." She said Emma's name like it repulsed her.

"Yup."

"You know she's a loser, right? Totally freaking weird. Jake says you've been nice to her, and I thought you should know what kind of person she is."

I shifted my feet and stared over her head and focused on the dance floor. I didn't want to give her the impression that I found her interesting. "And what kind of person is she?" I sounded bored. Mission accomplished.

"She's in love with Jake and wants to break us up. She's always trying to get between us. And she's super strange. She's into something like witchcraft or whatever. Everyone stays away from her. She has no friends. Zero. Nada. Nothing. You should stay away from her too."

"Why?" I asked. I should have shut down the conversation, but I was curious what more she'd fabricate.

"I heard you had a soft spot for her. I don't think your parents want you mixed up with someone so ... questionable."

Fucking Brett. "The only questionable thing here is your story."

Bianca's mouth gaped open for a second. I took a sip of my beer.

"You like her, don't you?" Bianca said with a sneer. Not a good look for her.

"I think she's a normal and nice human being. I can't say the same thing about all the people I know."

"OMG! You do like her!"

I shook my head and rolled my eyes. "So what if I like her? What is the big deal? Am I not allowed to be friendly to her? Do you make the rules?"

"You're a fucking idiot, you know that! People like her can screw up your dad's re-election."

"Thanks for the valuable insight."

"I'm trying to help you."

I'd had enough of her shit. I stared her down, planting myself in front of her. "I don't need your help. Last time I checked, it's you who needs me."

She knew exactly what I meant. She retreated and her shoulders dropped. "Is that what I get for giving you a heads-up?"

"Yeah, so leave me alone. Leave Emma alone too."

She stomped off and I was glad to be rid of her. I turned to Brett who'd been dismissed by the brunette. He was scanning the crowd for his next victim.

"What'd you tell Bianca?" I asked him.

"About what?"

"About Emma."

Brett thought about the question and shrugged. "Who's Emma?"

"Emma from the cabin. I took her home. Remember? How many times do I have to remind you who she is?"

"Oh yeah, the weird one. Nothing." He paused. "Oh wait, I told her you were texting her."

"Why'd you do that?"

"She came up in conversation. Something about Bianca going around to her job and giving her a hard time."

"Wait, what? Going to her job?" My blood pressure was rising. I could literally feel it ticking up by the second.

"She and Becca went by the place she works and gave her a hard time or something." Brett looked at me and the smile on his face vanished.

"You're an asshole, you know that, right?"

"Hey, it was sort of funny."

"What was funny about it?"

"Why are you getting so bent out of shape?"

"Because she didn't do anything to you, to Bianca or to whoever else was there."

"Jake laughed, too, and he's her friend."

"Then that makes you all assholes." I gulped back the last of my beer and slammed the bottle down on the bar. "I'm out of here. I'll walk home."

THE BRIGHT SPOT OF my night out with the guys was that I was home early and up looking fresh and bright-eyed when the entourage arrived for our Christmas card photos. Clothes were picked out and after a quick hair and makeup session, I was sitting with Dad on the sofa, waiting for Genie and Mom.

"You're keeping up those grades?" Dad asked.

"I know how important these next two years are. I won't screw it up."

"No more distractions."

"I know."

"We'll talk more about this after breakfast," he said once Mom and Genie appeared.

I would have killed someone for breakfast, but Mom didn't want to look bloated in the pictures. Normally she wasn't vain, but this Christmas card went out to thousands of people and she wanted to look her best. The second I was out of my sweater, slacks, and tie, I'd be chowing down on pancakes, eggs, and bacon. Louisa had promised it all.

For an hour the photographer placed us in various positions while his assistants moved various Christmas decorations around—all decorations I know weren't ours. By the time the last few pictures were snapped, my stomach was growling and Genie was fidgeting.

"How much longer?" she asked. "I'm about to eat one of these Christmas trees."

"We're done," the photographer said.

"About time," she said. "I'll let Louisa know we're ready to eat. Let's meet in the dining room in five minutes."

She rushed out of the room to change and I was close behind. I threw on jeans and a T-shirt and when I got to the dining room, Louisa was putting out plates of apple pancakes, bacon, sausages, eggs, and cubed potatoes. I didn't wait for the rest of my family before I dove in.

"Coffee?"

"Yes, thank you, Louisa."

She touched my shoulder and squeezed it. Louisa had been a part of our family for so long we couldn't survive without her. She kept us fed, watered, and moving in the right directions. And when she finished putting out all the various plates of food, she took her seat next to me. Unlike other the help at other homes, Louisa always ate with us. We'd have it no other way. If it wasn't for Allen, Dad's communications director, laying down his veto, Louisa would have her place in our Christmas photo shoot.

"We should wait for everyone else," Louisa said.

"No way," I said, passing her the plate of pancakes. "You snooze, your food is cold."

Louisa smiled and pinched my cheek the same way she did when I was five. "You're a little devil, aren't you?"

Dad, Mom, and Genie filed in moments apart. Mom had Christmas on the brain and wanted to discuss arrangements for the party that was two months away. She let Louisa in on all the details, often running ideas past her. Dad was busy with the newspaper so Genie fixed her attention on me.

"I need a favor," she said.

"What's that?" I asked, pouring more maple syrup on my pancakes.

"One of Steve's friends is getting married and he's the best man. He wants to throw a big party and I thought you could help."

"Zach has retired from party planning," Dad said.

"What Dad said." I wouldn't help Steve plan a party if it was the last party I'd ever attend.

"You could give him some ideas."

"I've never thrown a bachelor party so I can't help."

She huffed. "If you got to know him, you might actually like him."

"Doubt it."

"You could at least give me some leads."

Dad lowered his paper. "Genie, your brother has already told you he can't help you. Let's move on."

I tried not to smile. Dad hated Steve as much as I did.

"We'll talk later," she said under her breath.

Not if I had my way.

We finished up breakfast and I hung out with my parents for a bit before heading back to the apartment. I passed Julian's on my way home and thought of Emma, wondering if she was inside. For a split second I considered turning around, but stopped myself. I couldn't hang around Julian's all the time. The girl loved Jake, despite how shitty he'd treated her. I could try to make her see reality, but my gut told me I'd be wasting my time.

But somehow, I didn't think that was going to stop me from trying.

CHAPTER NINE

EMMA

I didn't have classes until the afternoon, so I spent my morning making éclairs in Julian's kitchen. I finished up, grabbed a coffee, and ate my lunch in an empty booth. I was looking through notes when my phone pinged

Zach: You free at all?

Me: I am until 1pm. Having lunch at work.

Zach: I'm five minutes away. I'll stop in. Save me an éclair.

Little did he know that I'd tucked one away for him at the bottom of the cooler. We'd already sold two dozen of the three dozen I'd made. I'd also baked pecan and butter tarts which were selling briskly.

As promised, Zach showed up five minutes later. He got a coffee and took the empty seat across from me. His éclair was waiting for him.

"I could eat these for breakfast, lunch, and dinner."

"I don't recommend it. You do want to keep your physique, don't you?"

"I guess so. How do you stay in such great shape when you're surrounded by all this food?"

"Tennis."

"That'll do it."

"So what brings you by?" I asked, closing my books. I cherished the diversion.

"I haven't seen you in a few weeks and thought I'd say hi. How are things? How'd the weekend go with your dad?"

"Great. I cooked up a storm once I discovered that my dad and grandpa have been eating pizza practically every night. The freezer is restocked with tons of healthy meals. And I found out my grandpa has a girlfriend!"

"That's cool."

"How about your weekend?"

"Went to FIXX on Saturday night. I ran into Bianca."

I groaned. "Lucky you."

"I hear she came by and it wasn't a friendly visit."

Every muscle in my body tensed. I'd tried to forget about that. "Yeah, she was here. And no, not very friendly."

"Did you tell Jake?"

"Why? He wouldn't believe me."

Zach smiled and his brown eyes warmed me like hot cocoa. Why did I trust him? Why did I feel like I could tell him anything? What if he was the enemy, infiltrating my life and taking everything I said back to Bianca?

"If I tell you something, will you believe me?"

I leaned back in the booth and crossed my arms over my chest. I'd read somewhere that we did that instinctively to protect ourselves when we felt threatened. "I don't know."

He pushed his coffee to one side and folded his hands on the table. "I thought about this for a long time before I came over here. I know Jake's your friend and I know you're kind of in love with him, and before you protest," he said in response to my opening mouth and attempted objection, "I think you should hear me out."

"Fine," I muttered.

"I'm not going to bother telling you what she said to me because a lot of it was BS, but I will tell you this. Jake knows she was here, he knows what she did, and whatever it was, he thought it was funny. I know this because one of my buddies was there when Bianca told the story. Emma, Jake's not your friend. I think you should seriously consider getting away from him. He's a first-class asshole. If you need a place to stay, I can help you find one. I know some people you can get in touch with."

He was still talking, but my mind couldn't move on from what he'd already said. Jake knew? Not possible. And even if he did, he wouldn't have laughed, not after everything that had already happened. Jake learned his lesson and wouldn't do that again.

"Who told you this?" I asked, a chill coming over me. I didn't believe him. My reaction took Zach by surprise. Why would I believe him? Because he said so?

"A friend who was there with Bianca and Jake."

"So you weren't there. You're just going to believe someone who was?"

"He wouldn't lie about it. Emma, why are you pissed at me?"

"I'm trying to figure out why you would do this. Do you think if you sway me that I'll sleep with you or something? That you'll be my hero? Sorry, but I don't want to be another notch on your bed post."

His eyes grew wide. "What? Are you kidding me?"

He was good at feigning indignation but I wasn't falling for it. "Is this a game to you? Do you think it's funny? Jake is sorry for what he did and I seriously doubt this friend of yours heard him say anything at all. And I thought you were a good guy, but all you're trying to do is drive me and Jake further apart. Well, I'm not falling for it. I'm not that stupid."

"Wow! I don't know what just happened here. I guess I should have kept my mouth shut and let you continue thinking Jake is some saint. Anyway, I'm done with this conversation. One day you're going to realize I'm right, but for now you can go on hoping that one day Jake will see the light. Good luck with that."

He snatched his coffee and left.

I STEWED ALL DAY AND when my last class finished later that afternoon, I took the bus to the Taylor Tennis club. I'd joined a few weeks before, mostly because it was the closest to the apartment. The courts were well kept and the rates affordable.

I changed and was happy to see it was a quiet afternoon. I needed to get out my frustrations and the ball machine and an empty court were the perfect companions. I hit balls for a while before an older woman, probably in her forties, came and stood alongside my court. Was my time up already? She watched me and I got a bit self-conscious. I hit a few more and stopped despite the machine continuing to spit balls at me.

"Are you next?" I called.

"You have another twenty minutes. I was admiring your forehand. And your backhand, for that matter. You're pretty good."

"Thanks. I can quit now if you want the court," I said, trying to catch my breath.

"I was going to hit balls too. If you want, we could rally or play a mini game. I'm not nearly as good as you, but I'm sure you'll be kind to an old goat like me."

The thought of company didn't appeal to me, but playing against someone other than a ball machine was a nice idea. "Sure, why not."

We pushed the ball machine off our court and rallied for a few minutes which turned into more than an hour. Helen, my partner, was pretty good for her age. She had me all over the court, working up a good sweat and feeling refreshed. We probably would have kept playing if it hadn't been for a group of four waiting for our court.

"You look familiar," she said, as we went into the changing rooms.

"My dad has an antique shop in Pine Falls. Does that ring a bell?"

She shook her head. "No. What's your name?"

"Emma Andrews."

She nodded and smiled. "I remember you now. You were quite good, then all of a sudden you quit. Injury?"

"Sort of. My grandmother died. Tennis was our thing and with her gone, I lost my desire to compete."

"You were damn good. Didn't you reach number one in the state?"

"Number two."

"You should have gone down south to all those fancy academies. I bet you could have gone professional."

"I wasn't that good."

"I think you were. How often do you come here? I'd love to play with you again. It'd be my honor."

A warm, fuzzy feeling came over me. "I go to school full time, but I try to get out here a few days a week. It's hard to pin down times."

"Tell you what, I'll give you my number. Call me when you're coming out and we can play a few sets."

"Sure," I said, taking the card she produced from her gym bag. I took a quick glance at it. She was an accountant.

"Have you ever considered teaching here? They could use some better instructors."

"I already have a job and with school, I wouldn't have the time."

"Just throwing it out there. The club would be lucky to have you."

"Thank you, Helen. For the game too."

We parted ways and I took the bus home and found the apartment empty. Again. I made a quick dinner, did a little homework and went to bed.

ZACH DISAPPEARED FROM the face of the earth. He didn't text or come by Julian's. Each time I made, saw, or sold an éclair, I thought of him. Yes, I'd been too hard on him. I still didn't believe his story, but I was pretty sure he did. I could have called him and tried to patch things up, but I didn't know what to say. And what if I texted him and he didn't reply? All these thoughts went through my mind as I went through the motions at work. It was Friday night and I was closing with Jessica. The crowd was light with everyone off drinking in celebration of the weekend. My weekend plans consisted of a tennis game with Helen and lots of working and studying.

The night was uneventful until about nine forty. Bianca showed up again with Becca and a few friends. This time Jessica was at my side and told me to get some medium sized cups from the stockroom even though we didn't need them.

I hung around back there, hoping to give Jessica enough time to fill their orders. When I returned with the cups, Bianca and her three friends were seated at the booth closest to the door. They were all decked out in bar clothes, complete with miniskirts, stilettos, and enough makeup for a Broadway musical.

My phone trilled a text. I pulled it out and read the text from the unidentified number.

000-000-0000: Too scared to serve us?

How did she get my number? I turned my phone off and put it away. Giggling and loud laughing emerged from their table. I glanced at my watch. In less than ten minutes they'd be kicked out and we could close and go home. Just a few more minutes.

"I'll clean tables and you tidy up the front end," Jessica said. We usually did the reverse, but her kindness was immeasurable. The only problem with this plan was that she left me alone. The second Jessica was at the other end of the shop, Bianca bee-lined for me.

"Why so rude? Don't you reply to texts?" she asked, leaning over the counter with a big smile on her face.

"I'm working. I'm not supposed to text."

"Well, I ordered a medium skinny latte and it's gross," she said, slamming her cup on the counter. Half of it spilled in my direction but missed hitting me.

"I can make you another one," I said with forced calm.

"You should probably clean this mess up first." Her valley girl voice nauseated me.

"Do you want me to make another one or not?"

She squinted her eyes and smiled again. "You really shouldn't be rude to customers. I could tell your boss."

"I'm not being rude. I'm asking you a question. Do you want another one or not?"

"What I want is for you to leave Jake and Zach alone."

I laughed. I couldn't help it. "Seriously? Is that what you came here to tell me? You can have both of them, Bianca."

"And I want you to move out," she said, poking me in the shoulder.

I stepped back. Her touch felt like a tetanus shot. "I'm not moving out."

"Yeah, you are, because Jake is going to tell you to."

"No, he won't."

"If I tell him I'm going to break up with him if he doesn't get rid of you, he will, because, unlike how he feels about you, he actually likes me. And then you will have to take your sorry-ass, nasty self and go back to whatever cave you came from. So save yourself the embarrassment and go away now."

"I'm not going anywhere."

Bianca's face tightened as the frustration mounted, mostly because I wasn't getting upset, at least not outwardly. "Newsflash—you are. I know you think Jake gives a shit about you, but I don't think he'd care if you dropped dead. You're like a rash that won't go away. You're this gross, disgusting boil he wishes he could pop. Why don't you do us all a favor and go kill yourself. Pills work fast and I hear it's painless."

"You're sick."

"No, you're sick. I think you have some serious mental health issues. Everyone who meets you thinks you're some crazy-ass witch.

Do you brew things in your cauldron at night? No, wait, I forgot, you'd rather hang around with your pack of mangy stray dogs. Tell me, did you ever have friends, or were you always pathetic?"

Images and reminders came back to me of when I was a kid. I was in grade one, in a different class from Jake, and a girl named Victoria Parry used to make fun of my clothes and hair. She called me stinky and her friends would laugh and so would the other kids in my class. After that no one wanted to be my friend. At the time, Dad and I were living alone in an apartment because Grandma and Grandpa wanted to teach him to be responsible. Responsible meant not combing my hair before school, or sending me in clean clothes. It wasn't his fault. He was twenty-two with a six-year-old daughter. He didn't have a clue what to do. School lunch consisted of peanut butter and jelly sandwiches and an apple, if he remembered to buy them. Ms. Granger, my teacher, didn't treat me much better than the kids did. Because dad enrolled me late and forgot to buy me school supplies, she always treated me with contempt, like it was my fault. She made me sit at the back of the class even though it was configured in alphabetical order. I hated her because she made me want to cry. At recess and lunch Jake would let me play with his friends, some of whom were in my class, but once we were back in our room, suddenly they forgot to be nice.

My only solace that year came when we had meet-the-teacher night. Ms. Granger took one look at Dad and was putty in his hands. I may have been six years old, but I wasn't stupid. She took Dad under her middle-aged wing, flirted with him like crazy, and lied to him about how much she adored me. Dad asked her why I was sitting at the back of the class, because Dad wasn't stupid either. Ms. Granger claimed it was a mistake and promised to rectify it, which she did the following day. As for the other moms, who were at least five to ten years older than Dad, all chatted with him—even horrible Victoria Parry's mom. They loved him, so why couldn't they love me?

"Uh, freak show, I'm talking to you."

"Why don't you leave me alone?" Now I was upset. She'd broken me and I had to calm myself down.

"I will once you disappear."

"I've already told you that I'm not going anywhere."

I took a nearby rag and cleaned up the mess she'd made hoping she'd shove off, but Bianca kept talking.

"Jake told me how in the fifth grade this guy Justin beat the shit out of you. He said that all these kids watched while Justin kicked and punched you. You know how Jake knows? Because he was watching. Bet you didn't know that. And then after Justin beat you up, you sat on the ground like a loser and wouldn't get up. Jake took off before you saw him because he didn't want to help you. Even then he wanted you to go away. Why can't you take the hint?"

I could barely breathe. He'd told her that story? I'd never told Jake about that. Justin Havers was another person who'd taunted me and he beat me up because I got brave one day and told him to leave me alone.

"He said the worst thing that ever happened to him was when you decided to go to Western. He knew he'd have to let you live with him, that his brother and your dad would make him. It's so strange that your dad and his brother are friends, but then Jake told me you were a mistake. That your horny parents had sex and out came you."

"You better go," I warned.

"Or what? Like I'm scared of you, you stupid bitch. No wonder your mom took off. I would too if you were my kid. You're so gross."

Something came over me, like some demon possessing my body. With one swing, my fist connected with her face. I could hear the crunch of something. Her teeth? She screamed and I took a step back as blood spurted from her nose.

"Oh my God, oh my God!" she kept screaming.

It was all so surreal. Her friends came running from their booth, Jessica dropped her mop and rushed over. People were yelling, maybe at me, I couldn't tell. Bianca, clutching her nose and mouth as blood trickled down her hands, sobbed like I'd handed her a death sentence. My first instinct was to smile, but then I realized how depraved that would look. This wasn't me. I didn't do things like this.

"I'm pressing charges!" Bianca shrieked, spitting out blood at the same time. Tears were streaming down her face and I didn't feel a thing. Not an ounce of remorse. "My parents will sue!"

Jessica grabbed me by the arm. "Go to the stockroom and don't move," she commanded.

I did as I was told and waited. I pulled out my phone, switched it on, and sent Jake a text telling him what I'd done. Then I put my phone back in my pocket and waited.

CHAPTER TEN

ZACH

I was in a deep sleep and jarred by the ringing of my phone. I felt around for it and mumbled a hello.

"Emma's been arrested. I'm not going down there to bail her out. If you don't go, I'll have to call her dad and I know that'd kill her. Not that I really care about her right now."

I rubbed sleep from my eyes. "Who is this?" I grumbled.

"It's Jake," he spat.

Like I was supposed to know it was that asswipe. "What's going on? What are you talking about?"

"Emma attacked Bianca. I'm heading to the emergency room right now. She's going to be fine, but Emma was taken to the police station. I'm trying to talk Bianca out of pressing charges, but she won't listen to me. Look, someone has to go down there, at least to bail Emma out."

"And that's supposed to be me?" When did I become her keeper?

"Well, it's not going to be me. Right now I'm so pissed off, I don't care if I never see her again."

I sat up in bed and tried to absorb everything. "Well, she lives with you."

"No, not anymore. If you can go get her, bring her to a hotel or something, I'll pay for it for a few days, but she's going to have to find another place to live."

"So you're throwing her out? Where do you expect her to go?"

"I don't care where she goes. She can go back home! Are you going to bail her out or not? They took her downtown."

"Why'd you call me?"

"Aren't you her friend?"

I thought of the last time I spoke to her. She was so naïve, but I hadn't wanted to argue with her any further. Either she would eventually come around, or she wouldn't. Only now she'd apparently beaten the shit out of a no-doubt deserving Bianca.

Well, everyone had their limits.

"Fine, I'll go get her. She can stay at my place until she gets things sorted. You know, Jake, you're a real piece of shit."

I hung up before he could say another word. I changed and sent Genie a quick text to let her know of the potential new living arrangements, not that it would matter much to her. I got into my truck and drove the short distance to the precinct. I spoke to the officer on duty. He told me to sit and wait. I texted the asswipe to have Bianca phone me ASAP. She did a few minutes later.

"How are you?" I asked.

"How do you think I am?" she cried. "I've lost a tooth, I have a broken nose and two black eyes. I'm fucking fabulous."

"I'm sorry this happened to you, but I don't want you to press charges." My tone was matter of fact. I didn't want her to think I cared about her face.

"Not you too! No fucking way that bitch is getting off."

I kept the calm approach. "Bianca, it would be in your best interest to drop this. I'm going to guess you did something to provoke Emma, and while that doesn't excuse her actions, I know that you've also done some pretty stupid things in the past. Stuff you wouldn't want dredged up. So I want you to call whichever officer took your statement and tell him you've had an epiphany."

A long silence followed. She knew what I meant. "I really hate you," she seethed, finally. "You better tell her to watch her back. I mean it, Zach."

"Bianca, let it go. It's over. Let's call this even."

"She ruined my face. We aren't even. She crosses me again she won't know what hit her."

The line went dead.

CHAPTER ELEVEN

EMMA

While I regretted what I did to Bianca, I still thought she deserved it as I was hauled away by two less-than-impressed police officers. It was then that I realized I was in some serious trouble. I was booked, fingerprinted, and escorted to a holding cell.

That's when the waterworks started. I sobbed alone, thinking of Dad and Grandpa and what they'd say when they found out. I hadn't called Dad yet. It was nearing three in the morning and I wasn't about to scare him and Grandpa half to death by calling in the middle of the night. I was going to spend a night in jail, like a criminal. I'd have a record that would follow me forever. I'd be unemployable and living with Dad and Grandpa while working the rest of my life at Andrew's Antiques.

Wailing like a two-year-old without her pacifier, I hadn't seen the officer standing in front of me. I hadn't even heard the cell door open.

"Andrews, stop crying," he said somewhat sympathetically.

My chest heaved and I sniffled a few times. The officer shook his head and huffed. "Charges have been dropped. You're free to go."

"What?" Did I hear him right?

"Charges were dropped. You can go home. So, off you go. Collect your belongings and please stay out of trouble."

"She isn't going to press charges?"

"That's what I said. Consider yourself lucky."

"I can't believe it."

"Believe it. You dodged a bullet, young lady."

In a fog I filled out some papers and had my watch, purse, and phone returned to me. I wandered out to the main hallway, checking my phone for messages, and there he was. I nearly walked into him. Why had I even considered the idea that Jake would be the one waiting for me?

"Hi, Zach," I said meekly.

His brown eyes were staring back at me, firing imaginary bullets that hurt as if they were real. His jeans and white shirt looked disheveled, as if he'd dressed in haste. A five-o'clock shadow had already formed on his face.

"Hi, Emma."

"Were you in the neighborhood?" I asked, attempting some bad humor.

He frowned. "This is hardly the time to joke."

My cheeks flushed with shame. "I know."

"You're really lucky, you know that, right? I had to persuade Bianca to drop the charges."

"You did that for me?" I asked. His gesture touched me to the point of tears. He cared, at least a little.

"Yes. Emma, what is wrong with you? Why would you hit her?"

I opened my mouth to protest, but stopped. He was in no mood to listen to my defense. "I don't know. She provoked me and I snapped. Did you talk to Jake? Is he really mad?"

"Yes to both your questions. He's kicking you out and you have until morning to collect your stuff from the apartment. I can take you there now to get your things."

My jaw dropped. My stuff? Kicking me out? This was happening too fast. Where would I go? How would I tell Dad? Seeing the panic on my face, Zach continued.

"You can stay with me until you have things figured out."

My suppressed tears sprang from my eyes. I quickly wiped them away not wanting Zach to see me as more of a mess than I already was. Jake had finally turned his back on me and our lifelong friendship for Bianca. She didn't love him the way I did and now I was out of the apartment, the way she wanted it.

"Emma, don't worry," Zach said, dropping the edge from his voice.

I shook my head. "Jake will never forgive me for this."

"I won't lie; he was pretty pissed off."

We stepped out into the cool early November air. I wrapped my jacket tightly around myself as the remaining tears on my face froze. My feet crunched through the leaves as I followed Zach to his SUV and got inside. We set out for my apartment. Well, my former apartment.

"What did he say?" I finally asked.

"Not much. He told me you punched Bianca in the face and that he was meeting her at the hospital. He was flipping out and told me that he wanted you out of the apartment and that if I didn't help you, no one would."

That summed it up all right. "How did you convince her not to press charges?"

"I asked her not to."

His tone was casual, like he'd asked Bianca for a cigarette. "And it was that easy?"

"Bianca and I have an understanding."

It sounded ominous, but I wasn't about to pursue it. "Jake's never going to speak to me again, is he?"

"Sure he will. Once Bianca dumps him."

"Why can both you and I see that, but not him?"

"He's in love. Sucker."

I stole a glance at Zach. His focus was firmly on the road. "Thanks for helping me. I owe you big time."

"I think you're being unfairly treated."

"No, you feel sorry for me."

He looked over at me. "As much as I don't condone what you did tonight, I'm sorry I wasn't there to see it."

I stifled a giggle. "I shouldn't laugh. My life is going to the shithouse. If I didn't have you, I'd be out on the street. Thanks for giving me a temporary place to stay." Suddenly nothing seemed remotely amusing anymore. "Oh, God. I don't know what I'm going to do. I guess, I mean if I can't find something, I might have to drop out—"

"Hey, don't worry about that right now. You can crash with me for as long as you need. I have a spare room that my sister never uses. So don't even talk about dropping out."

"You'd do that for me?"

"I'd do that for any friend."

"I'll pay rent. I can pay you what I paid Jake."

"Em, my parents own the place, so you don't have to give me, or them, a dime."

"I can't do that. I'll pay utilities and buy food."

"How about you cook? I'll agree to that."

"And I'll buy food."

"Okay, fine, if that will make you happy."

Despite everything that had happened, I finally felt a moment of security. The constant anxiousness, like a snake coiling itself around me, finally loosened a little, but when we reached my apartment block, the suffocation returned. What if Jake was inside? I couldn't deal with a confrontation. Zach switched off the truck and I grabbed his arm. "What if he's up there?" I asked.

"I'm sure he's not. He told me he wouldn't come back tonight."

My heart raced and I felt hot and sweaty. "You're one hundred percent sure?"

"I'm positive."

The muscles in every limb tightened as I climbed out of the truck. We headed to the entrance. I was aching for sleep but functioning on necessity. I used my key and then it hit me. What would

I do with my keys? I turned to Zach and before I opened my mouth, he spoke.

"Leave them with me. I'll give them to Jake."

I nodded and we proceeded to the third floor in silence. It was three thirty in the morning, so what did I expect? We reached apartment 310 and I slipped my key into the lock. We entered the darkness of the apartment and I switched on a light. No one was there.

"Do you just want to pick up what you most need? We can come back later for the rest."

"That's probably a good idea."

I looked around the room. The home I'd known for the last two-and-a-half months immediately felt foreign, like I didn't belong anymore. It was so instantaneous. I wanted to collapse on the sofa and not leave. This was my second home, the place I shared with Jake, and I didn't want to go. Perhaps it was the earliness of the morning and the lack of sleep, or that the events of the night were finally sinking in. I'd hit bottom. I had no one...except a guy I barely knew who for some reason was willing to give me a place to stay. My head was a jumble.

"Do you want me to help or should I wait?" Zach asked.

"I'M JUST GOING TO PACK the essentials. It won't take long."

In less than an hour I'd packed all I needed into my luggage and a duffel bag. Zach took them from me and tossed them in his truck. It was nearing five now and I could barely keep my eyes open for the ten-minute drive. Zach's building was much nicer than mine, but then, he was a senator's son. I followed him down the manicured cobblestone path to the glass double doors. He lived on the top floor and like my building, it was still. It was early Saturday morning. Who needed to be up?

"You can take Genie's room. I don't think she's used it since September," Zach said.

Genie? A girl? "Who's Genie?"

"My sister."

"Where is she staying?"

"Her boyfriend's place mostly. Other times she stays at my parents'."

"Why aren't you there?"

"I wanted to be on my own. If they are going to ship me off to their Ivy League school of choice, I told them I wanted a few years on my own without being under their thumb."

His place put ours to shame. The apartment was modern and spacious, easily twice the size of Jake's place. I would have taken more in, but I was falling asleep on my feet by this point.

"Genie's room is on the left. I'm sure you want to crash."

"I do."

"We'll talk in the morning."

I SLEPT UNTIL NOON and when I awoke to my unfamiliar surroundings, it took a minute for reality to set back in. I wasn't in my own room, but in some foreign bedroom with a double-sized bed, a warm and comfy down duvet, a flat-screen TV on the wall, and a cherry wood dresser complete with a huge mirror and matching nightstand. Zach's sister may have rarely used the room, but she sure had it decked out.

I showered and tried to wash away the night before. I padded into the kitchen to find it empty. I peeked down the hall to see that Zach's bedroom door was still closed. I silently went through the cupboards making mental notes of where he kept everything. The kitchen was bare bones and missing all sorts of small appliances. I'd be retrieving those from Jake's the first chance I got. What Zach did have was all top of the line and expensive, brand names I could only wish to own one day and now had full access to. His stove had more features than a Cadillac, and when I pulled the oven door open, it looked pristine. Either Zach didn't cook or he was the tidiest man I'd ever met.

I found the coffeemaker and some coffee. While it was brewing, I searched through his fridge. There wasn't much to work with. I sprang into action and used what little I had. By the time Zach joined me in the kitchen, I had a hybrid lunch ready to eat. I also had the table set in the dining room.

"Wow! I could really get used to this," he said, stretching and letting out a huge yawn. "What are we eating?"

He hadn't changed from his plaid pajama pants or the wrinkled white T-shirt that hugged his chest just enough to show off the ripped muscles beneath. I had to force myself to stop gawking.

"It's really nothing fancy. I made some open-face sandwiches with sunny-side up eggs, cheddar, and tomatoes, and I lightly sautéed the sliced ham you had. And there's coffee," I added as an afterthought.

"Thanks, Em. You didn't have to."

I was starting to like the way he called me that.

"You grocery shop like my dad, so I'm used to working with limited resources."

Oh, no—Dad. I'd have to call him at some point but I didn't know what I'd tell him. The truth? I couldn't. I put those thoughts aside. I'd deal with it later.

"It all looks delicious."

"It's the least I could do after all you've done for me. I thought I'd pick up some groceries today. Is there something nearby that I can walk or take the bus to?"

He nodded as he tore into breakfast. "There's something close by. I can drive you there or you can take my truck."

"Really? You'd let me? Jake had a huge issue with me taking his car."

"I don't have any particular attachment to my truck, so feel free to use it anytime."

Zach was nonchalant about it, which was such a refreshing change from Jake's constant uptight attitude. "Thanks. I'll use it only when necessary."

"Sure, whatever."

I watched him devour every morsel on his plate. His face now had full-on stubble and it looked good. I could see why every girl at Western wanted to be with him. Simply put, he oozed coolness. The sultry brown eyes, wavy, unkempt dark brown hair, and killer physique didn't hurt either. I didn't know what was wrong with me. He was the total package, and yet my heart broke for a guy who'd thrown me out of our apartment and sided with a she-devil.

"How come you never mentioned your sister?"

"She didn't come up."

"How could she not love living here?"

"Because she loves living with her stupid boyfriend instead. If she needs to sleep here for some reason, we'll figure it out."

I sipped my coffee and watched him grab seconds. My stomach felt full even though it had been so long since I'd eaten. Mostly I was worried that Bianca would still come after me, that I'd be charged with assault. What if she saddled me with her medical bills? Or sued?

"Your face just got ten shades whiter. You feeling all right?"

"What if she sues me?"

He cocked his head. "Sues you? Bianca?"

"She could. I don't have money to defend myself."

He fought hard not to smile. "She's not going to sue you. That's cute."

"What makes you think she won't?"

"I'm clairvoyant."

"This isn't funny," I said, my body going through two emotions at once. Not only were my hands clammy from a possible heart attack, but my cheeks were flushed from feeling silly at the prospect of Bianca's imaginary lawsuit.

"Let's bet on it. I bet she won't sue you. If I lose, I'll pay all your court costs. If I win, you make éclairs one day a week for the next ten years."

I rested my head on the back of the chair and grinned. "So you have something really horrible on her, don't you?"

He pointed to his lips. "These are sealed."

I could see him eyeing my plate so I passed it over.

"You sure?" he asked.

"I've been nibbling," I lied. I traced a finger around the rim of my coffee cup. "How long have you known Bianca?"

"Too long."

"She's a rich kid too."

"You bet. Her family is old money."

"How do you know her?"

"Us rich kids find each other," he said and winked. "A bunch of us hung out in high school. My private boys' school and her private girls' school. We have tons of mutual friends and when we started college, we all still hung out."

"And why don't you like her?"

He chuckled. "She's a vulture. She picks away at your dead flesh and when there's nothing more, she moves on." Zach paused. "Look, Jake is crazy about her, and when she dumps him, and she will, he's going to come slinking back to you, but not for the reasons you want."

I rolled coffee around in my mug. I'd never once told him how I felt about Jake...I'd never told anyone. Was it really that obvious? "I'm not sure what you mean."

"I think you're a funny, smart, and gorgeous girl who can get any guy she wants, but you don't put yourself out there. The problem is that the one guy you do want doesn't want you back. You've got to stop pining for him. Truth be told, he's a loser."

My back went up. "He's not a loser."

"He totally is and he'd be lucky to have a girl like you."

"Are you BSing me to make me feel better?"

"I've dated a lot of Biancas. I really need to be dating more Emmas."

"I think we Emmas would prefer you date only one of us at a time."

Zach rose and grabbed both our plates. "See what I mean? You have a sense of humor. Jake likes drama and high maintenance. I also think he likes a trophy, hence him being a loser."

"He's not a loser," I mumbled.

"Yes, he is," Zach called from the kitchen.

"You should put that superhuman hearing of yours to better use."

Zach ignored me. He came back from the kitchen and grabbed his phone from the coffee table. It buzzed for a second as he fired it back on. He scrolled through his messages and rolled his eyes a few times. "I guess I'm going to be monkey in the middle for a while. Jake wants to know when you're picking up the rest of your stuff. What should I tell the asswipe?"

My heart deflated. Jake was taking this seriously. Not once had he made an attempt to contact me. I'd only checked my phone a million times. "I could go over there later, if you don't mind helping me."

He expertly tapped on his phone and sent a text within seconds.

"I'm going to hit the gym and we can go after that. I'm sure he'll make himself scarce."

"Yeah. I don't think he wants to see me anytime soon."

"I'll check if there's room in storage if you need a place to put your things."

"Honestly, I don't have much other than some appliances. I figure we can use them here."

His phone buzzed and he scanned the text. "He says if we tell him a time, we can go get what's left."

"You pick the time. It's not like I have anywhere to be."

Zach furiously tapped again then tossed his phone back where he found it. "When I get back, we'll go. Remember, I want you to make yourself at home." His gaze was intense and I knew he meant it. Right now, Zach Walker was my only friend in the world.

CHAPTER TWELVE

EMMA

I sent Jake a few texts that went unanswered. I envied the control Bianca had on him. I envied Bianca because Jake loved her so much. I would have killed for him to look at me the way he looked at her. I would have given a limb for him to be with me, hold me, kiss me, and love me.

Those thoughts rambled through my head as I unpacked the occasional thing in between checking my phone. I was actually hoping that in the next few hours Jake would calm down and call, telling me what a horrible misunderstanding it had all been, but the only peep my phone made was a text from Dad. I texted him back, not wanting to call him yet. There was still a chance Jake would see the proverbial light.

Zach returned from his workout and shed his jacket. He hung it in the closet and I noticed again what a clean apartment he kept. Everything was neatly arranged and organized. The furniture was dusted and the hardwood floors polished. He was a rich kid and if I knew anything about kids of privilege, they didn't clean.

"I'm going to grab a quick protein shake and we can head out," he said.

"Sure, no problem. When does the cleaning lady come?" I asked.

"Every other Wednesday morning," he called back.

I smiled. Mystery solved. I followed him into the kitchen. Despite a cleaning lady, he was still neat and tidy. He'd done all the dishes, if you counted loading them haphazardly into a dishwasher.

"It shouldn't take me long. Like I said, I didn't leave much behind."

"It's not like I have anything better planned."

On the short drive reality slowly sank in. Jake wasn't changing his mind. Once again the apartment was empty, but this time, as an added insult, Jake had left some of my items next to the door, including some books I'd loaned him and a personalized pocket knife I'd gotten him for his birthday. I stared at the items, my heart crushing. For Jake to have done this, he was serious. And in the split second it took to get sad, a switch went off making me angry. After all the insults Bianca had hurled my way, and despite his complacency in it all, he still had the nerve to punish me. My cheeks burned and the adrenaline flowed. I wanted out of the there as soon as possible.

I grabbed Zach's arm and pulled him to my bedroom.

"Hey, I'm usually game, but now isn't a good time," he joked.

I wasn't interested in humor. "I want us to be out of here within an hour. Start putting everything in garbage bags. I'm going to pack up my appliances." And that would include the coffeemaker I'd paid for, and the grinder too. Jake could get his own.

Four trips later we had Zach's truck packed up.

"Let me buy dinner," I said. "You pick the place."

"Let's go to Ben's."

"Ben's Burger Barn? Really? I owe you more than that."

"I'm craving burgers."

I smiled. Zach had that effect on me. I felt completely at ease with him, even more so than I did with Jake. Or...used to with Jake. Maybe because I wasn't in a constant state of worrying how he saw me. I didn't need to impress Zach.

Ben's Burgers was quiet for a Sunday evening. We took a booth and I perused the menu. I was starving, having not had a good meal in almost twenty-four hours. I decided to go full force with a cheeseburger and fries, including the gravy. I set down my menu and stole a glance at Zach. He was still a bit of an enigma. Why was he so nice to someone like me? Sure, he'd been friendly from the moment I met him, but based on Becca, I knew the kind of girls he liked and they weren't anything like me. They were knockout beauty queens, not girls who barely wore makeup, didn't fuss over clothes, and actually ate food.

The server came around and took our orders. Zach settled into his seat and fixed his gaze on me. Was this the look he used on all the girls? If so, I could see how it worked. He had me thinking I was the center of his world, and it was flattering. My skin tingled a little and although I wanted to look away, I kept my eyes on his. The difference, though, was that I was immune to his charms.

"So," he said.

"So," I replied.

"I realized today that I don't know a whole lot about you. If I'm going to live with you, I should have more details."

"Like what?"

"You never talk to your mom."

I groaned. "Not her again. You're so obsessed with her."

"I'm trying to wrap my head around this. She never calls?"

"You know how often Halley's Comet comes around? That's how often I hear from Meredith. When I was twelve, she got married and me and Dad were invited. She asked Dad not to tell guests who I was, so they made up a lie that I was her cousin. I felt like she didn't want me around, which was probably true. Her husband knows about me but I don't think anyone else does."

"What about your other grandparents?"

"The last time I saw them was that day. I don't remember them saying hello. Pretty much all I remember is sitting near the back of the church with Dad and wondering why I wasn't part of the wedding. After that I wrote her off. She sends birthday and Christmas presents, but I don't care. You know, she didn't come to a single of my tennis tournaments. She was too busy with her new family. I have two little brothers I've never met."

Zach leaned over the table, engrossed in my not-so-entertaining story. "I still can't believe she walked out."

"She was fifteen when she had me. She didn't want to be tied down. To be honest, neither did my dad. He didn't always get the parent thing because he was so young himself. My first day of kindergarten he had to tell my teacher more than once that he was actually my dad and not my older brother. He'd barely turned twenty and he had a five-year-old. Think of yourself right now. Can you imagine towing around a five-year-old?"

"Sometimes I can barely take care of myself. So what was it like not having a mom around?"

"My grandma was a pretty good substitute. She died two-and-a-half years ago."

"Sorry to hear that."

"She wasn't sick for long, or at least she didn't let on. I miss her a lot."

"And your dad. Did he have a tough time?"

"I don't know. He finished high school, but didn't go to university. I think he may regret that, but he's never said so. He and my grandpa have an antique shop. My dad does a lot of buying and selling online too. He's been successful."

"So if Jake's brother and your dad are best friends, now what happens?"

"I'm not sure. I'm going to call my dad later. I'll have to tell him something."

A thoughtful expression spread across Zach's face. "I've said it before and I'll say it again: I think you should tell the truth."

The truth was that I had a history of telling the truth and it getting me into trouble. When I was eleven I made a good friend. Her name was Leslie and we hung out 24/7. She was the first true friend I'd had besides Jake. Then one day we were sharing a candy bar on one of the schoolyard benches and she told me a secret. She made me vow to keep it to myself, but I couldn't. It was too horrible. I told Dad and a day later I lost my friend. Leslie was pulled from school for a while and when she returned, she never spoke to me again. At the end of sixth grade her mother divorced Leslie's stepdad, moved her and her two little sisters away, and I never heard from them again. While Dad maintained that I'd done the right thing, and today I know what I did was right, it had cost me Leslie.

"I don't want to tell him what I did. It's not like he'll hear about it. I don't want him to know what Jake did either. It's too humiliating and not only that, he'd get so angry and I don't want him to take it out on anyone."

Zach shook his head and rolled his eyes. "Why are you still protecting Jake?"

My cheeks flushed. "I'm not, but I don't want to upset my dad."

"I think your dad deserves to know what kind of person Jake is."

"I'll tell him, but not today." Or tomorrow. I wanted to put if off forever.

The server came around and slapped down our platters. Maggie, the name on her nametag, wasn't friendly, but I understood why. Ben's was a college hangout and students weren't exactly the best tippers.

I attacked my burger like I hadn't seen food in weeks. For a few minutes we ate in silence. People wandered in and Zach gave them a wave. He knew half the school, but then I guess a senator's son was on everyone's radar.

"So about Monday," Zach said, "I wanted to give you some advice."

I put down my nearly finished burger. "Why?"

"Bianca knows a lot of people. I'd keep a low profile."

Concern masked his face and nerves bubbled up in my full stomach. "What's going on? What have you heard?"

"Let's just say that she's connected. I've put out there that she better not seek any retribution. I'd like to think I have more reach and pull than she does, but watch your back. Don't put yourself in a vulnerable position."

I pushed away my plate and wanted to throw up. "Is she coming after me?"

"No, no," he said, his voice light but unconvincing.

"I'm worried. She has tons of friends. Some of them are nasty bitches."

"Don't be worried. I talked to Jake, and the deal was that everyone stays away from each other. Bianca agreed, but I'm not sure I trust her. So the first few weeks we should go to and from school together. If we can't go together, we'll figure out something else until I can be sure this has blown over."

My skin prickled. "I'm freaking out." My voice may have sounded calm and collected, but any second I thought I'd pass out.

"I'm sure they're not going to try anything crazy, but I don't want them to harass you either. If they see you with me they'll back off. So starting Monday, we go to and from school together."

"My own personal bodyguard," I said, trying to sound upbeat.

"And if they bother you, I want to hear about it."

"How long do you think I have to live this way?"

"Not long. Something else will happen and you'll be a memory."

I groaned. "I hate this."

"Next time keep your fists to yourself."

CHAPTER THIRTEEN

EMMA

My last day of freedom before school started. I decided to stay in bed a while before heading to the tennis club to meet Helen. I still hadn't told Dad anything. We spoke after Ben's Burger Barn and I pretended that the world was wonderful and everyone was happy. Today I would try to call Jake and if he didn't answer, I'd leave a message that I had to tell Dad something. If he ignored me, I'd come up with some kind of story.

I heard Zach get up. I could have dragged myself out of bed and offered to make breakfast, but I preferred feeling sorry for myself. I heard him talking to someone on the phone before heading back to his room to take a shower. I read for a bit before pulling myself out of bed and just as I was about to leave my room, there was a knock on the front door. I retreated. Whoever it was, I didn't want to see them.

"You're late," Zach said.

The door was ajar and I could hear the conversation perfectly.

"Slept in. Is she here?" The voice was male, and it dropped to nearly a whisper when I came up in conversation.

"She's sleeping."

"Man, you're crazy. Why are you getting mixed up in all this?"

"Because she's a nice girl and didn't deserve what happened to her."

His friend snorted. "Sure. There's only one reason you'd help her. So have you been in her pants yet?"

"Cut it out."

"Of all the chicks to get a hard-on for, you pick her? Every girl at Western will kneel at your dick, and you find a nutter."

"Stop being an ass. Let's go."

The front door opened and shut. Silence. I sat on my bed and tried to absorb what I'd heard. He didn't confirm or deny it. Could someone like Zach really like me? I shook my head. No, not possible. His stupid friend was right, he could have his pick of any litter, so why would he choose me? The simple answer? He wouldn't. Would he?

I CALLED HELEN AND apologized for standing her up for our tennis match. More lies spewed from me about a friend being rushed to hospital. She bought the story and we settled for a rematch that afternoon. It gave me the opportunity to blow off some steam and forget about Zach's conversation with his friend and my first day back at school after the Bianca affair.

"I was thinking," Helen said, huffing and puffing after an hour of intense rallying. I felt bad making her run all over the court. "The club is holding a tournament in the New Year. I'm looking for a partner for the ladies' division. How about you?"

"Me?" I asked. I pulled my duffel bag from my locker and fished for a change of clothes.

"Yes, you. We could practice a few times this week and I'll do all the paperwork. I'll even pay the entry fee."

I sat on the bench and slid off my sneakers. She was going to a lot of trouble to get me to agree and the thought of playing in a tournament again did sound appealing. "Am I eligible?"

"Of course you are," she said, scoffing at the idea. "I already asked the tournament organizers. The prize money for the winners is a thousand dollars. If we win, I'll give it all to you."

Something wasn't adding up, including her complete inability to stand still. She was like a firecracker about to go off. "I'm guessing there's more to this than entering a tournament."

She sat next to me, scooting in close. "I have to beat Sally Carruthers. Every year she kicks my butt. She finds these amazing partners and wins. No one else has won in years. With you on my team, we can beat that bitch!"

I'd never seen her so animated before, in fact, I'd never heard her curse. "How do you know we'll win?"

"Because there is no one better than you. Together we can wipe the court with her."

The money was attractive, although I would insist on splitting it with Helen. The problem I had was that I wasn't as convinced as she was that we'd win. Helen's tennis game was good, but she was far from great. Her serve had no power or speed, her backhand needed hours of work and at five foot nothing, her forehand wouldn't give a woman my height and strength any trouble at all.

"Prepare yourself for the possibility that we'll lose," I said diplomatically.

"Oh, we will win. You'll make up for my lack of talent."

"It does sound fun. It's a weekend?"

"And some qualifiers."

"I'll do it only if we split the money."

"I don't care about the money. I want the trophy."

"Sign me up then."

"You made my day," she said, shaking with giddiness. She hugged me and skipped to the showers.

Helen was added to the friend column.

I MADE ONE LAST CALL to Jake. He didn't answer. I left my final message telling him that I would be calling my dad that night and I had to tell him something. Within an hour Jake called me back. Hearing his voice for the first time made my heart blip a few beats, but his tone was flat and unforgiving.

"Hello, Emma."

"Hi, Jake. How are you?"

"Good."

"And Bianca?" My voice went into a phony high pitch. Did he pick up on it?

"She's fine."

"Tell her I'm sorry."

"I will."

I took a deep breath in an attempt to calm my nerves. I was alone in my new bedroom and glad that Zach wasn't nearby. He'd see how school-girly nervous I was and he'd hate it. "I haven't told my dad anything. I assume you haven't told Ron either."

"No."

"Zach thinks I should tell Dad the truth."

"I'm sure Zach thinks a lot of things," Jake said bitterly.

"I can't keep lying to him."

Jake let out a deep sarcastic sigh. "I don't want you to tell him the truth."

"I don't want to either, but I can't keep doing this."

"It's not like your dad will figure out we aren't living together anymore. It's not like he visits."

"He hasn't, but he might."

A long silence followed. It gave me time to think about what he said. Why didn't he want me to tell Dad the truth? Was it because he may come off as a jerk? That Dad would be so disappointed and disgusted with him? That Ron might get mad?

"I think you should tell Paul that you have a boyfriend and decided to move in with him."

My jaw dropped and I was at a loss for words. I hated how easily that plan would work, but Dad, and more importantly Grandpa, wouldn't be impressed. And this way Jake would have no blood on his hands.

"Okay." I can't believe how quickly I agreed to it. "I won't tell him right away because he won't believe it."

"Fine, do whatever you want."

"Jake, I am so sorry the way things happened. I hope that we can work it out."

"Emma, I have to go."

With that he hung up. I stared at my phone for a while and wanted to cry. Jake severed ties with me and didn't care one bit.

I sat for a few minutes before putting down my phone and finding Zach in the living room watching hockey. I plopped down next to him.

"How'd it go?" he asked.

"Jake talked to me all of three seconds. He doesn't want me to tell Dad the truth. He wants me to tell him that I met a guy and moved in with him. Presumably you. Not sure my dad will fall for that one."

Zach tore his eyes off the game and scowled at me. "You do realize what he's doing, right? This way he comes off like an angel. I've told you before, tell your dad everything."

"He'll be gutted."

"I think he'll be outraged and proud of the fact you stood up for yourself." He shifted his body to face me. "You want to know what I think the real reason is? If you tell your dad, it officially ends whatever it is you think you have with Jake. That's why you're worried. If Jake is half the guy you think he is, if you tell the truth he'll come around and you'll be friends again."

I hated that Zach was right, but telling Dad now would serve no purpose other than starting trouble. "I know you aren't going to believe me, but I want to tell Dad in person. The last thing I need or want is for him to flip out on Ron. They've been friends their entire lives and I think if I tell Dad face to face, I can keep him calm. I'll go down in a few weeks and tell him."

"And until then?"

"I'm going to pretend that everything here is going along smoothly."

CHAPTER FOURTEEN

EMMA

The first day back at school was a cold one. I wrapped my pink wool scarf tightly around my face and walked, then nearly ran to my building. Zach followed closely behind and when we reached the glass double doors he grasped onto my arm. "We meet back here at three?" His intense stare said it all. Watch my back.

"Is that when the Zach train leaves?" I said for levity.

He smirked. "Yes, so don't be late. This train leaves on time."

I stuck to large crowds. I couldn't believe how paranoid I was. I went to class, ventured to the library, and hit the cafeteria. I made no other stops and saw none of Bianca's crew. Campus was enormous, I had no classes with any of her friends, and the odds of running into them were remote. I trudged back to our meeting spot at three and saw Zach there with a perky blonde. I kept my distance, not wanting to interrupt, but something tugged at me. The way they laughed and how she playfully touched his arm bugged me. If he was possibly into me, why was he flirting with other girls? Reality hit. Because he wasn't into me.

They each pulled out their phones and obviously exchanged numbers. She was blushing now, having scored the number of Zach Walker. There couldn't be another guy on campus who was a bigger catch. They said a few more words and she scampered off. I approached him and pretended that I hadn't seen a thing.

"Hey," he said, a smile still plastered on his face. "How was your day?"

"Exciting," I deadpanned. "How was yours?"

"Not too bad. Ran into Genie. She's coming over for dinner. Hope you don't mind."

"The girl you were talking to? That was your sister?"

His eyebrows furrowed. "No, that was someone from class."

Of course it was. "Oh. Well, I'm looking forward to meeting Genie."

"I thought you'd make some awesome meal to show off your skills."

I was still thinking about the cute blonde and only half-listening to what he was saying. He rambled on some more as we walked back to his truck. When he fell silent, I realized he was waiting for me to say something.

"Well?"

"I missed that last part."

"What time should I tell her to come?"

"Six. We can eat around six-thirty."

He texted her and I got into the truck and sulked. It had been nice to think that Zach had some interest in me other than pity. That dumb friend of his, the one I hadn't even seen and didn't know the name of, had gotten my hopes up that maybe, just maybe, a member of the opposite sex under the age of eighty and over the age of ten found me attractive. I hadn't thought I was interested, but I couldn't deny that Zach was gorgeous, smart, and had an amazing personality. What woman wouldn't want him?

"So what are we having?"

I hadn't even thought about it. I went through my last grocery run. "How about pork Wellington, roasted potatoes and a salad? Is that enough?"

"I'm foaming at the mouth just thinking about it, but Genie won't eat pork."

I know who else was foaming at the mouth. The blonde with his number. "I don't have any other protein. How about a vegetarian lasagna?"

"She'll love that."

We chatted about school until we got back to the apartment. While he stationed himself in front of the television, I got to work. Dinner was pretty simple because I was doing some cheating. I wasn't making the lasagna noodles from scratch, but I did have homemade sauce, and a variety of cheeses to add to it. A little ricotta, mozzarella and asiago for punch. If I'd had more time, I would have attempted a dessert, but after a long day at school and a whole lot of watching my back, my heart just wasn't in it.

Zach dragged himself from sports highlights to set the table as I was putting everything into the oven. I really was looking forward to meeting Genie, the sister I knew so little about. She had a boyfriend that she lived with; beyond that she was a mystery.

The front door swung open suddenly and I nearly jumped out of my skin. A young woman, her thick mane of dark brown hair flowing behind her, breezed in. Her enormous brown eyes fixed on me, and wide smile spread across her face. "You must be Emma," she said.

"Yes. Genie?"

"The one and only."

Zach waved over his shoulder from the position he'd resumed on the sofa. "Hey, Genie."

"It's great to meet you," she said, scooping me into a hug. I was tall, but Genie was easily an inch or two taller. I put her at five foot ten. Good looks apparently ran in the family. The Walker family seemed to be blessed with everything life could offer them. "I've heard so many great things about you," she said, releasing me and hanging her coat.

"You have?"

"Don't be so surprised. You seem so sweet."

Sweet? I'd never been called that before. "Uh, thanks."

"And I hear you're an amazing cook," she said, standing in front of me. She was stunning, but still somehow approachable.

"I like to cook. And thank you for letting me have your room."

She waved it off like it was nothing. "No problem. At least now Zachy isn't all alone."

"Zachy didn't mind being alone," he said.

"Don't listen to him. He loves having you here."

Zach and Genie started catching up on family drama, which I didn't feel comfortable listening to. I checked on my lasagna, then began working on the salad. A few minutes later I had everything on the table ready to eat. Zach and Genie took their seats as I plated food. Genie looked at her plate and whistled.

"This looks delicious. If you eat like this all the time, how to you keep that figure of yours?"

"I have my dad's metabolism."

We all started to eat.

"Emma, this is to die for," Genie said after her first bite. "Where did you learn to cook?"

"My grandma taught me, and I like to find recipes and play around with them."

"I think I might need to come around more often."

"Technically, you do live here," Zach said wryly.

Genie turned her attention back to me. "I hear you had a run-in with Zach's cohorts. You're welcome to hang out with my friends any time."

"Really? I'd like that," I said, feeling a bit giddy.

"There's a reason I never hang out with Zach's friends. They're all idiots."

"Not all of them," Zach said, going for seconds.

"Most of them. Emma, Bianca used to be one of my friends, in middle school, so I know the kind of person she is. You don't know how happy I was to hear you broke her nose."

"I'm not proud of it. It's the first time I've ever hit someone."

"She deserved it, especially after what she did. She's always been a jealous bitch."

My body stiffened. She knew? Zach told her? I didn't want my total humiliation broadcast throughout Minnesota. If Genie knew, how many others knew? My cheeks burned, more out of embarrassment than anger, but I was pissed, too.

Zach shot Genie a look and I saw the pity set in on her face. "Oh, I'm sorry, Emma. Zach told me everything. I haven't told a soul. I promise. My brother and I are tight and neither of us gossip with anyone else, right Zach?"

I wanted to get up, go to my room, and hide under the bed with a box of tissues. I tried so hard to forget all about that day, and here it was, thrown back in my face like a dirty diaper.

"It's okay," I said quietly. I wanted the ground to swallow me whole.

Genie gave me a sympathetic smile. "Look, Bianca didn't say all those things because she actually thought they were true. You're a beautiful girl and for whatever reason, you don't think so and trust me, she knows that. She can smell weakness. From what Zach told me, I'm gathering she's pretty jealous of your friendship with her boyfriend, so she had to knock you down. She probably didn't think you'd see those texts, but it was her way of diminishing you in the eyes of her lame boyfriend. So forget about what she said because it's crap. I see a gorgeous girl with a killer bod who cooks like a Michelin star chef. You're a catch. She's a skank. Right, Zach?"

"Right."

I smiled. "Thanks, guys. You're both fantastic liars."

Genie howled. "Liars! Put yourself out there, Emma, and the men will come. Right, Zach?"

"Right."

"Just don't put yourself out there with any of his friends. They are all Neanderthals. Except my little brother. He's a catch," she said, pinching his cheek.

"She's only eight minutes older than me," Zach said, shooing her hand away.

His statement made my eyes grow wide. "You're twins?"

"I got the looks and the brains and Zach got the jock thing."

"That's cool. To have a twin."

"We gave Mom and Dad a pretty hard time," Genie said, looking over at her brother. "We used to get up to some crazy shit, but once we got to college, that changed, at least for me. I decided to hit the books, while Zach..."

"Had his epiphany this year," Zach said, grabbing another helping.

Genie laughed. "Dad told him if he didn't get his grades up, he'd cut him off."

"You don't get into Harvard with those grades," Zach said, mocking his dad's voice.

"But I'll get into Yale with mine."

I loved their banter, and it was easy to see how much they cared about one another. Growing up I would have killed for a brother or sister. Jake was like a brother except that we didn't have this kind of relationship. Jake made the rules and I followed them. It had always been that way.

"Do you always tease each other like this?"

"Yes," they answered in unison.

"Do you have siblings?" Genie asked.

"Technically I have two little brothers, but I don't see them. My mom has another family."

"Bummer."

Zach's phone went off. He looked at the number, got up and took the call in his room. The blonde?

"A bunch of us are going out this weekend," Genie said. Did she notice I'd momentarily left the conversation, wondering who he was talking to? "Why don't you come? We like to go to Bravo's. Have you been?"

"No. I don't go out much."

"Then it's settled, you're coming out with us. We'll pick you up Saturday night. I'll call you with a time."

Zach returned and resumed his seat. "What did I miss?"

"Emma's coming to Bravo's with us this Saturday. Care to join?"

A hint of a mischievous grin spread on her face as she waited for his answer. He shrugged. "We'll see."

Genie glanced at her watch. "I've got to run. I want to get in a few hours of studying before bed. Emma, thanks again for the wonderful dinner. Zach, I'll see you Saturday."

"I HAVE TO MEET BILLIE, my boss, after school. Would you mind dropping me off before you go home?" I asked Zach on our ride to school the next day.

"You think the axe is coming down?"

"Probably." I'd dreaded returning the call she'd left me Saturday morning. After some telephone tag, she summoned me to Julian's at my earliest convenience. Sure, I could have gone Monday, but I'd had enough to worry about that day, like Bianca and her friends finding me and pummeling me into next week.

"Tell you what, I'll hang out and wait. I have a feeling it won't take long and if it does, I'll get some studying in."

He was taking this whole not-letting-me-out-of-his-sight thing seriously. "Thanks. I'll probably need a shoulder to cry on afterwards."

"Mine is always available."

I sat through classes trying to formulate the perfect speech for Billie and why I should be able to keep my job, but in every scenario, I came up sounding lame. I punched a customer in the face. It was wrong on so many levels. I had to accept that I'd be fired. After my last class I ventured over to our meeting place and found Zach sitting on a bench reading a paperback.

His face lit up when he saw me. He stuffed the book in his bag and we headed for the car.

"Were you waiting long?"

"Not long. I finished my Modern Lit class and have been reading the last couple of hours."

I stopped walking. "The last few hours? When did your classes end?"

"Around noon."

"You've been hanging around for two hours waiting for me?"

"No, I've been reading this damn book. It's called studying," he said and winked.

"Zach, you don't have to wait for me. How many hours a week are you going to do that?"

"An hour here and there. Em, trust me, I need to study as much as I can. If I don't pull out straight As this year, my dad will have my ass."

Jessica, my soon to be ex-co-worker, popped into my head as we started walking again. "Can I ask you something?"

"If it's about *The Sun Also Rises*, I haven't finished it yet."

"Uh, no, smarty pants. I heard a rumor about you and I'm wondering how true it is."

"It's not my baby."

"Cut it out," I said, punching his arm.

"Okay, okay, shoot."

"Someone told me that you have a bit of a party reputation."

"I had a party reputation. All true. There are months I don't even remember. I had a lot of fun but then my parents found out about my less-than-Ivy-League grades so I decided to smarten up. Threatening to pull someone out of school and make him work in a fast-food joint for the rest of his life can really motivate a person."

"I can't see you as a party guy. You're so normal."

"No, I'm sober. A lot of alcohol was consumed and a ton of weed smoked my first two years at Western. Let me put it to you this way: I dropped out of so many classes that I'm a whole year behind. It's going to take me two more years to graduate."

I did a quick calculation in my head. "Wait, you're older than me?"

"I turn twenty-one in May."

"Interesting. And you turned it around just like that?"

"My dad can be a very persuasive guy. His pep talks get straight to the point. Here's the thing, Em. I don't want to live in Minnesota my entire life. I want to see the world. It's not to say I hate it here, because I don't. But I want to travel, start a life somewhere else, do exciting things. I can't do that here. So, if I continued to be stoned and hammered all the time, that pretty much sealed my fate of never getting to leave."

Leaving? He was so adamant about it. "And you don't miss all that fun?" I asked as we reached the car.

"I did at first. I missed hanging out with the guys, and I do catch up with them now and then, but I look back on those days and can't help but think what an idiot I was. And honestly, we only had fun because we were wasted."

His trip down memory lane made me forget about my meeting with Billie, at least until we drove up in front of the building. My heartbeat picked up at the thought of going inside. My first job in the city was about to be no more.

"Get it over with," Zach said. "We'll drink beers after. Sorry, but I don't have any weed."

I laughed nervously. I hopped out of the truck with Zach close behind. We entered Julian's to the familiar sound of the bell above the door. Jessica and some new girl were standing behind the counter. Jessica and I made eye contact and she smiled. At least she seemed to have forgiven me for the scene I'd caused.

"Want a coffee?" Zach asked, stepping into Jessica's empty line.

"No, it will only remind me of what I'm about to lose."

Jessica half-waved. "Hey, Emma," she said, her voice a bit solemn. "How are you?"

"I'm good. I'm here to see Billie."

"I know. Keep your head up high."

"Thanks."

She looked at Zach then back to me. "I'll get her after I finish up your friend's order."

I nodded. Like she didn't know who my friend was.

Zach ordered a plain coffee and Jessica handed it to him before disappearing. "It'll be fine," he said, giving my shoulder a squeeze. "If you need me, I'll be reading Hemingway in the corner." He tilted his head to the side. "That sounds kind of literary. I sound smart for once."

He wandered off and I took in a few deep breaths. How long would this take? Did I try to defend myself? Billie came out from the stockroom with Jessica. Her face, expressionless, motioned for me to come behind the counter. I followed her into her office and she shut the door behind us. My heart was now pounding so hard I could barely hear anything else.

"How are you?" she asked.

"I'm good. And you?"

"Good. I asked you here today to talk about what happened Friday night."

"I know."

"Emma, we can't have employees assaulting patrons. You put Julian's at risk and we could have gotten into some serious trouble. Fortunately, the victim decided not to pursue anything against us. I think you're a great girl—punctual, hardworking—but I can't keep you out on the floor. It would set a bad example."

"I understand," I said, my lip quivering. I wanted to bawl my face off, but that would have to wait until later.

"Jessica told me that this girl has been in here a few times harassing you. Is that true?"

I shuffled my feet. "Yes."

"Jessica also put in a good word for you, but I can't take the risk of this happening again."

"I know. For what it's worth, I'm so sorry, Billie. I don't know what came over me. I've never behaved like that before."

Billie's expression mellowed. "I thought long and hard about this, and while I can't let you work the floor, I can have you in the kitchen baking, if that's something you still want to do. It won't be the same hours, but it's the best I can do. You're the best baker around these parts."

"Really? I'd be happy to keep that part of my job." She'd made my day! Sure, it would be a third of the hours, but it was still a job and some kind of income. Without it I'd have to find another job fast, or ask Dad for money which meant ...

"And when things die down a bit, maybe we can put you back out on the floor. But we'll have to see. No promises."

"Thank you, Billie. You don't know how much this means to me."

"You're welcome. We'll set up a baking schedule. How does that sound?"

"Amazing!"

I wanted to skip out of the office, but had to keep my composure. Billie stayed behind and when I saw Jessica, she pulled me aside into the empty hallway.

"So?"

"She'll keep me on as a baker."

Jessica let out a huge sigh. "I fought for you! That little bitch deserved that punch."

"Thanks for going to bat for me."

"Before you go, what's up with Walker?"

"It's a long story, but my roommate kicked me out and Zach took me in."

Jessica's jaw fell wide open.

"It's not what you think," I said quickly. "He and I are not together. Just roommates."

She gave me a disbelieving look. "Next time you're in I want the full details."

My cheeks got hot and I excused myself, telling her I'd see her soon. I walked over to Zach's table. He was so engrossed in his paperback, he didn't even see me.

"I get to keep my job, well, sort of anyway," I said unable to hide my excitement.

He jumped at hearing my voice, then a wide smile spread across his face. "That's awesome, Em."

"It's baking only, but it's better than nothing."

"Sounds like everyone around here likes you."

We got up to leave and I waved goodbye to Jessica. She waved back and patted her heart a few times. Thankfully Zach didn't see a thing.

CHAPTER FIFTEEN

ZACH

"Man, what the hell has happened to you?"

"What are you talking about?"

We were on our way to a Wild game. Both our parents had season tickets, but tonight we were using my dad's.

Brett kept up his grumbling. "Since this broad moved in with you, I barely see you anymore. What's so special about her? Are you already banging her?"

"Are you for real? You know I have to hit the books this year. That's about the only thing I've been hitting lately."

"And did I mention that you're touchy all the time?"

I sighed. "Look, I'm under tons of pressure. I know you want to go party and have a good time but I can't do that anymore. Sorry if I'm boring."

Brett shrugged. "Yeah, I know. It just seems that ever since this girl came along you don't have time for me anymore."

I wanted to roll my eyes but actually felt a bit sorry for Brett. Not too long ago he and I would party four or five nights a week, now I saw him once a week and that was for workouts. Brett didn't take school quite as seriously as I did. His parents weren't as invested in his future as my parents were in mine. There'd always be a job for Brett in the family business, but Mom and Dad expected me to work for my future and not have it handed to me.

"It's not about her, you know that. When winter break comes you and I will be hanging out every night. I promise."

Brett sulked a bit. "I guess so."

The Wild won the game and we stopped for beers on the way home. We had fun once he stopped razzing me about Emma, and when I got back to the apartment, she was already asleep. I got into bed pleasantly buzzed and scrolled through my texts. I had to stop giving out my number. There must have been twenty or thirty texts from the previous couple of hours, and all from girls I barely knew, except for the five from Genie.

Genie: Emma would be good for you.

That was the first one which came from out of nowhere. Fifteen minutes after that one she'd sent another.

Genie: You like her, don't you?

Then, five minutes later:

Genie: Stop dating trash. You want a good girl, not just a girl good in bed.

Then, about an hour ago:

Genie: Fine, ignore me, but I can tell you have the hots for her. Does she like someone else? Is that the problem? This Jake guy?

Finally, clearly annoyed that I hadn't responded, she'd sent one more.

Genie: No need to reply. I texted her myself. So if she isn't pining for this idiot Jake, what's the problem? She's a great girl, Mom and Dad would love her, she's smart, she can cook, just don't rush her into anything. Take your time. Girls like this don't come along that often. I'm assuming you're coming to Bravo's? That would be a great chance to get to know her better. We can arrange to give you guys some alone time. Do not sleep with her though.

Alone time? I lived with Emma. I had plenty of alone time with her.

Me: Stop texting me!

I loved Genie, but she could be such a nag and I couldn't stand her rambling texts. As for not replying, I'd been with Brett all evening and if I'd dared to pull out my phone, he probably would have tossed it in our pitcher of beer.

I put my phone on the nightstand and closed my eyes. My phone buzzed. Against my better judgment, I grabbed it.

Genie: So you DO like her.

I switched off my phone and fell asleep.

"YOU'LL ALL ALONE."

I looked up from my Politics and Economy textbook to find Heather, a classmate of mine, standing at the opposite side of the table I was occupying in the cafeteria. She had a coffee cup in her hand and her school bag over her shoulder.

"I'm getting in some studying before class," I said, glancing at my watch. There was still about a half hour to go. "You killing time? You can join me."

"I'd like that," she said, flashing a smile. Heather smiled a lot—almost too much. It gave off a phony vibe, but unlike all the other plastic girls I knew, I think she did it mostly out of insecurity.

"I could use a break anyway," I said, drinking the last of my cold coffee.

She sat down across from me. "This class is pretty intense, but I need it for my major."

"I need it for my minor."

"Any big plans this weekend?" she asked, tapping the side of her cup.

"I'm hitting Bravo's with my sister and some of her friends."

"A night out with the girls," she said, giggling and running a hand through her hair. "Is your girlfriend going too?"

"My girlfriend?"

"Yeah, the girl you go home with after school. I noticed you meeting up with her after our class is over."

"Right, that's Emma. She's my roommate."

Both corners of Heather's lips lifted. "I assumed you were dating. It seemed like you were."

"It did? It does?"

"The two of you look like you're together. I don't know how else to describe it."

"We aren't."

The frequency of the tapping on her coffee increased. "Then maybe the two of us could go out sometime. Catch a movie?"

"Sure. I'm focusing on school right now, but we could do that. Later, though."

"Yes, I totally understand. School first." She paused. "A few of us were thinking of doing a study group. You're more than welcome to join us."

"I'd like that. I can use the help."

"Good. I should go. I have to pick up a book from the library before our class. See you in a bit."

I chuckled to myself. She was a sweet girl, but not my type.

CHAPTER SIXTEEN

EMMA

Genie picked out an outfit for me, something I'd normally never wear. She took a simple fitted knit black dress from the closet and flung it at me. The spandex hugged every inch of my body, leaving nothing to the imagination. Yes, I'd pranced around tennis courts wearing less, but that was different. This kind of dress would attract attention I didn't want.

Genie ignored my objections. "You have fabulous legs. I'd kill for those legs."

"Tennis legs."

"Do you even have an ounce of fat on you?"

"But you have curves. I'd kill for those."

"Nah, you've got it all. You look great."

I was having my first girl's night out at the tender age of nineteen. Genie did my makeup, which was kind of fun. I sat on the edge of the bathtub, closed my eyes and let her do her magic. Normally I didn't wear much more than a bit of concealer, some blush, and a tinted lip gloss, but Genie was doing the works. She moved on to my hair and did a messy updo that looked spectacular. I stared at the reflection in the mirror and didn't recognize myself.

"All the guys will go crazy when they see you."

"Do you think?" I asked, twirling in front of the mirror.

"I guarantee it."

I came out of the bedroom and Zach's eyes went wide. "Wow, you look hot."

"Doesn't she?" Genie sounded like a proud mom. "I told her we'd find a guy for her tonight."

"We didn't say that," I said, my skin tingling from the compliment.

"Zach, you still coming with us?" Genie asked, grabbing our coats.

"I better come as the chaperone," he said, still staring.

Zach became our designated driver. We picked up Genie's friends Lucy and Andrea.

"I thought this was a girl's night," Lucy said, climbing in. She was the last stop. "What's Zach doing here?"

"He says he's our DD."

Lucy, the bubblier of the two, pressed her pink glossed lips together and looked over at Andrea with eyebrows raised. Did Zach not normally hang out with them? What was I missing?

"Genie says it's your first time at Bravo's," Andrea said. "The guys party pretty hard, but we've got your back.

"Thanks."

"We never abandon one of our own," Lucy said with a smile.

"But we're all underage. How are we going to get in?"

All eyes fell on Genie.

"So I may have an in, there. Zach and I know all the right people."

"It helps when your dad is a long-serving senator for the great state of Minnesota," Lucy said.

"I never hear any of you complaining," Genie said, playfully punching Lucy in the arm.

The attention turned back to me. "Do you have a boyfriend?" Andrea asked.

"No. Do you?"

"Yes, he's my high school sweetheart," she said, her face beaming. "And before you ask, he totally trusts me. He knows I go out to have fun, nothing else."

"How about you, Lucy?" It was weird. I was asking questions, actually getting to know someone without it sounding awkward and forced.

"I've been dating Eric a few months. We met at a summer camp we both worked at. He goes to Western too."

"And what are you taking at Western?"

"I'm pre-med," Andrea said.

"I'm in civil engineering," Lucy threw in.

These were women I could relate to. They both had aspirations that didn't include landing the right husband or belonging to the best country club.

"This is your first year?" Andrea asked. She had amazing curly red hair that bounced all around her. She could have come out of a shampoo commercial.

"Yes. I'm still not sure what I want to major in."

"You have a few more months to decide," Lucy said. "Until then, just enjoy yourself."

I was a part of something. Genie and her friends seemed to like me. By the time we got to the club, Jake, Bianca, and everything else that had happened the past few months were the furthest thing from my mind.

Our first stop once inside the crowded club was the bar. The noise was so loud we had to yell at each other.

"What do you like to drink?" Genie asked.

"I don't know. I'm not much of a drinker. Surprise me."

She ordered me something fruity with a kick. It tasted pretty good.

"Pace yourself," Zach warned. "You may not notice right away, but those drinks pack a punch."

A few drinks in it was time to dance. A little liquid courage went a long way. Lucy, Genie, Andrea, and I danced up a storm. After a while some random guy jumped in, dancing with us and asked my name.

"She's got a boyfriend," Genie said before I could answer. "So bugger off."

"He was kind of cute," I said once he'd found other girls to dance with.

"He's bad news. He's always here flirting with the cute girls. Trust me, you don't want anything to do with him."

We danced some more and when I looked around for Zach, who'd already met up with a bunch of friends and seemed to know half the crowd, he was standing near the bar where we'd left him, cradling a soda and chatting with the blonde from school. She was here? How did she know we'd be here ... unless he'd invited her? Did he like her that much? The drinks started bubbling up in my stomach.

"Let's get another round," Andrea suggested.

I wasn't sure I could handle another drink, but before I knew it, we were back at the bar, a few feet from Zach and the blonde, and Lucy was ordering drinks.

"Who's the girl?" I asked Genie.

She looked over at Zach and his friend. "I don't know. I've never seen her before. Zach's a chick magnet. He walks into a room and all the girls are ready to hop into bed with him."

I watched them some more. He was so fixated on her that if someone shouted fire, I'm not sure he'd notice. He leaned over and whispered in her ear. A huge smile spread across her face and she nodded.

"Drink up," Lucy said, thrusting the drink in my hand. "The night is young."

I did. And then I kept drinking. I lost count and became the drunk girl, the girl I loathed. Zach and Genie helped me to the car at the end of the night. My head was spinning and my stomach was ready to heave at any moment.

"Please don't throw up in the car," Zach said.

I nodded, too afraid that if I opened my mouth, I'd hurl. We dropped Lucy and Andrea at their dorm and Genie at her place. She was going to pick her car up later.

"Zach, you can handle this?" Genie asked.

"I'll be fine."

"And don't take advantage of her!" she added with a laugh.

By now I was lying flat out on the backseat, clutching my stomach and moaning in discomfort.

"You're a lightweight," Zach said when we got to the apartment. He opened the door and helped me to my feet.

"They tasted good."

"I warned you."

"I know."

A few seconds passed. "Who was the blonde you were talking to earlier?"

"Heather? She's in my Poly Sci class."

"You like her?"

"She's nice. Why do you ask?"

"You talk to her a lot."

"I do? I didn't notice."

"She wants to have sex with you." Oh. Had I said that or just thought it?

"Yup, you're drunk."

Crap. I'd said it. "She was undressing you with her eyes." My lips were moving before my brain had time to stop them.

"Really drunk."

"Don't you want to meet someone nice? Why do you chase after all these vacuous girls? Don't you want something meaningful?"

This coming from someone who couldn't stand straight. I stumbled along to the lobby with Zach propping me up.

"Sure I do."

"No, you don't," I slurred. "You want the Biancas, Beccas, and Heathers of the world."

"No, I've never wanted the Biancas of the world."

"I'm dizzy."

"And drunk."

I leaned up against him in the elevator and when we reached the apartment, he poured me some water.

"You should probably eat something too. It will help with the hangover."

I waved him away and took only a few sips of water. "I need to go to sleep."

I staggered to my room and collapsed onto the bed. I closed my eyes and was out within seconds.

A FEW HOURS LATER I raced for the bathroom. I made it just in time to throw up what little was in my stomach. My throat burned from alcohol and bile. My eyes teared as I slumped to the floor. I looked down and realized I was still wearing the black dress. I must have looked a mess.

Zach appeared in the doorway, shirtless and wearing pajama bottoms. I couldn't help but stare at his chest. It was there on display, all muscular with a light sprinkling of chest hair, begging to have my hands run through it. I shook my head and let out a groan. What was wrong with me?

"You are a train wreck."

I nodded.

He pulled a washcloth from a drawer and ran some water. He handed it to me and it felt cold but refreshing against my cheek.

"Do you want me to get you something?"

"A cure for this hangover would be nice."

"How about some water? Or I could make scrambled eggs or something."

"No food. The thought of food makes me want to throw up again."

"I'll get the water."

He left and I closed my eyes and put the cloth completely over my face. If I hadn't changed, I hadn't washed my face either. My makeup was probably all over the place. I was worse than a train wreck.

Zach returned and sat next to me, handing me the glass of water. I took a few gulps and put it down. I leaned my head against his hard, bare shoulder. The action was involuntary and I liked it. I didn't touch people much, and I made sure my hands didn't leave my side. He smelled heavenly, a mixture of cedar wood, bergamot, and sandalwood.

"I'm never doing that again."

"You were funny."

"I have never felt this crappy in my life."

"Well, tomorrow will suck too. Then you'll start feeling better."

I closed my eyes and took in the moment. It was nice despite the circumstances. "Thanks for the water."

"You're welcome."

"Thanks for everything. I'm not sure what I would have done without you."

"Pay it forward some day."

"I will."

"Should we get you back into bed? I think you could use the rest." He helped me to my feet and to my room. "Goodnight, Em. Sweet dreams."

I BARELY RECOGNIZED the face staring back at me the next morning. Black mascara and eye shadow ringed my eyes and my hair was matted on one side. The pounding headache didn't help matters.

I took a long, hot shower, letting the water pound against my skin. Despite how awful I felt now, the night before had been one of the best of my life. The only thing that came close was finally beating Melanie Peters in a three-set marathon to win my only title against her. And while the satisfaction of beating her was euphoric, this was entirely different. I had fun. I hadn't wanted the night to end. I met two new people who liked me, who wanted to hang out with me, and I owed it all to Zach and Genie.

I dragged myself out of the shower and got dressed in my most comfortable yoga pants and oversized t-shirt. It was almost noon, and I was dying for some good old-fashioned bacon and eggs.

I found the kitchen empty. I put on a pot of coffee, pulled out a medium frying pan then grabbed the eggs and bacon from the fridge. I sliced a few tomatoes and seasoned them with a bit of salt and pepper. They went onto a baking sheet while the oven heated. I peeled and cubed a few potatoes and seasoned them with oregano, basil, salt, pepper, and a hint of spicy paprika. I tossed them around in warmed coconut oil and threw them into the hot frying pan. They'd have to cook for a bit before I tackled the bacon and eggs.

Zach appeared and pulled a chair up to the opposite side of the counter and watched me work. He had a shirt on this time.

"Coffee?" I asked.

"You bet. You look chipper this morning. No hangover?"

"Nothing some Aspirin can't fix," I said, pouring coffee in his favorite South Park mug.

"I'm starving. What are we having?"

I relayed the menu as he hopped off the chair and grabbed some plates and cutlery. I finished up our breakfast and we dug in.

"I think I've gained ten pounds since you moved in."

I highly doubted that. "I do make healthy food," I said. "Except for this breakfast."

He chowed down on his sunny-side up eggs, the way he liked them, and I thought about all he'd done for me. Without him I would have never met Genie and her friends—all of whom accepted me. But most of all I had Zach himself in my life. I owed him so much and other than some home-cooked meals, what did he have to gain?

That's when I felt it. A little tickle in my heart and it made me gasp. I'd only ever felt that once before ... and look how that turned out.

Zach looked up from his plate and caught my stare. "What's up? Something on my face?"

"No," I said, darting my gaze away. Were my cheeks flushing? I grabbed my coffee cup to hide my face just in case.

He smiled, that killer smile that made every girl trip all over her feet. And then I thought of the blonde. Heather. I hated my mind sometimes, and how quickly it could take a beautiful moment and crush it into tiny jagged, tear-your-skin pieces.

"For someone who was so wasted last night, you throw together an amazing breakfast."

"Thanks."

"Genie and her friends liked you."

A shy smile spread across my face. "Really?"

"I wouldn't tell you if it wasn't true."

"They weren't feeling sorry for me, were they? Do they know about the whole Bianca thing?"

"They don't know about it. Besides, our campus is huge. Not everyone knows Queen Bianca."

"I hope they invite me out again."

"I'm sure they will."

Yes, life was definitely on the upswing as long as I kept myself in check.

CHAPTER SEVENTEEN

ZACH

I had a couple of hours between classes and met Brett at the gym. We had an upper body workout planned. He was already waiting and chatting up a brunette at the free weights. The guy was clueless when it came to girls. He had a way of striking out every time. He wasn't a bad-looking guy, average height, sense of humor, but the second he opened his mouth, crap came flying out. I gave the guy advice, but not once did he take it.

The brunette saw me coming and her green eyes locked on me. Shit, Brett would be pissed. I nodded to her, trying to act disinterested at the same time. Brett followed her stare and when he saw me, he frowned. Double shit. The girl said a few more words and wandered off, but not before giving me a pouty smile.

"Really? Wear a fucking bag over your head next time. I almost had her."

Right. "Sorry. Must be my magnetism."

"Shove it!"

We got to work. I only had an hour before I had to meet Genie. I promised to have a quick lunch with her before my Economics class. There was an urgency to her text, like she had something important to tell me. If she was pregnant, Mom and Dad would kill her.

"How was your night out with the girls?" Brett asked, his tone mocking.

"Jealous that I got to spend my Saturday night with four beautiful ladies?"

He let out a huff. "Wanna invite me next time? I'd tap Andrea or Lucy."

And that's exactly why I didn't invite him. "Haven't they already shot you down a million times?"

"I figure if I wear them down, they'll submit to my charms."

"What charms?"

He gave me the finger.

We did some reps and took a short break. I loved the burn, it made me feel like I was accomplishing something.

"And Emma? Man, I can't believe I just asked about her."

I bristled. "Then why did you ask?"

"Curious, I guess. Like watching a car crash."

I took a swig of water, carefully formulating my thoughts. If I sounded too pissed off, he'd get on my case. Treading carefully was the right approach. "Look Brett, you want to be on Team Bianca, I don't give a shit. Go shove your nose up her ass. Makes no difference to me. But leave Emma out of it. She's a nice girl and doesn't deserve all this shit from you guys. I've said it before and I'll say it again: what has she ever done to you?"

Brett took a step back and looked up at me. I was easily four inches taller than him. He narrowed his eyes and crossed his arms over his chest. So much for treading carefully. "What is it about this girl?" he asked. "I don't get it. It's like she's got you by the balls."

Brett had been my best friend since forever, and we were tight, but for some reason I knew I needed to be on guard. "I see things in her that you don't. It's that simple."

"So you want to do her?"

His face was twisted in confusion and disbelief. He seemed so lost. I felt like his Dad trying to explain why his favorite hockey team had to trade their star away. He couldn't grasp the concept that not everything was about sex. "She was down-and-out. She had no one."

"So you feel sorry for her?"

"No, I just ... I needed to help. I can't explain it."

A flash of understanding came over him. "You're always picking up strays, you know that? Sometimes you gotta walk away. You can't be the good guy all the time."

"Why not?"

"You want to be lawyer or a politician some day? You have to be cutthroat. You won't be able to hide stray dogs in your basement, hand money to bums on the street, or give the clothes off your back to some homeless guy. And you especially won't be able to let random sketchy chicks crash at your apartment."

Yes, I'd done every one of those things and never regretted any of them. That's what made me different from Brett and most of our other friends. When I handed the homeless guy my wool Burberry scarf and leather gloves on a bitterly cold January night, I didn't think twice, not even when my hands froze so bad I wanted to cry from the stinging pain.

The dog reference had been about the shepherd mix Mom discovered cowering in our laundry room. I can still remember her yelling my name across the house. I knew I'd been discovered and reported to her immediately.

"Why is there a dog in our basement?" she asked.

I explained how I'd seen it for a couple of weeks wandering the soccer field at my middle school. Kids had been throwing things at it and chasing it away while I'd been secretly sharing my lunch with it. One day a kid threw a rock so hard the dog yelped. It made me so angry that I picked up a rock and hurled it at the kid, hitting him hard in the chest. He cried like the spoiled piece of shit he was. A hush fell over the field where we'd all been playing around, kicking soccer balls. Even the dog had stopped whimpering. All eyes were glued on me.

"Any of you hurt this dog again, I'll fucking kill you."

I was thirteen, and that's the day I decided not to care what anyone else thought of me. Apparently, that's also the day I became cool, the "it" kid for more than just my dad being a senator.

So I told Mom all this. A part of me was frightened that'd she'd kick the dog out, or worse, bring her to the vet to be put to sleep. Instead she took me to the pet store and made me buy a leash and collar from my allowance. We then took the dog to the vet. Other than some worms and a little malnutrition, she was healthy. Mom then made me post signs around the neighborhood in case her owners were looking for her. After two weeks, she and Dad called me into the living room. I sat on the sofa with Mitzy by my side. Yeah, I was stupid and named her.

"What are we going to do about the dog?" Mom asked.

"I dunno," I said, my voice quiet and sullen. I'd grown so close to her and the thought of giving her up killed me. She slept with me at night, on the bed, even though she wasn't supposed to. I couldn't let her go.

"Well, this is what's going to happen. You're going to take her for walks before and after school, you're going to feed her and take her out at night before bed. If she makes any messes, you are going to clean them up. Is that clear?"

I thought I'd explode with excitement. "Yes, I'll do all that!"

"And don't bring anymore dogs home," Dad added.

Mitzy died last summer. The vet said she had bone cancer. I was so grateful to have her for six years. Man, I loved that dog.

"I'm not sure why any of those things are bad," I said, picking up a pair of thirty-pound dumbbells.

"I'm just saying that you can't always be the saint. One day someone is going to fuck you over."

"Thanks for the sound advice."

"If this girl goes psycho and cuts your throat in the middle of the night and you bleed to death, don't come crying to me."

"I won't. I'll be dead."

"Smartass."

We finished up our workout, and I took a quick shower before meeting up with Genie at the coffee shop in her building. She had secured a table and was tapping furiously on her phone. I sat across from her and she didn't look up.

"Hey, loser," she said.

"What's up? Why the ominous text?"

"Talked to Mom this morning. They are having their Christmas party at the beginning of the month and I thought you should know."

"You could have put that in a text."

She put her phone down with a thud and let out a sigh. "Here's the thing; I want to bring Steve and she said no."

"No surprise there."

"I thought you could talk to her."

"Me? No way. Why would I want to jump through that minefield?"

"Because you're my brother and Mom's favorite."

"And you're Daddy's little girl."

"Not when it comes to Steve."

It was no secret we all just barely tolerated Steve. He was a bolded capital 'C' conservative, but that wasn't the problem. It was that he enjoyed butting heads with Dad on the rare occasions Genie brought him around. He was also the reason Mom and Dad still thought that Genie lived with me. If they had any idea she was spending every night at his place, they'd blow a gasket. The last time Steve had graced us with his presence, he'd gone on a rant about gun control that nearly sent Dad into orbit.

"Sorry, Genie, I'm not touching this one."

She frowned and tried her puppy dog eyes on me. "If you do it, I'll owe you big time. I know you can sway Mom."

"Maybe, but I can't sway Dad."

"Okay," she said, folding her hands together, "let's negotiate. What do you want in return?"

"There's nothing you can offer that will persuade me to stick my neck out for you on this."

"I'll do all photo-ops with Dad."

"I'm sure he won't want you in pictures if you're associated with a righty like Steve."

"I'll do all the campaign work for the next three months."

Her desperation had hit rock bottom. "It's a losing battle. They won't come around."

Her face lit up like some imaginary light bulb had gone off. "I'll help you with Emma."

"Help me? What are you talking about?"

She leaned in close. "Are we going to play this game? You like her."

"She's a great girl."

"No, like her in the biblical sense."

I grimaced. "Did you just say that?"

"I think she likes you back. The way she stares at you. She wants you. And the way you look at her. Don't even try to deny it."

"She's in love with Jake."

"Ah ha! You admit it," she said, pointing her finger at me. "I knew it! You talk to Mom and Dad and I'll talk to Emma."

"And that would be a *no*," I said, laughing and shaking my head.

"You worried Mom and Dad won't like her? I told you they would."

"No. What I'm worried about is all this shit you just made up."

She tapped her fingers on the table and I knew her mind was working overtime. "You're afraid of two things. One, she doesn't like you back, and two, you'll actually stick it out with her which might lead to some kind of serious relationship. Let me give you some sisterly woman advice: she does like you back and you'd be lucky to have her in your life for as long as she can put up with you."

"Wow, thanks for all the unsolicited advice. Anything else? I've got class in fifteen minutes."

"Please talk to Mom and Dad." All the kidding around was replaced with sincerity. She needed me.

"I'll make one try. Don't expect any miracles."

I got up to leave and she grabbed onto my arm. "I think you should invite Emma to the party. I mean that."

"I'll see."

"She's a good one, but I think you already know that."

CHAPTER EIGHTEEN

EMMA

Another week went by and I hadn't told Dad a thing. He still thought Jake and I were living together and neither of us had done anything to clear it up. In fact, I had heard little from Jake other than the occasional text to remind me to cover up our lies. How much longer could we keep this going on? With only a few more weeks until Christmas break, would we just avoid each other? And how would I get home? Dad and Uncle Ron would know something was up if we didn't arrive together. All these thoughts funneled through my head while I waited for Zach. It was Friday and I was looking forward to the weekend.

Then I spotted him. He was twenty feet away, chatting with Heather again. Every time I saw them, they were laughing, and twice she touched his arm. My first instinct was to walk over there and barge in on their conversation, but then I realized how crazy that would look. It's not like he belonged to me. So I waited, irritated that they were taking so long. What was so interesting? Couldn't they talk later? The longer they talked, the more it picked away at me and then it hit me. Was I jealous? No, not possible. Besides, what was there to be jealous of?

Finally she waved goodbye, a huge smile imprinted on her face. Zach caught sight of me and jogged over.

"Ready?" he asked.

"Yup."

He didn't say a word about Heather on our walk across the parking lot to his truck.

"You should just date her," I said.

"Date who? Heather?"

Really? Did he think I was that stupid? "Yes, Heather."

"Why would I date her?"

"You talk to her all the time and she likes to touch you. I think she wants to go out with you."

"Wow, that's a lot to digest. But what if I don't want to date her?"

"Then you should tell her. You shouldn't lead her on."

He chuckled. "It's sweet that you're being such an advocate for her."

"Are you making fun of me?"

"Not at all. I think it's adorable that you care so much about Heather and her feelings."

"So you are." I was officially annoyed.

"To make you feel better, I'll call her tonight and ask her if she wants to marry me."

I wanted to punch him really hard in the arm. He glanced over at me and laughed.

"You aren't funny," I said.

"If you could see your face right now, you'd laugh."

"No, I wouldn't."

"Look, if I wanted to date her, I would. If she thinks I'm leading her on, too bad for her."

"Maybe she doesn't know because you keep talking to her."

"Then she's pretty dense. When I like a girl, she knows."

"You might want to tell her," I mumbled.

"Sure, Miss Lonelyhearts."

We got back to the apartment to find Genie there. She was watching television and leapt to her feet and followed Zach into the kitchen. He got himself a beer and jumped when he found Genie right behind him.

"Did you talk to them?" she asked.

"You only asked me the other day. I'll call tomorrow."

"Ask what?" I decided to stick my nose into the conversation.

"It's less than three weeks away. I know you think it's a long time, but it's not. Especially if they say no to you. It doesn't give me a lot of time to work on them."

"Ask what?"

"You're setting yourself up for major disappointment. Why do you want him there anyway? He's not good for Dad's image. And you can't even control him," Zach said, peeling the tab on his beer. He tried to sidestep Genie, but she wasn't moving.

"He promised to be on his best behavior."

"And the minute someone brings up something he disagrees with? You know he can't help himself."

Zach successfully got around the Genie blockade but she followed him as he collapsed onto the sofa. He had the remote in hand and tuned into ESPN. The highlights were old, but he didn't care. He took a few swigs of beer and tried to ignore his sister.

"He knows how important it is for Mom and Dad to like him."

Zach rolled his eyes. "Fine, delude yourself. I'll talk to them tomorrow."

"About what?"

They both looked at me like I'd just materialized. Genie flew from the sofa and grasped onto my hand. "There's this fundraiser my parents have every year. It's also their Christmas party. I want to bring my boyfriend, but his political views are a bit different from Mom and Dad's."

"A bit different? Try radically different," Zach added.

"To make a long story short, my parents don't like him all that much, so Zach said he'd ask them if I could bring Steve. In return, I told Zach I'd help him out with something. Right, Zach?"

She shot Zach a knowing look. Whatever it was, it appeared to be none of my business.

"And I told Genie that I didn't need any help."

I had no idea what they were talking about.

"Anyway, he's going to ask tomorrow. And I'm sure he'll get the desired results."

"Genie's a dreamer."

She turned back to me. "Emma, would you like to come to the party?"

"Me?" The question took me aback. I was never invited to anything, especially a fancy party.

"Yes, of course you. You could go as Zach's guest."

This all felt a bit awkward. Zach hadn't invited me, so how could I go as his guest? "I don't know. I don't have anything to wear."

"I can loan you something."

I kept looking over at Zach, but his full attention was on the TV. Had he invited me as his guest, I would have accepted, but Genie asking didn't feel right, like she was making him do it and I didn't want him to feel obligated. "I don't think so." My voice dropped off and sounded pathetic, like I was feeling sorry for myself. I hated that I'd done that. I didn't want Zach thinking I'd guilted him into an invitation.

"Why not? We'd have lots of fun."

"You don't have to invite me," I said to Genie. "Zach should ask someone he really wants to the party."

"Oh, I see," she said. She hopped over to Zach and slapped him on the arm. "Ask Emma to the party."

"Hey, what'd you do that for?" he said, massaging the spot.

"Well, ask her."

"No, no, Zach, you don't have to," I protested.

"Yes, he does and he wants to."

I hated that she put him on the spot and now I was on the spot, too. "I can't go anyway," I said, even though I had no idea when the party was. "I'm sure I'll be going back to Pine Falls if it's end of term, and if it isn't, I'll still be going home. I've got some studying to do, so I'll leave you guys to figure this out."

I slunk to my room. It was clear Zach wanted someone like Heather on his arm and not someone like me.

I DECIDED TO DO LAUNDRY the next morning. Zach's door was shut, and I knew he'd been out late with his friends. Genie had stayed for dinner and while we chatted, I was a bit reserved. I didn't intentionally do it, but I was a bit down. I tried to keep up with the conversation, but secretly I wanted him to hurry up and go out with his friends and for Genie to go home so I could hole myself up in my room and have my own personal pity party followed by a little Jane Austen.

Instead of going back to the apartment, I sat in the laundry room and read a book. Oddly, I found the thumping of the washing machine soothing. Maybe it reminded me of tennis balls hitting the hard court? Other tenants came in and out to use other machines, but my fantasy novel was far more interesting than any of them.

When I got back to the apartment, Zach was back in front of the television watching sports highlights again. At least these ones were new. He was hunched over, coffee in hand, his hair a little disheveled from sleep.

I put the laundry basket in my room and went to the kitchen. I was starving.

"Are you hungry?" I asked.

"Famished. What are we having?" he asked without diverting his attention.

"Pancakes?"

"Love pancakes."

I made them from scratch and decided to add blueberries. I pulled out a pan and got to work. Ten minutes later we were eating while he read the newspaper. I thought about my day. I'd study the rest of the morning and then meet Helen at the tennis club. I couldn't wait to smash some balls and whip her into shape. The evening consisted of my boring history paper.

"About my parents' Christmas party," Zach said, putting down the paper, "now that my sister is gone, I'd like to invite you as my guest." Nothing in his tone sounded the least bit sincere. It was like he'd rehearsed it a million times trying to make it sound as natural as possible.

"I think you should invite someone else."

"Why?"

"I don't want you to think you have to ask me. It's okay, my feelings won't be hurt."

He rubbed the back of his neck. "Look, I was going to invite you anyway, but Genie brought it up before I could. I do want you there and I think you'd have a great time."

"I think you should ask Heather."

"Oh my God, Heather again? I think *you* should date Heather. You're so obsessed with her."

"I still think you like her."

"Why do you think that?"

"You're nice to her. You laugh at everything she says. And she's pretty."

"Based on that criteria, I'd like half the girls on campus. I don't have time to date them all."

I used my fork to swirl around the remaining maple syrup on my plate. "I don't want to be your mercy date for the evening."

I looked up and his gaze was fixed on my face. "Em, I asked you because I think we'd have a great time together. By the way, I don't do mercy dates, whatever the hell that is."

"You aren't just saying that, are you?"

"No, I promise. I really, really, really want you to come."

I shrugged. "Okay, when is it?"

"December second. You can stay the night in case it goes late. My parents have a million extra bedrooms. You can go home the next day."

"All right."

He smiled. "We'll have a blast.

CHAPTER NINETEEN

EMMA

The end of term came and except for a few easy exams, I was free of school. My worry now was the Walker Christmas party. Genie had convinced me to spend an extra day at her parents' home before the big party. We'd go Friday night, have a spa day Saturday, and then attend the Walker Christmas party that night before I grabbed my things and took the bus home on Sunday.

And on the subject of getting home, Dad was highly suspicious. He asked a hundred different ways why I wasn't going home with Jake. That prompted me to send Jake a text, our first correspondence since Thanksgiving, when he'd decided to spend it with Bianca and not return to Pine Falls. We had to come up with something, otherwise all I had left was the truth.

As I packed the last of my things for the weekend at the Walkers', my phone rang Jake's familiar bullhorn tune. I stared at my screen, Jake's name popping up. My hand shook. Why was I so nervous?

"Hello," I said.

"Hi, Emma, I got your text. Instead of texting back and forth, I figured I'd just call. It's quicker that way."

"Well, you read my text so you see the dilemma."

"Tell your Dad that I'm staying through my exams and that's why I'm not coming home right away."

I knew he wanted to rush me off the phone, but I wanted to talk. I loved hearing his voice again even though it had an edge to it, like I'd been bothering him from something really wonderful like a hot steamy bath with horrible Bianca.

"You know that Dad is going to ask me more questions when I get home. I'm going to have to tell him something soon."

Jake cleared his throat. "Haven't we already been through this? You said you'd tell him Zach is your boyfriend and you moved in with him."

His words hit me like a hammer. "I never agreed to that. And Dad won't believe it anyway."

"Then you need to convince him. I think he needs to know you're living with Zach now." I could hear bitterness. Was he mad that I was living with Zach, or did he just dislike Zach in general? I couldn't read him.

"I don't like that idea at all."

"It has elements of truth to it."

He was so smug and it pissed me off. The old me, the girl from six months ago, long before the cabin incident, would have gone along with Jake's BS, but in those short few months I'd grown up a lot, and my epic punch to Bianca's face had a lot to do with it.

"Why should I protect you?"

"Excuse me?"

"You heard me. Why should I protect you? In your scenario you and Bianca come off unscathed while I have to explain to Dad why I not only didn't tell him about my imaginary boyfriend, but now I've moved in with said imaginary boyfriend. How does that work? Maybe I should just tell Dad everything, right down to all those nasty texts."

Jake let out a huff. "Yeah, why don't you tell Paul the truth? Tell him how you ruined my girlfriend's face by breaking her nose and knocking out her teeth. I'm sure he'd be really impressed."

"If he knew what kind of bitch she was, he might be."

"You know what, do what you want! Sounds like Zach has been a great influence on you. Does he feed you what to say?"

"What are you talking about?"

"This isn't you, Emma. It's not you talking. You go ahead and let Zach manipulate you because I don't give a shit. Goodbye."

He hung up and I slammed the phone down on the nightstand. I wanted to throw it against the wall, but the phone didn't deserve the abuse.

"I didn't mean to eavesdrop, but that was awesome."

I jumped at hearing Zach's voice. "I didn't know you were there."

"I heard you talking and I figured it was to Genie. Now I'm guessing it was the asswipe."

I plopped down on the bed and air-punched an invisible Jake. "He really wants me to go with this lie about moving in with a new boyfriend. That way he comes off smelling like roses."

"I still think the truth is a better option."

"I'd rather not think about it and focus on this weekend instead."

"I'm waiting for Genie to call and then we'll go pick her up. Speaking of lying, don't mention that Genie is living with Steve."

"This web of lies..."

I zipped up my overnight bag and set it near the front door. Zach was on the phone with Genie and he gave me the thumbs up that we were ready to go. When we pulled up at Steve's, my jaw dropped at the assortment of designer bags and luggage on the curb.

"I have way too much stuff," she said.

"And half of it is still back at my place," Zach said.

"Are you looking forward to the weekend?" Genie asked me, ignoring her brother. I'd taken the backseat, insisting Genie sit up front.

"I'm a bit nervous. What if I say or do anything stupid?"

"We have Steve for that," Zach said.

Genie beamed. "And I have my little brother to thank for making it happen."

"Just make sure he doesn't say anything too stupid."

Genie waved him away and turned to face me. "I thought tonight we'd have a nice relaxing evening. After dinner we'll have a soak in the Jacuzzi and a quick swim in the pool. We don't want to stay up too late because our appointment at the spa is at eight a.m."

Jacuzzi? Pool? "I don't have a bathing suit and isn't it a little cold to go swimming?"

"Oh, it's an indoor pool. I thought you knew. As for a bathing suit, I have a million of them. I haven't even worn half of them. You can take your pick."

"Thanks." To say I was a bit overwhelmed would be an understatement, but I kind of appreciated that Genie had everything planned out.

"Zach, you going to join us?"

"We'll see."

We chatted about nothing really for the next forty-five minutes. We drove into Forest Park and I took in the huge estates. I'd driven through Forest Park when Dad had the odd delivery to drop off, but I'd never been in any of the homes, or even on a front doorstep—I'd always just waited in the car for Dad to finish the transaction. All I knew about this area of town was that the richest of the rich lived here in multi-million-dollar houses.

Zach pulled up to a tall metal gate. I couldn't see beyond it, but when he put in the pass code and the doors swung open, my mouth gaped open in awe. The house was magnificent, the kind you see on television that celebrities lived in. Lights illuminated the stone face and as we drove up the long driveway, I wanted to yank out my phone and take pictures to show Dad and Grandpa.

"This house is so beautiful," I managed to get out.

"Wait until you see the inside. I'll warn you now," Genie said, "don't touch anything. The party planners and decorators are setting up and if you move a thing they get really pissed off."

Zach parked the truck and I followed them inside. The house was filled with people looking busy, but I looked past all that. The house was even more amazing on the inside. The winding staircase, the marble floors, the priceless works of art adorning perfect walls, the antiques and all the collectables. Dad and Grandpa would fall all over themselves to see them. And the indoor pool? I couldn't wait!

"I don't get why you'd want to live in an apartment near campus when you could live here every day," I said, doing a three-sixty turn.

"I like living five minutes from campus and not with my parents."

I couldn't wipe the awestruck look from my face. I wanted to dance around the main entrance which was nearly the size of our apartment. And then the kitchen. The thought of all the fancy appliances that called that room home. To have a few hours alone in there would be pure nirvana.

"We better find Mom and Dad," Genie said.

I followed them down various hallways, but my attention kept getting diverted by artwork and antiques, some of which I recognized from the books Dad kept around. He'd never had any of these artists in the shop and would salivate just to see them in the proverbial flesh. I snapped some pictures and quickly caught up to Genie and Zach whenever I fell behind.

We travelled to the back end of the house to a large family room that was untouched by party planners. There we found Genie and Zach's parents. I recognized them because I'd googled them. Mr. Walker was reading the paper and Mrs. Walker was on the phone, an iPad in front of her. Mr. Walker glanced up and smiled at the sight of his children.

"Look who's finally here," he said, setting down the paper and rising.

Genie gave her dad a big hug while Zach just nodded. Mrs. Walker continued her conversation about the upcoming party, but smiled and waved. She put her finger up, indicating it would only be another minute, then left the room to finish her call.

"Daddy, this is Emma," Genie said.

Mr. Walker extended his hand. Like Zach, he was tall, easily six foot two, and had Zach's same chocolate-colored eyes and strong jaw line.

"A pleasure to meet you, Emma," he said with a firm handshake. He sounded like a politician with his strong confident voice. "I hear you will be joining us this weekend."

"Yes, and thank you so much for the invitation."

"We are happy to have you."

I had to ask about the Grant Wood in the hallway. My meek little self didn't want to, but if Dad knew I'd seen it and not asked, he'd kill me.

"Mr. Walker, the oil painting, is that a Grant Wood?"

He looked at Genie and Zach then back at me. "Why, yes, it is. Very impressive. These two wouldn't know a Grant Wood if American Gothic was hanging right in front of them."

"My dad and grandfather have an antique shop in Pine Falls, so I've been around antiques and art my entire life. I saw the oil painting and hoped it was a Grant Wood. It's gorgeous."

Zach whispered to Genie asking who Grant Wood was. She shrugged.

"Well, thank you. My wife is more of the art connoisseur. She's also been to her fair share of antique shops, so I'm sure she'll want to have a chat with you."

I glanced over at Zach, not quite able to read his expression. Was he proud of me?

"I'm going to show Emma to her room," Genie said. "I'm guessing we have access to the Jacuzzi and pool?"

"Yes, but don't make a mess. Zach, don't disappear. I want to talk to you about a few things."

Genie and I set off, leaving Zach behind.

CHAPTER TWENTY

ZACH

Dad led me into the study. What had I done now? Or worse, what had I not done? I took my seat across from him as he shuffled through papers on his desk. He took off his glasses and set them down.

"I see you got your marks up. Your mother and I are pleased."

The threat of being cut off could scare anyone straight.

"I've been working hard."

"Good. We're proud of you."

"Thanks, Dad." I knew he meant it. Dad was out of town for most of the year, but he still tried to be around for us. I had to give him credit for that.

"About Steve."

"I know. She insisted on having him here."

"If he steps out of line, I want to know. That bastard will not embarrass us tomorrow."

"I'll let you know if I see anything untoward."

"I thought Genie might tire of him, but clearly I was wrong. How serious are those two?"

"I don't know for sure." I couldn't tell him she was living with that idiot.

Dad leaned back in his chair and tilted his head. "About this Emma. Who is she?"

"A friend."

Dad nodded. "A friend who lives with you."

My mouth fell open. How the hell did he know? "Who told you?"

"Your sister."

Shit! Genie and her big mouth. Could she not keep a secret? And here I was covering her ass while she was blabbing any chance she could get. "Dad, it's not what you think."

"Zach, I was once twenty years old. I know how this works."

"Really, it's all innocent. I'm helping her out because she fell into some trouble."

Dad's eyebrows raised. "What sort of trouble?"

Right, optics. I gave him the shortest version I could of the story regarding Jake and Bianca. "She needed a place to stay," I finished. "It's temporary."

"That Smythe family drives me crazy. They are supporters, but those kids of theirs are uncontrollable."

Meaning, especially, Bianca's older brother, the cokehead. "I know. Bianca isn't a nice person."

Dad grunted. "That's putting it mildly. But back to this girl, Emma. She doesn't have any baggage we need to worry about? If people find out about your situation with her, they may get the wrong idea. We don't need any trouble."

"She's a small-town girl, nothing more. And like she said, her Dad owns an antique shop. Her mother is out of the picture." Did I tell Dad more? "Look, her parents were very young, teenagers, when they had her. Her mom walked out and her dad raised her with the help of his parents. Nothing else."

"She seems like a good kid. Don't let her distract you."

"I won't."

"And if you're wondering, I know about Genie's living arrangements too. She's not fooling anyone."

I fought a smile. Nothing got past Dad. "I'm not sure what you're talking about."

Dad smirked. "That's all then. If you're hungry, Louisa made dinner."

For once I left a meeting with Dad unscathed.

Next up was Mom. She was off the phone now and enjoying a late dinner with Louisa. They were gabbing about the party and Mom motioned for me to sit next to her. Louisa pulled out a plate and filled it with rice pilaf, pork tenderloin and a generous serving of salad. Louisa was big on making sure we ate our vegetables.

"Tell us about Emma," Mom said, a sly smile on her face.

"Not you, too."

"I want to know everything," Louisa said, pouring me a glass of water with a slice of lemon. I've never had the heart to tell her how much I hated lemon in my water, but because everyone else drank it that way, I suffered through it.

"She's a girl I met from school."

"She's living with Zach," Mom told Louisa.

"She is?" Louisa asked, her ebony eyes growing wide.

"It's not what you think," I said, throwing my hands up in protest. "She had nowhere to go."

"She's sweet," Mom said. "I like her. Pretty, too."

"I haven't seen her yet. Zachy, do you have a picture?" Louisa asked.

"No."

Louisa turned to Mom. "He likes her but he doesn't have a picture? That's not right."

Mom shrugged.

"This conversation isn't happening," I said, wanting to get up and leave.

"Not a denial," Mom pointed out.

"If the two of you gang up on me, I'm eating upstairs."

Mom put her arm around my shoulder. "We're only teasing, but I think we can agree this is the first time you've brought a young lady around."

I scratched my head. I had no idea how to deal with this. "She's just a friend."

"If you don't tell us everything, we'll ask Genie. You know she'll spill all."

Like with Dad only moments ago, I relayed the story to Mom and Louisa. They listened, barely blinking, as I recounted it all. "Now don't go repeating it, please. Emma's sensitive about it."

"I hate those Smythes," Mom said.

"I look forward to meeting this young lady," Louisa added. "I know you say you don't like her, but I think she sounds special."

Mom grinned. "We've waited a long time for you to bring home a nice girl."

I rolled my eyes. "Okay, I'm eating upstairs."

Mom and Louisa giggled as I gathered my plate and the putrid lemon water. I went to my room and collapsed on the bed. I took out my phone and googled Grant Wood. Man, I was an idiot. That Grant Wood.

A text popped up.

Genie: We're going down to the pool in ten minutes. Emma is going to look hot in her new bathing suit. Made sure to give her a choice of ones that will make her look amazing.

I rolled my eyes.

Me: Okay?

Genie: Did I mention how hot she'll look? Try to keep your boy parts in check.

Me: Did you really just text me that?

Genie: Yup!

Me: Nice of you to tell Dad she was living with us.

Genie: Oops. That kind of slipped. And she's living with you. And you like that.

Me: Goodbye!

Genie: See you in ten. Take a cold shower before. And after, lol!

CHAPTER TWENTY-ONE

EMMA

"Great mention of the Grant Wood," Genie said. I think Dad loves you."

"It was all right that I asked? I felt like I was overstepping and being nosy."

"Dad lives for that shit. It impresses him."

Genie showed me to my room and told me she'd be back with some bathing suits for me to choose from. I put my bag down on the bed and took in my room for the weekend. It was huge—twice the size of our living room in Pine Falls—and I had my own bathroom! I'd always assumed that Zach's family was well off, but this was far more than anything I could have expected. And not once did Zach or Genie give off the rich-kid attitude like Bianca and her bratty friends.

"Found three brand-new ones that should fit you," she said, tossing them on the bed. "Sorry, they are all bikinis. I don't have any one-pieces."

Bikini? I'd never owned one in my life, mostly because I didn't think I could pull it off. I certainly didn't have Genie's cleavage or much in the way of hips. I looked through my choices and picked a plain navy blue one with white polka dots. It had the most material. I might have been slim, but I was more muscular, not anything like Genie's hourglass figure.

"Great choice. If you want to keep it, and the other two also, you're welcome to them. They're all too small on me. There should be a robe and towels in your bathroom along with some flip flops. I'll meet you downstairs when you're ready."

She left and I went into the bathroom to change. I carefully removed the tags from my new bikini and put it on. I looked at my reflection in the mirror. The top pushed up my boobs making them look larger than their barely B cup. The bottoms fit like a glove and I had to admit I looked pretty good. I'd even consider wearing it again. I slipped into the white fluffy robe and it was so soft against my skin. I wrapped it tight around me and rummaged through the various sizes of flip flops until I found mine. I took one towel from the stack piled high in one of the cabinets. The Walker home was the poshest of hotels.

I went downstairs and Genie was waiting for me in the family room. She grasped onto my arm, leading me down another hallway and down a set of steps that led to the pool and Jacuzzi. There was no one else there.

"I've been looking forward to a soak for weeks," she said, shedding her robe and revealing a tiny pink bikini. I tried not to stare, but her body was fabulous. I was a bit jealous. She eased into the water and let out a moan of satisfaction.

I removed my robe and piled it neatly off to the side on a nearby chair and set my flip flops underneath. I put one foot into the water and the heat enveloped me. It was glorious. I sank deeper into the water as the jets massaged each muscle of my body.

"I don't ever want to get out," I said, resting my head on the edge and closing my eyes.

"I know. Let's just stay here until morning."

We relaxed in silence for a few minutes, the only sounds coming from the thrusting jets. Thoughts of Jake and my upcoming predicament with Dad floated away. I intended to enjoy every single second of this weekend.

"So Zach convinced your parents to let Steve come to the party?" I asked, breaking the silence.

"Yes, and now I owe the bastard. He's making me go with Dad to visit some hog operation next month. It goes against all my principles," she said in a sleepy voice. "I'm going to want to take all those pigs home. I hate factory farming and Dad knows that. But if I can sway a farmer or two on letting pigs live better lives before slaughter, it won't be a total waste."

"I didn't know you were an animal activist. That's great."

"And I didn't know you were a tennis ace."

"Zach told you that? I'm not exactly a tennis ace."

"Ranked second in the state? I'd say you're an ace. We have a tennis court out back. This spring you could give me some pointers."

"You guys have your own court?" Why did that surprise me?

"Yup. Mom plays and so does Dad, occasionally. Even Zach's pretty good."

"What's Zach good at?" he asked, breaking the tranquility of the moment. I opened my eyes to see him standing next to the Jacuzzi in his blue and black swim trunks, holding a towel.

"You're good at ruining a girl's night," Genie said without flinching.

"Is there room in there for me?" he asked.

"Sure," I said, scooting over. There was room for ten people.

He got in and sat across from me and stared. I was getting a bit self-conscious. What was so fascinating about my face? That's all he could see.

"What did Dad want?" Genie asked.

"Nothing important."

"Did he grill you about Steve? I did promise them he wouldn't embarrass anyone."

"It wasn't about Steve. Why are we talking about Dad when I'm trying to relax?"

He shut his eyes and stretched out, one leg brushing mine. I thought to move, but didn't. Even though it was only a passing touch, my heart skipped a second. Any girl with a pulse would be attracted to Zach, but I kept telling myself to keep it strictly platonic. Any feelings or secret crushes on Zach would lead to heartache. Besides, I didn't want a boyfriend. Boys were trouble. The single life was fine with me.

An intercom blared through the pool room, startling me. "Genie, we need to talk about tomorrow. Please come see me in the study."

"Great," Genie muttered. "Let me guess, it's about Steve." She got out of the Jacuzzi and into her robe. "If I'm not back in ten minutes, please come get me."

"Have fun," Zach said, not moving an inch.

She gave him the finger and was gone. It felt strange being alone with Zach. Sure, I was alone with him all the time, but never this close. I took the opportunity to take him in, his broad shoulders, the scruffy face, his placid, peaceful expression.

"Can I ask you something?"

Zach's eyes opened, a sleepy gaze. "Sure."

"When you're at school, don't you miss all this?"

"Nah. It's nice and all, but this belongs to my parents. Besides, I kind of like communicating with people directly and not through an intercom."

I stifled a laugh which made him smile.

"I've only been here an hour, but this is pretty amazing. Thank you again for inviting me."

"You're invited anytime."

I was dying to hit the pool. It would mean getting out of the Jacuzzi and putting myself on full display, but a nice swim on a cold December evening sounded attractive.

"How cold is the pool?"

"Compared to this? It's like jumping into a frozen lake."

"You make it sound so appealing," I said with a laugh.

"If you don't believe me, try it."

"I'll see that as a challenge." I got out of the Jacuzzi and was greeted by room temperature air that felt like a gust of cold wind. Compounding that was the feeling of Zach's eyes trained on me, possibly checking me out in a bikini I never thought I'd wear. I acted fast and dove in. The water slapped me like a bag of ice. I surfaced and let out a mini shriek.

"Told you," he called out.

"At least I did it. I think you're being a wimp."

"Them's fighting words. Are you daring me to jump in, Miss Andrews?"

"I am."

"What do I get if I do it?"

"I'll make you dinner for a week."

"You already do that. Something better."

"I don't know."

"Tell you what, we'll determine it later as long as it's within reason."

"I'll take that bet."

He climbed out of the Jacuzzi took a running start then cannonballed into the pool only feet from me, sending up a wave that soaked me again. He surfaced and then laughed at my stern expression.

"Did I splash you?"

"Yes!" I splashed him back and he swam away.

"It's too cold in here. I'm heading back to the Jacuzzi," I said.

"Told you it would be freezing in here," he said and winked.

I rolled my eyes and got back in the warm water. Zach followed seconds later. "What's tomorrow going to be like?" I asked.

"Lots of people and lots of BS," he said. "I tow the party line all evening while wishing I could get drunk."

"What if I say the wrong thing?"

"You're a guest, you can say what you want."

"If that's the case, why is everyone worried about what Steve will say?"

"Because he's an idiot and an attention whore."

"Why does Genie like him so much?"

"I don't know. He's good in bed?"

"TMI."

"You asked."

I put my robe back on and wrapped the towel around my wet hair. "Does it go late?"

"Yeah, but I usually only put in a few hours then watch movies the rest of the night."

Genie breezed back in, unscathed by whatever she'd just experienced. "Are you guys hungry? There's some food for us."

"I'm going to hit the sack. Long day tomorrow," Zach said. "Goodnight, ladies."

I watched him go, and when I looked back at Genie a wide smile was on her face. "What?" I asked.

"Nothing," she said.

"No, what? I want to know."

"Never mind. Are you hungry or not?"

"No, not really. What time to we have to be up?"

"I want us up and out before seven."

"Then I better go to bed too."

"See you in the morning."

She was still smiling. I couldn't help but wonder what was going on.

GRANDMA HAD TAKEN ME to get a manicure and pedicure done at the mall when I turned sixteen. The Ivy Spa was no afternoon at the mall. We got our own robes, even softer than those at the Walker house; a tall glass of sparkling juice; various mini muffins, cookies, and cakes; and an assortment of fancy teas I'd never heard of. Before they'd even taken us in for our manicure, pedicure, facial, and whatever else Genie had planned, I got the most relaxing and mind-blowing head and neck massage. I didn't want it to end. I felt all my tension evaporate.

Next came the facial, the seaweed body wrap, a light lunch, and then our manicure and pedicure. With all that done, we moved on to hair and makeup.

"Is this how celebrities live?" I asked, as Pamela, my hair stylist, worked on my updo.

"This and more," she replied.

"I could get used to this."

By three p.m. we were all done. Pamela presented me with the mirror and I barely recognized the face staring back at me. I looked like a movie star. I felt like I could walk any red carpet. Even with my subdued makeup—I'd specifically asked for my neutral tones—Pamela had made me look flawless. I actually looked pretty.

"You're gorgeous," Genie said. "The guys are going to fall all over you tonight, especially when they see you in the dress I picked out."

"You think so?"

Genie hugged me, something foreign to me. "Emma, I just love you. You're so adorable! Now let's get out of here. We still have to get dressed."

A car picked us up and took us back to the Walker house. We meandered through the serving staff and party planners up to Genie's room. We had about an hour before guests arrived.

"Here it is," she said, holding up the dress. The navy gown with navy embroidered beads and crystals looked like nothing I could ever afford. Already Genie had done so much for me by paying for our spa day and giving me the bathing suits, but this dress? It was fit for a princess. "Try it on."

I took it from her and went into her bathroom. I slipped it off the hanger and slid into it. It fit perfectly, hugging every subtle curve of my body. The v-shaped neckline didn't plunge too much, but showed just the right amount of cleavage. The slit up my right leg went mid-thigh revealing my toned legs. They were definitely my best asset.

"Let me see," Genie called.

I came out of the bathroom and she whistled. "Holy shit! You look gorgeous."

"Thanks," I said, my skin tingling with excitement.

"Let me find you some jewelry," she said, going through her massive collection. She picked out a strand of pearls and teardrop pearl earrings. "These will complete your look."

I took them from her, feeling my eyes well up with tears. "Genie, thanks so much for everything."

"No crying! We just had our makeup done," she said, hugging me again.

"It's just so much..."

"Don't worry about it. Now let me get dressed and you can help me with my jewelry."

Once we were ready, it was time to make our grand entrance. I was so nervous that I couldn't get my hands to stop shaking. What if I said something stupid? Or fell flat on my ass in the heels Genie lent me? What if I threw up all over Genie's pretty dress? I told myself to pull it together.

Light dinner music was now playing through the house. I followed Genie through the main entrance where a few of the servers had set up a bar. We drifted into the main living room which I now saw for the first time. It was a wide, open room as large as our house in Pine Falls and filled with expensive art on the walls and antiques on full display. There we found Mr. and Mrs. Walker and Zach, who was dressed smartly in a black suit and grey tie looking as handsome as ever. They all looked at us when we entered.

"Wow," Zach said. "Em, you look beautiful."

My cheeks burned. "Thanks," I said shyly.

"I told her the guys would go crazy the moment they saw her. Zach, you might want to keep an eye on her."

"I think I will," he said with a wink.

"About Steven," Mrs. Walker said to Genie, who retreated to a corner with her mother while Mr. Walker was ushered away by one of his aides.

"So, come here often?" Zach joked.

I giggled. "Come on, stop teasing."

"Genie's right. The guys will be all over you. I think I should be your personal bodyguard."

"If you think I need one," I said, trying not to giggle some more.

"Everyone, gather around," a tall man in a pinstripe suit boomed. I had no idea who he was, but he sounded prickly so I did as he said. "Remember, don't mention the pipeline or the upcoming election. Let's keep this a light evening and where are the Walker kids? I only see Zach."

Genie popped her head out and waved. "I'm here. Mom is just grilling me."

"Right. Walker kids, take lots of photos. We want to see you working this room. Handsome children get their mothers and fathers re-elected. And don't forget to smile." The man focused on me, his black eyes like laser beams. "Who are you?" he asked.

"I'm Zach and Genie's friend."

The man looked at Zach then back at me. "Is Zach your boyfriend? Zach, is this your girlfriend? Will her political affiliation be problematic?"

"Allen, she's not my girlfriend, and her politics don't matter."

"You aren't a radical, are you? Either left or right?" he asked me.

"No. I don't really get involved in politics. I haven't even voted yet."

He rolled his eyes. "Zach, brief your girlfriend. Everyone else, let's have a good time."

"Who was that?" I asked when it was all over.

"Allen, my dad's campaign manager. Micromanager freakshow."

"What are you going to brief me on?"

"Here's my brief. Have a good time and don't mention the pipeline or the upcoming election."

A short time later guests arrived and so did the photographers and media. Zach and Genie did their jobs and took pictures with everyone, but Zach never strayed too far. It was nice knowing he had my back.

"Let's get a picture together," he suggested. He called over a photographer who took a picture, but then three more appeared. It was the paparazzi. "I'll be doing this all night," he muttered through a smile.

Zach put his arm through mine and the next stop was the bar. "The best way to make it through one of these evenings is with a little alcohol. What can I get you?"

"I only drink the occasional beer. Well, except for that one memorable night."

He turned to the bartender. "White wine for the lady and a whiskey sour for me. No beer on tap," he said to me. "Too pedestrian."

With our drinks in hand we hit the refreshment table where Genie was with the infamous Steve. I did a double take at first. Steve was older than Genie, easily in his late twenties and slightly balding. I'd assumed that Genie would be with an Adonis, but Steve was so ordinary, right down to his wrinkled grey suit.

"Steve, this is Emma," Genie said, her face beaming.

"Hey," he said obviously disinterested. He quickly turned his attention back to the phyllo pastry appetizers.

"And a hello to you too," Zach said.

More guests filed in, which meant Genie and Zach had to make an effort to greet them, at least for the first little while. I stood back, away from Steve, and watched them both work the men and women who donated to their father's campaign. They looked so natural, laughing at jokes, handing out compliments, and saying words of support for their father. Many of the ladies took long glances at Zach even with their husbands standing by their sides.

"You're Zach's latest girlfriend?" Steve asked, licking from his fingers whatever remnants of food were still on them.

"We're just friends."

He snorted. "Good ol' Zach likes to play the field, so don't say you weren't warned."

Where had this guy come from anyway? I thought I'd left him safely with the refreshments. "Like I said, we're just friends. How long have you and Genie been dating?" I thought changing the subject was a good idea.

"Two years. Met her in one of my classes. I was her TA."

Kind of gross. "Oh. Are you still in school?"

"Getting my PhD in poly sci."

"That's good."

"Thought I'd scope out the party and see if there are any prospects here."

"Job prospects? I thought you were a conservative. Aren't you barking up the wrong tree?"

"You never know who might show up to one of these things."

Mercifully Zach finished the schmoozing and rescued me from Steve. He had another glass of white wine in his hand and a drink for himself. "I can guarantee that talking to that guy will make you stupid."

"So, I have to ask, what does Genie see in him? And don't say he's good in bed. That's not enough."

"I don't know. He's a way to rebel from my parents? He's a doofus."

"He's not what I expected."

Zach groaned.

"What?" I asked, following his gaze.

"Bianca's parents are here."

My body froze. Did that mean she was here? "Her parents?"

"Yeah, they donate to Dad's campaign. They've always been supportive."

The wine began to burn in my stomach. "Is she here?"

"I'm sure she couldn't be bothered and besides, she wouldn't set foot in this house."

"Why not?"

Zach smiled mischievously. "Let's just say that she wouldn't want to poke the bear."

"That sounds ominous."

"Let's leave it at that."

I titled my head to one side and stared at him. He tried to ignore me. "What do you have on her?" I asked.

"It's better you don't know," he said and laughed.

"You've got me curious."

"All I can say is that Bianca has some skeletons and I happen to know where all the bones are buried."

"Are you the reason she's keeping her distance?"

"Maybe. At least I know she's not as stupid as I once thought she was. Look, let's not talk about Bianca. Let's circulate."

He had to know that people would think I was his girlfriend. He introduced me to the mayor, business leaders and other politicians. I'd never be able to remember all the names. We drank more expensive wine and ate fabulous appetizers of duck, lamb, and cheese-filled pastries. By the time the last of the guests had left, I was on a euphoric high. I could have run laps around the estate despite my aching feet.

"Did you have fun?" Zach asked, walking me to my room.

"Tonight was amazing," I said with a little skip to my step.

"I'm not sure you'd say that if you had to go to dozens and dozens of them a year."

"Pretty sure I'd still say that."

We stopped at my bedroom door and he gazed down at me. Even though he was only a few inches taller than me in my heels, I still felt small under his stare.

"You looked beautiful tonight."

"Stop saying that or it will go to my head."

He took hold of my hand, squeezing it gently. My heart picked up a million beats as a rush of warmth flowed through my veins.

"I'm glad you were here tonight. I couldn't dream of spending it with anyone else."

I looked up, and at that moment, when our eyes met, I knew I'd given him all the reassurance he needed. He leaned in and I closed my eyes, anticipating the kiss. At first his lips barely grazed mine, but as I got up on my tiptoes, he slipped his arms around my waist and pulled me closer, the kiss growing more intense. A flush of warmth enveloped me, making me want to bury myself in his embrace. He gently bit down on my lower lip and broke the kiss, leaving me wanting more.

"I should probably get off to bed before we get caught," he said.

"Uh, yeah."

"Goodnight, Em."

Never in my life did I so desperately want to run after someone and tell them not to go, but so many things stopped me—most of all my crippling fear.

I went into my room and closed the door behind me. I wanted to laugh, scream, and cry all at the same time.

I SPENT THE WHOLE NIGHT thinking about that kiss. In fact, I don't think I ever fell asleep. Over and over again in went through my mind like an old movie reel. At one point I'd even had a panic attack, gasping for air and barely able to breathe. The most amazing kiss of my entire life–not that I'd had very many–had reduced me to a muddy, messy puddle of confusion.

I didn't want to leave my bed and the limited security it offered. Getting up and dressed meant I had to face Zach. What was he going to do? How was I supposed to act? The kiss had been a mistake; it was going to ruin everything. My heart picked up beats again and my hands shook a little. I could deal with this; I had to.

I showered and put on some clothes. Thankfully I'd packed all my stuff before the party, so I didn't have to worry about that now. I brought my bag downstairs and braved the breakfast table. Only Mrs. Walker was there.

"Good morning, dear," she said. "Sleep well?"

"I did. Thank you for having me at your party."

"We love friendly faces. Help yourself to breakfast. I should probably wake the other sleepyheads."

I wanted to throw up. As I looked through all the chafing dishes, even the sight of eggs Benedict turned my stomach. Knowing I had to eat something, I scooped some scrambled eggs and speared a slice of French toast. What if I couldn't keep it down?

One of the staff came around and asked me what I wanted to drink. I prayed they had chamomile tea to settle my nerves and was thankful when the server said she'd be right back with it.

I nibbled the eggs, pushing them around my plate more than anything else. Mrs. Walker returned and resumed her seat across from me. I wanted to die right there. I couldn't handle whatever would come next. I liked my life the way it was; completely uncomplicated. No kiss, no friends, no life. It was easy and all I'd ever known.

"I've woken everyone up. They should be down shortly."

The server returned with my tea and I longed to drink it as fast as I could. I needed something, but I'd stopped filling my anti-anxiety meds a long ago and hadn't even refilled the prescription when the whole Bianca thing went down. I was definitely longing for a Paxil right now, though. A kiss was a prelude, and I didn't want to know what came after that.

"I hear you like to cook," Mrs. Walker said, starting up conversation.

"I do. I find it relaxing."

"I must confess I'm not much use in the kitchen. I have two older sisters and they and my mother did all the cooking when I was growing up. Do you have siblings?"

I couldn't figure out if she was fishing for information, or if she genuinely wanted to know. Was she sizing me up to see whether or not I was good enough for her son? My stomach gurgled. "I have two younger brothers."

"I bet they are picky little eaters. Zach used to be so picky when he was young. Now he'll eat just about anything."

"I don't live with my brothers."

"Your parents are divorced?"

I panicked some more. Did I tell her the truth and risk her looking down on me, or just perpetuate a lie? I hated lying and I'd done enough of it with Dad.

"Actually, my parents were never married. My dad and grandparents raised me. My mom was a teenager when she had me...fifteen."

I expected Mrs. Walker's expression to curdle like all the other people who couldn't, or wouldn't, understand. Or, she'd give me that pitying look I hated even more. But Mrs. Walker did neither.

"I bet your father and grandparents are lovely people. We should have them over for dinner one evening. Not to sound sexist, but was it your grandmother who taught you to cook?"

Mrs. Walker didn't care and I couldn't believe it. "Yes, she was a great cook. She passed away three years ago."

"I'm sorry to hear that, dear. Well, if you ever want to take over our kitchen, you can make us something anytime. I can even try to help."

I was now convinced Zach's family were the Waltons and while that should have made me happy, it made me feel worse. I sipped tea. I needed a vat of it.

"Morning," Zach said, entering the dining room and grabbing a plate. He filled it high with eggs, potatoes, bacon, sausages and a generous helping of grilled tomatoes. He took a seat next to me and I felt my head fog. I could not have a panic attack at their table.

"I was just getting to know Emma," Mrs. Walker said. "I'd like to invite her family to dinner. How about after the holidays?"

"I'd like to meet them too," Zach said.

I sipped more tea, pinching my leg under the table to divert my attention from the looming panic attack. Pull it together, I told myself. I was not going to make a fool of myself in front of Mrs. Walker. I had to quell the butterflies fighting around in my chest. I focused on my breaths and felt the panic subside. I could do this.

"And we won't make you cook," Mrs. Walker joked.

I smiled. Yup, I could do this.

Genie, Steve, and Mr. Walker joined us. The conversation was light, mostly about the party. I had a few refills of tea and listened absently to the chitchat. I kept timing my breathing, focusing on my calm place.

"We should get out of here," Zach said, glancing at his watch. "Emma has to catch a bus back to Pine Falls early this afternoon."

"Dear, it's been a pleasure and we hope to see you again soon," Mrs. Walker said. She reached out to hug me and I hesitated for just a second. Hug me? She scooped me into her arms. "Now you tell your father and grandfather that we are expecting them in the New Year."

"I will."

I put on my jacket and boots and Zach grabbed my bag. We went to his truck without exchanging any words. How long could I put him off? I was sure he was going to bring it up.

"You know my mom is serious about having your dad and grandfather over."

"I'll tell them." Why hadn't I taken tea for the road?

"And you had a good time?"

"I did. Thank you."

He acted so cool, like nothing had happened. I knew he'd kissed a thousand girls, but he was only the second guy to ever kiss me, and the only guy to ever kiss me like *that*...so it was kind of a big deal. I couldn't just forget about it; the kiss changed everything.

He talked about neutral stuff for most of the ride. His dislike for Steve, some guests he liked, others he couldn't stand but pretended to be nice to. I half-listened and when we pulled up to the apartment, I felt a sense of relief. I needed to finish packing for Pine Falls and then I'd call a cab. Even if I was at the bus station early, I didn't care. I needed space.

Did he notice I was acting weird? I had to act as normal as possible for maybe another half hour. I packed quickly, stuffing things into my suitcase without even folding them. I pulled out my phone and called a cab. I rolled my luggage do the door and Zach looked up from the sofa where he'd been scrolling through his phone.

"You're leaving already?" he asked, surprised. "Don't you have a couple of hours?"

"I figured I get there early."

He got up and as he got closer, I stepped back. He stopped, staring at me quizzically. "What's wrong?"

"Nothing." My heart raced again and the fog was setting in. Keep calm.

"You've been acting strange all day. Is this about last night?"

My stomach bottomed out. Oh, geez. "No, no. I have to go, I've got a cab coming."

He grasped onto my arm before I could make my escape. "Are you mad at me?"

"I'm not mad. You have to let me go. I'm sure the cab is waiting."

"He can wait." Zach's face was marred with confusion and concern and his hold on my arm was unwavering.

"But they make you pay, and I don't want to get hit with a huge fare."

"I'll pay for it. You can give me a couple of minutes."

I set down my backpack and he let go of my arm. I dared to meet his eyes and then immediately looked away. "I don't have a lot of time."

"Emma, what's going on?"

"Nothing is going on. I'm anxious to go home."

"Is this because I kissed you? I did that because I wanted to."

His words were a knife to my heart. "You shouldn't have."

"Why? Is this about Jake?"

"No!"

He let out a grunt. "This is about Jake. My God, are you still pining for that asswipe? When are you going to get that he doesn't give a shit about you?"

"It's not about Jake!" I screamed. I'd turned all out hysterical. I felt like one of those cornered and wounded animals fighting for its life. I needed to escape before I did something stupid.

"Then what is it?"

"It's you!" I could feel my eyes welling with tears. I hated letting him see me cry. "It's all about you. If we start dating everything we have together will be gone. In a few months some hot girl will come along and you'll dump me. Then I lose you and Genie. I lose everything." I wiped the tears from my eyes and felt angry. Why was he doing this?

"That won't happen," he said, sympathy etched on his face.

"Oh please! Are you serious? I know that right now I'm this little puppy you feel sorry for, but then I'll stop being so cute and you'll wonder why the hell you ever got mixed up with me. I don't want that. If we're just friends, then it's different. Then everything can be okay."

I could feel his eyes on me, but I couldn't look at him. He reached out for me, but I jerked away.

"None of that is true and I don't want to be just your friend," he said, his voice just above a whisper.

"Well, that's all I want and you should respect that."

He retreated, possibly hurt by my words. "Go, then," he said.

I scooped up my belongings and bolted from the apartment. I didn't like how I'd left it, but he had to know how I felt. I couldn't lose him too.

CHAPTER TWENTY-TWO

EMMA

Dad picked me up from the bus station and I tried to act like everything was great, but he was my dad and he saw through all my bullshit. Instead of taking me home, we stopped at Harriet's Diner, the restaurant Jake's parents owned, for a burger. We ordered, and then Dad's ice-blue eyes were trained on my face and I was withering under his silent cross-examination.

"What's going on? No more sugary crap, just the truth."

"Nothing's going on."

"And you think I believe that?"

So many lies and all I could think to do was stretch the truth. "I met a guy but I don't think it's going to work out."

Dad shifted in his seat. The conversation of boys clearly hit a nerve. "Why not?" he asked, trying to sound sincere, like he wasn't unhappy about this revelation.

"He's not right for me. I like him, but it just can't work."

"You're young and have lots of time to meet boys," Dad said relieved. "I was worried this had to do with Jake."

"No, nothing to do with Jake." At least that part was true, right at this particular moment. I was too upset about Zach to even think about Jake.

"Do you want to tell me what happened?"

The food arrived, buying me a few more seconds of stalling. I grabbed a French fry and dipped it into my ketchup a million times until it resembled a limp noodle. "Do I have to?"

"I suppose not, but you seem down. Did he hurt you?" Dad asked, his eyes narrowing.

"No, he's a really nice guy."

"Then what's the problem?"

I dropped the fry onto my plate, but didn't look up at Dad. "When I meet the right guy, I want it to be real. I'm not sure he does real."

"He's a player," Dad deduced.

"Pretty much."

"I was one of those. Stay away from them. Look, Kiddo, you'll meet other guys. If you don't have a good feeling about this one, then it's best to walk away."

But part of me did have a good feeling about Zach, and that's what was eating me up. The other part of me was issuing a constant reminder that I didn't want to end up like the Beccas of the world. At the end of the day Zach's word didn't mean all that much. He could say anything he wanted, but that didn't mean three months from now he'd still want to be with me.

"Can we talk about something else? Having the boy talk with my dad is kind of weird."

He laughed. "Let's talk Christmas. I should probably tell you that Dad has invited Wendy for dinner. She's nice enough, but I kind of like when it's just the three of us."

That was it? End of interrogation? Boy, I'd gotten off easy.

"Do you like her?"

"I do, but I guess it feels like Mom is being replaced."

"You know that he's not trying to replace her. He just doesn't want to be lonely. And sorry, Dad, you just aren't cutting the mustard."

"I suppose."

We finished our burgers and I was anxious to get home. I needed the safety of our house, a place that was my own. The short drive from Harriet's had me edgy. I couldn't keep my feet still and their constant tapping resulted in a look from Dad. I stopped. I nearly jumped out of the moving car when Dad pulled into our gravel driveway. Grandpa met me at the front door and gave me a big bear hug. I missed this so much.

"My girl is home! We missed you, Emma," Grandpa said, kissing the top of my head.

"I missed you guys, too," I said burying my face in his shoulder. If I cried now, they'd never leave me alone.

"Did your dad tell you about Wendy?" he asked.

"Yes, and I'm happy she's coming."

"Are you sure?" I didn't know why they thought I'd be so bothered by it. Of course, they couldn't know that I was more concerned with our Christmas Eve dinner at Jake's parents' house. He and I would be in the same room for the first time since he'd kicked me out.

"Yes, of course. It'll be nice having another woman around."

Grandpa beamed. "I hoped you'd say that. Now let's get inside before we get a chill."

Yes, being home was exactly where I needed to be.

A PART OF ME HOPED that Zach would call or even text. Days, then weeks, went by without a word. I was getting ready for dinner at the Bennetts' house and wished to hear some comforting words from Zach. I pulled out my phone and hesitated for a long time before sending him a text.

Me: I wanted to wish you a Merry Xmas. Hope all is well. I'm going to Jake's tonight so that will be super awkward. Say hi to your parents.

I waited, not that he'd text me back instantly. But what if he didn't text at all? I sent Genie a text too and finished getting ready. What would I say to Jake? Would we just pretend it was all happy times? What if Bianca was there? My phone buzzed. I ran for it, excited for a response from Zach.

Genie: Merry Christmas to you too. See you in a couple of weeks.

I wanted to text her back to see if she was with Zach, but instead I put my phone in my pocket and met Dad and Grandpa downstairs.

"Ready to go?" Dad asked, getting into his coat.

"You bet." It was now or never.

The Bennetts lived less than a block away. I'd walked this route so many times I could recognize every imperfection in the sidewalk. The three of us trudged through the newly fallen snow and I longed for my phone to sing to me. It didn't.

"Emma, what do you know about Jake's girlfriend? Ron asked me and I said I'd ask you."

Just the subject of Bianca raised my already sky-high blood pressure. What if she was there? The whole afternoon I'd vacillated between all-out panic and then a minute or two of calm once I temporarily convinced myself she wouldn't be. Then I'd think of her again, and my hands and body would shake. I tried to busy myself with laundry, baking a pie for the Bennetts, and some reading, but all the words melted into each other. I didn't even remember what book I'd attempted to read. Mercifully, the pie and laundry were unscathed.

"Not much." More lies.

"I'm getting the impression the Bennetts don't care for her. This is the first time Jake hasn't spent Christmas with his family."

I skidded to a stop. "What?"

Dad glanced over at me looking puzzled. "You knew that, didn't you?"

"Right, sorry, my head was in the clouds."

Dad took a long hard look at me but resumed walking. "Ron was so pissed off. You don't bail on a Bennett family Christmas."

I wanted to let out a gasp of relief. This news couldn't be any better. I wouldn't have to face Jake, and Dad wouldn't be able to use his super-parent power to figure out something was amiss.

"The only thing I know for sure is that Jake really likes her." Finally, some truth out of my mouth.

"Ron and his parents are going to grill you."

"Dad, I don't have much to add. I barely know her."

"Apparently she's all Jake talks about. Not with you?"

"No, not really."

I checked my phone again. This time there was a text, one I hadn't heard.

000:000:0000: Merry Christmas Bitch.

I gasped. Who would send me this? I stopped again to reply.

Me: Who is this?

"Something wrong?" Dad asked.

"Just someone from school," I said in a fake voice. Dad had to know I was full of it.

This time I heard the chime as the response came in.

000:000:0000: The person who's going to fuck you up.

My insides tightened. Bianca. Who else? I didn't know whether to be worried or angry, so I chose neither. The best course of action with a person like Bianca was to ignore her. If she kept it up, then I'd go to Jake. He'd stop this. She wanted to ruin my Christmas even though she had Jake safely in her clutches. I deleted the two texts and put my phone away. Bianca Smythe could shove it up her ass.

CHAPTER TWENTY-THREE

ZACH

I saw the text from Emma. Nearly three weeks without a word. No, I wasn't replying. Screw that. She'd walked out and I wasn't about to forget it.

"Cider?" Genie asked. "I spiked it."

I hated the holidays. I would have rather stayed at my apartment and invited some of the guys over to drink beers and play poker all night. What I didn't want to do was spend Christmas with a bunch of people I didn't give two shits about, all new donors—I mean, new friends—of my parents. I'd have to be a phony bastard all night long. I could feign sickness but Mom would kill me.

"I'm going to need about a dozen of these."

"Tell me about it. Why didn't you invite Emma?"

"Why would I invite her?" I snapped.

Genie scowled. "Relax, I was just asking a question. I thought she might like it."

"I told you she went home."

"Isn't it just her dad and grandfather? You could have invited them all. It's not like we don't have enough strays here."

"After the last party, I think she'd probably say no." Shit, I'd said too much. Genie's eyes narrowed and she zeroed in for the kill.

"What are you talking about? She had a great time."

"But then I fucked it up."

She pulled me to a corner away from other guests. "What did you do? Did you sleep with her and then blow her off?"

"No! I wouldn't do that."

She rolled her eyes.

"I wouldn't do that to Emma."

"Ah, the qualifier. So what did you do?"

I briefed her. I didn't relish revisiting it.

"You kissed her. That's so cute and so last century. Later you can go around to her dad's and ask him if you can court her."

I groaned. "Really, Genie? That's not helpful. You're being a bitch."

She stopped immediately. "Hey, sorry. I shouldn't have been a jerk. I didn't mean it. I was trying to make light of it because I can tell you're bummed. I'm sure it was a nice moment for both of you and then she just got spooked. Give her some time. I can talk to her."

"No, do not talk to her. You do enough talking." I paused. "What if it's for the best?"

"You're a weenie, you know that? You're stressing that maybe you might like her a little more than all those bimbos you chase after. She's the real deal. Being a big boy is kind of scary, isn't it?"

"Not what I meant. If we did try this out and it didn't work, what if we didn't stay friends? She's right about that."

"And what if I'm right that you're a big weenie?"

"You should probably stop drinking."

"She's an awesome girl, perfect for you. When I see the two of you together, it's so natural. Have you ever felt that way about a girl before?"

"No," I said begrudgingly.

"Exactly. Give her a little space to come around. I don't think she's ever had a boyfriend before and she's apprehensive."

"There's something else. The guys already give me a hard time about her." Genie was about to open her mouth and I stopped her. "Yeah, I'm the biggest weenie you've ever met, I get it. It's just that I don't want them to give her a hard time. I can handle it, but I'm not sure she can."

"Other than Brett—and I don't like him anyway—none of these guys are going to be friends when you go off to law school, so why do you care about them? If you like her, and it's obvious that you do, why does it matter what those guys think? Man, Zach, I thought you'd be tougher than this. Where are your balls?"

"Don't you have some of Dad's friends to impress?"

"Sure, but only after another glass of my special cider."

She wandered away and I pulled out my phone.

Me: You know he's just an asswipe, right? And it's only awkward if you make it that way.

I finished my cider and looked for the wine. I had a two-drink limit before I'd start getting the look from Mom. Little did she know I'd really need about ten drinks to make this evening bearable. I'd slip out early anyway. Brett rented a rink, and the guys were going to play a late-night game of hockey.

My phone buzzed.

Emma: Jake's not here! How did I get so lucky? Uncle Ron's asked me about Bianca all night. Somehow she convinced Jake to stay in the city. How is your night going?

Me: Not bad. Hanging out with my family and about thirty other people I don't know. Playing hockey tonight with the guys before doing a repeat of this tomorrow.

Emma: Have fun! And see you soon.

"WE HAVE TO GO," DAD said, pounding on my bedroom door as he passed it the next morning. Genie's would be next. I wore a light blue cotton dress shirt that I didn't care about. If it got stained, I'd toss it. I grabbed my phone and wallet and met Mom and Dad downstairs. Genie was MIA.

"The only bad part of this whole thing in the photo op," Mom said, fiddling around with his purse. "I don't want them interfering," she said to Dad.

"I made it clear to Allen that we'd take a few pictures then we wanted them out."

"Good."

Genie came bounding down the stairs, dressed in a heavy wool sweater she'd regret. It amazed me how quickly she forgot.

"We're all here. Let's go," Dad said.

We piled into the car for our annual Christmas tradition of serving lunch at Saint Anthony's soup kitchen. We'd been doing it for ten years, two years before Dad won his first election. Genie and I were kids then, more of a nuisance than anything else, but even then we'd worked hard, serving and cleaning up. We also spent time chatting with our fellow lunch guests, learning more about their lives, how they'd come to Saint Anthony's. Mom and Dad's mission had been to support any initiative to help get people off the street, but every year the lines looked longer and longer. They weren't winning the battle.

"How is Emma?" Mom asked. "She's a sweet girl. We should have invited her along."

I stared at Mom who was sitting across from me. She wore a pleasant smile, but she was fishing.

"She went back home," I said.

"I bet she would have been in the kitchen helping them cook up a storm."

Mom didn't miss a thing. Knowing her, she remembered every detail about Emma. "Yeah, probably."

Mom shifted her attention to Genie. "And Steve? Where is he?" she asked, all joy vanishing from her voice.

"With his family," she said. "I assumed he wasn't invited."

"You assumed correct," Dad said.

More boring chitchat for the twenty-five-minute ride. My mind wandered to the New Year's Eve party Brett had planned. I needed a night out, away from bullshit. The thought of drinking and hanging out with my buddies was what all that was keeping me going right now.

People were lined up outside when we drove around the back of Saint Anthony's. The people who used Saint Anthony's were always polite and never gave anyone trouble. They were down-and-out, good people who had either lost their way or were unable to change their circumstances. My heart went out to them and never once did I dread our Christmas tradition.

Jill, the executive director, met us at the back door. She escorted us to the kitchen area where we'd find our hair nets, aprons and latex gloves.

"The presents for the children arrived?" Dad asked her.

"A few days ago."

"And the socks, mittens, and scarves for the adults?"

"Yes, thank you, Mr. Walker. You've been so generous."

"That's my wife you should be thanking."

Mom was the main breadwinner; it's a detail not many people knew and a secret Mom wanted kept.

"We should get started," Jill said. "We have a lot of people to feed today."

I was on mashed potato duty while Genie got to hand out dessert. I tried to speak to everyone, but I could see how that held up the line. I chatted when I could and when I scooped my last spoonful of potatoes, I took bags of wrapped presents and started handing those out. Genie, Mom, and Dad did the same.

The mom of a little girl who was no older than four or five couldn't stop smiling when I started to hand her daughter a gift. All the wrapped gifts had identifying tags on them and when I saw the doll, I yanked off the tag and knelt down in front of the girl.

"What's your name?" I asked.

"Molly," she said, looking down at her feet.

"Molly, I think this is for you," I said, handing it to her. She was tentative at first but when I held it closer to her, she took it from me. With great care, she peeled back the paper revealing the brown-haired doll who looked a little like her. I'd lucked out with that one.

"Mommy, look," she said, holding up the doll for her mom to see.

"That's very nice. Did you thank Mr. Walker?"

"Call me Zach," I said.

"Thank you, Zach," she said, her face coming alive.

"You're welcome." I turned to Molly's mom. "Is there anything I can get you? We have care packages for everyone."

"I'll get mine on my way out," she said. "I'm Diane," she said, extending her hand.

"It's a pleasure to meet you." I wanted to ask her how she got to Saint Anthony's, but I couldn't do it in front of Molly. Something about Diane set her apart from the others. As if reading my mind, she satisfied my curiosity.

"We're staying at Katie's House," she said.

I nodded. A shelter for abused women. "I understand."

"We wanted to spend the holiday with some of the people from Katie's House, right, Molly?"

The little girl nodded, but her focus was on her new doll.

"You have no family here?" I asked, keeping my voice low.

"Just my husband's. My parents have passed and my sister lives out of the country. She doesn't even know about this."

"You don't want to tell her?"

"I couldn't, it's too humiliating."

Diane's eyes welled up with tears. I took the seat next to her and grabbed a hold of her hand. "He's to blame. Not you."

"I picked him," she said, forcing a smile.

"Now you've unpicked him. Have you sought legal advice?"

"I've contacted Legal Aid, but the process is slow."

"I know someone who can help you pro bono. A great lawyer. Then you can get back on your feet."

"Thank you, Zach. That would mean the world to us," she said, her eyes glistening with tears.

I pulled Dad's old law firm's business card from my wallet and handed it to her. "Graham will help you. Tell him the Walkers sent you."

"Bless you," she said.

"I wish you well, Diane. And Molly, I will see you later," I said, calling out to the little girl. She smiled and waved goodbye.

I handed out the last of my gifts and we all sat down at different tables to enjoy the dinner with other Saint Anthony guests. I listened to their stories and wished I could help them all. And when we drove home a few hours later I was exhausted—not from serving food all day, but drained from the emotional toll all the stories I'd listened to. I was lucky for what I had and tried my hardest to never take it for granted.

"Why did I wear such a heavy sweater?" Genie complained when we'd gotten home. "I was dying in there."

"You make the same mistake every year," I said, following her upstairs. A quick change then on to our own Christmas dinner.

"You could have reminded me before we left."

"I got Christmas cheer watching you suffer."

"Since you're being such a jerk, I'm not going to tell you who I met."

"I'm sure I don't care."

"I think you should since she asked about you."

I stopped in the hallway and so did Genie. "Okay, I'll bite. Who did you meet?"

"A lady named Meredith. She's says she's Emma's mom."

CHAPTER TWENTY-FOUR

EMMA

Dad attempted Christmas breakfast with Grandpa as his accomplice. I wasn't allowed to help, but I did supervise by reminding Dad to turn over the pancakes before they burned and Grandpa to put a splash guard on the frying pan so he wouldn't get singed with bacon grease. Dad was a pro at making eggs so he didn't need any assistance there. They did let me put on a pot of coffee.

"Wendy was going to come over a little early to help us with dinner, if that's all right with you," Grandpa said.

He looked meek as if worried I'd erupt into a fit of rage. "Sure, that's fine. I could always use some extra help. Which reminds me, I've got to prepare the turkey once we're done opening presents."

"About presents...I thought we could open them this evening, once Wendy gets here."

"Oh, okay," I said. We were bucking tradition, but Grandpa seemed really excited about the whole Wendy thing.

We dove into breakfast and I was impressed with the pancakes. Dad had added chocolate chips to the batter. He was finally taking some of my advice and thinking outside the box...sort of.

Grandpa and I chatted about school while Dad flipped through the newspaper looking for the crossword. The rustling stopped and Dad stared at whatever had caught his attention. Someone die? Dad had a fascination with the obituaries.

He lowered the paper and looked at me, his face mired in confusion. Without a word he passed me the community section. I looked through the pictures and gasped. There I was, posing with Zach, my name in the caption as Zach's girlfriend.

"Care to explain?" he asked. He was a bit annoyed, and I couldn't blame him.

"He's not my boyfriend," was the first thing out of my mouth. And then I thought of Bianca. Did she see or hear about his? Was that why the texts started again?

"Let me see," Grandpa said, taking the section from me. "Oh, he's handsome and a senator's son. You could do a lot worse," he cooed.

"No, he's not my boyfriend," I protested. "He and his sister invited me to the party. Genie is a friend of mine." More truth-stretching. I was going straight to hell.

"Is this the guy you were talking about?"

"Dad!"

"Your grandfather is eventually going to find out. Why the secret?"

"Zach and I are friends, that's it. The photographer got it wrong."

"I think you make the cutest couple," Grandpa said. Now that he was in love, he wanted everyone to be.

Dad pressed his lips into a thin line. "Emma, you didn't even tell me about this."

My cheeks flushed. Busted. "It was a last-minute invitation. It wasn't a big deal."

"A party at the Walker house is a big deal," Grandpa said.

I shot him a warning glance. He responded with an apologetic shrug.

"I was going to tell you but I forgot about it. Really, it was nothing."

Dad's eyes stared hard at me. He was a human lie detector. "Why do I think you're not telling me everything?"

What did I do? He wasn't going to let it go. I bit down on my lip, trying to think of something fast, but nothing was coming other than the truth. "I did like him, but I knew right away that it wasn't right. Before anything got started, I shut it down. The caption is still wrong. He was never my boyfriend. That's it."

"Paul, cut the kid some slack," Grandpa said, rising from the table and grabbing our empty plates. "No need to pour salt in the wound."

Dad's hard stare softened. "If this changes... "

"I promise you'll be the first to know."

"Well, let's clean this place up. We have a guest coming," Grandpa said.

That was over, thanks to Grandpa. Next, I focused on dinner duty while Dad cleaned up our breakfast dishes. Grandpa disappeared to catch up on paperwork then ready himself since Wendy was expected in a few hours. I decided it was time to bake. Of everything in the kitchen, baking relaxed me most. With the few hours I had, I made Dad's favorite shortbread and Grandpa's gingerbread cookies. I was arranging them on a platter when Wendy arrived. I wandered over to the front door to see Grandpa taking Wendy's coat. Her eyes fell on me and she smiled.

"And you must be Emma."

"It's a pleasure to meet you, Wendy."

"Your grandfather's told so many great things about you. And I hear you're quite the chef."

My trusty old bullshit meter dove into action, this time on Wendy, but it wasn't going off. She seemed sincere. And though she'd never replace Grandma, she did have a grandmotherly quality about her. Grandpa had told me she was divorced with a son living on the East Coast. She wasn't spending the holidays with him and his family because she had a trip planned out there in the New Year. Or maybe she wanted to spend Christmas with Grandpa? And while she used to be a ruthless prosecutor—Grandpa's words—she had a straightforward simplicity to her. Black slacks, a fuzzy baby blue cashmere sweater, and although her nails were done, she didn't have on layers of makeup and her light brown hair was cut short—a style easy to maintain. She was elegant and gracious.

"Thank you for the kind words."

"And if you need any help, put me to work."

"Would you like some homemade eggnog?" Grandpa asked. "Emma made it herself."

"I'd love some," Wendy said, beaming.

I liked that Wendy seemed kind and soft-spoken. I'd been a little worried about meeting her, thinking I'd have to walk on eggshells or she'd make me wither under a barrage of questions, but it seemed she'd left that behind for small-town life.

"What are you taking in school?" Wendy asked.

"I'm in my first year so I'm still trying to sort things out."

"I got my English degree before I realized I wanted to be a lawyer. Just remember that you're young and you have lots of time." She sipped the eggnog. "Oh, this is divine."

Dad, who'd been loitering around but not saying much, jumped into the conversation. "Wendy, do you know the Walkers? What's his name? The senator."

"Oh yes, Daniel Walker. I don't know him per se; met him a few times and he has a good reputation."

"How about his kids?"

"Dad!"

Wendy's grey eyes looked from me to Dad. "I haven't heard a thing about them, and for a politician, that's a good thing."

I laughed nervously, wanting to throttle Dad. Time to make my exit. "I'm going to finish up dinner," I said, rising and giving Dad the stink-eye as I passed.

"Let me help," Wendy offered.

I wasn't entirely sure I wanted her help, but to refuse would disappoint Grandpa, so we got to work. The turkey needed a few more minutes in the oven before resting for at least a half hour. Wendy peeled potatoes and I stuffed mushrooms. I was attempting acorn squash for the first time and prepped them with fresh ground pepper, Himalayan salt, and a parmesan rub. Once the turkey came out, they'd go in.

"I don't mean to be nosy, but I'm guessing you're the reason your dad asked about the Walkers?"

"Zach and I are just friends. The stupid paper published a picture of us saying that we were dating."

"How'd they get a picture of the two of you?" she asked.

"I was at their Christmas party."

"And with the both of you at the party, I guess the paper assumed."

"So now Dad's all bent out of shape."

Wendy saw the paper lying on the kitchen table and glanced at it. "Well, he's certainly easy on the eyes."

My cheeks blushed and I made sure to keep my face hidden from Wendy. "Like I said, we're just friends."

"How did you get invited to a Walker party? Invitations like those are pretty exclusive."

"Zach invited me—I mean, Genie invited me. His sister."

If Wendy had a bullshit meter, it had to be off the charts.

"How many friends did the Walker kids invite?"

"I don't know, but I wasn't paying attention. Genie's boyfriend was there, but I guess the rest of the guests were donors and friends."

"I see. All your grandfather does is talk about you, so if I'm overstepping, you tell me to mind my own business, but usually a senator's son invites only special people to fundraisers like that."

My face was growing more crimson by the second. "Zach is a really nice person."

"I bet he is. How many potatoes should I peel?"

"I think six is enough," I said relieved that she'd changed topics.

"What is Zach doing for Christmas?"

Damn. "I don't know. I'm sure he's spending it with his family. He may have mentioned a ski trip with friends."

"And how long have you been friends?"

"Since the beginning of the school year. Do you like spinach in your mashed potatoes?"

"I love spinach and I've never had it in mashed potatoes before. Sounds intriguing." She peeled the last potato and brought them to the sink to wash. She glanced over at me as I coated the squash. "How did you meet him?"

"Jake, he used—he's a friend. He introduced us." Damn. I could see why she was such a good prosecutor. She had me tripping all over myself.

Wendy piled the potatoes in a colander. "Should I cube them and get a pot on for them?"

"Yes, thank you."

"Jake is your roommate? Henry mentioned that."

Grandpa sure did share a lot with Wendy. "Uh, yeah."

"Sweetie, I'm going to be honest with you. Your grandfather asked me to come early so that I could get to know you and talk to you about, you know, girl things. It seems your dad is really worried about you, and as much I want to help them out, I feel a need to be honest with you. Please don't tell them I told you. And if you want me to butt out, I'd understand fully."

In so many ways Wendy wasn't anything like Grandma. Grandma had doted on me, made quilts in her spare time, played cards every Sunday night with her friends, volunteered at the church, and didn't care about clothes or makeup—probably the exact opposite of Wendy. Grandma was a simple woman. Wendy was a lawyer, a woman who would have intimidated Grandma, but despite all that, I felt a kinship to her. She liked Grandpa a lot, it was obvious, and even though she didn't give off the warmth Grandma did, I was drawn to her. I made a split-second decision.

"Can you keep a secret?"

She nodded.

"Jake kicked me out of our apartment after I punched his girlfriend in the face. Zach took me in and gave me the spare room at his place where I've been living ever since. Jake and I no longer talk. Please don't tell Dad or Grandpa." I felt like those people who walk into sacred rivers and are cleansed. The burden was lifted, the lies out in the open.

Her eyes bugged open. "Well, I wasn't anticipating all that! You did what? You don't seem like the type of young lady to have that kind of outburst."

I told Wendy all about Bianca over another cup of eggnog. We sat at the kitchen table and I relayed it all, every last detail right down to the kiss. She listened, enthralled by every word. At one point she stopped me, telling me she needed another glass.

"You really should tell your Dad," she said, a thoughtful expression on her face.

"It will kill him. I figure I'll just let the school year end and come up with some story why Jake and I aren't living together next year. And you never know, Jake and Bianca could break up."

"They could, but is Jake still someone you'd call a friend?"

I deflated. "I guess not."

"I will keep your confidence, but at some point your dad is owed the truth."

"I know."

"And about Zach...he seems like a really nice young man. From one girl to another, you might want to give him a chance."

I looked at the clock. It was getting late for dinner. We mashed potatoes, plated food, and called Dad and Grandpa to the dinner table. As we all sat together, I wondered if I could trust Wendy and if she really intended to keep her word. Well, I'd know if she didn't. Dad and Grandpa would be all over me the second they found out.

CHAPTER TWENTY-FIVE

EMMA

I packed up for my return trip to Western. I sent Zach a few texts, including one on New Year's Eve, between batches of caramel popcorn and movies with Dad, but they all went unanswered. I felt a twinge of guilt and a bad case of nerves. Maybe he was still upset with me. I'd left so much up in the air.

"Let me drive you back to school," Dad said.

"It's an hour there and back on some pretty slick roads. The bus will be fine. Besides, I already got my ticket."

Dad frowned. "It was nice having you back, Kiddo. We're going to miss you. You'll call me when you get there?"

"I will."

"And keep me up to date on any developments with that Walker kid."

"Dad!"

"You're my girl and I worry."

"Well, don't!"

He took me to the bus station and a part of me didn't want to go. I wanted to stay behind with Dad and Grandpa, working in the shop, making dinners and living a much simpler life. The only problem was that Dad and Grandpa would have none of it.

I texted Zach a few more times from the bus with no response. I decided to put thoughts of him aside and pulled out a book to pass the time. As the bus pulled into the station in Minneapolis, a fleeting part of me hoped that Zach was there waiting, arms extended, and I'd run into them like in some sappy romance movie, but the only people there were waiting for other buses.

I did like him. I liked him a lot, but it was so complicated. It wouldn't last. I was not Zach Walker material. And then what? He'd dump me, I'd move out and have nothing. I cared too much about him to just throw it away on a two- or three-month fling. But I had a bigger problem. What would we do now? Forget about it, like it never happened? Or worse, try to talk about it. I cringed.

These thoughts floated through my head as I hailed a cab to the apartment. This would be the first time seeing him in a month and as the cab dropped me off, and I made my way to his apartment and put the key into the lock, I thought my chest would explode from the nerves. I opened the door and walked into darkness. Nothing and nobody. I let out a huge sigh of relief and went to my room. It was just as I'd left it. Next, I hit the kitchen and scoured it to see if we needed groceries. I found a few dishes in the sink. At least Zach had been here recently.

I opened the fridge door. Other than a few beers, a brick of cheddar cheese, condiments and limp celery, there wasn't much to eat. I grabbed my purse and keys and walked to the grocery store less than a block away. I bought only the essentials and whatever else I could carry. Some mixed greens, chicken breasts, milk, bread and a few other odds and ends. I got back to the apartment and this time a few lights were on. Zach was inside and he glanced up from the sofa when I walked in. He nodded and that's when I saw someone sitting next to him. My heart thudded to the floor.

"Emma, this is Heather."

"Hi," she said with a spastic wave.

"Hi," I said and scurried into the kitchen. Not Heather. I tried to keep calm as I set down the groceries. Heather, the one who'd been pining for him. A wave of nausea made me grip onto the edge of the countertop. No, no, no.

Zach came into the kitchen and gave me a funny look. I didn't bother trying to cover up why I was hunched over. Sure, I could have said I had cramps, hurt my ankle or some other excuse, but I didn't bother.

"You don't need to make food for us or anything. We already decided to go get burgers."

"Uh, fine."

"See you later."

I heard them leave and slumped down in one of the chairs. I should have gone with my instinct and stayed in Pine Falls.

I COCOONED MYSELF IN bed the next morning not wanting to venture out and see Zach. Fortunately, he'd come home alone, but did that really matter? And what if she ever spent the night? The thought gutted me.

I knew he liked to go to the gym Sunday mornings, so I waited until he left. Then I pulled myself out of bed and lumbered into the kitchen, making myself coffee and looking through yesterday's paper. I couldn't even think about food.

I'd asked for this. I'd pushed him away and he'd moved on. My only option was to deal with it.

I looked at the clock. I'd offered to take a shift at Julian's to make an assortment of cakes and cookies. It would be a nice escape from the apartment. I took a shower, got ready and left a note for Zach that I wouldn't be back until evening. With keys and purse in hand, I grasped onto my phone as I walked out the door. It wasn't until I was in the elevator that I saw the text.

000:000:0000: Watch your back you ugly bitch.

Me: Get a life.

Sure, I was defiant, but I was also a little frightened. I wouldn't put it past Bianca and her friends to try something. I doubted they'd try anything serious, most likely something more subtle. Harass me at school or work. Follow me around campus. Throw things at me. Trip me in a hallway. It wouldn't be the first time I'd been bullied.

000:000:0000: Why don't you string yourself up and end it already.

Dread came over me. It was nice that Bianca had left me alone for a few weeks, but now that classes started tomorrow, I guess she wanted to remind me what a monster she was. I thought to delete it, but keeping it seemed like the best thing to do. It would be good evidence to show Jake one day, if he ever came around.

"How were your holidays?" Jessica asked when I arrived at Julian's.

"Good. And yours?"

"Lots of eating, so try to make something healthy."

I laughed. "Students don't buy healthy."

"I've got some good news for you," Jessica said, struggling to hold back a smile.

"You won the lottery?"

"I wish. No, Billie told me to inform you that you're back on floor duty. No more hiding you in the kitchen."

"Really? That's great."

"You're the hardest worker we have. You never complain about hours, show up on time, do what you're asked to do...you're the best employee here. After me, of course."

"Of course," I said.

"When you're finished in the kitchen, get your apron and get back out here."

I spent half my shift in the kitchen and the other half on the floor. I made chocolate chip cookies, peanut butter cookies, ginger snaps, banana nut bread and chocolate oat squares. I wanted to make carrot muffins, but ran out of time. The showcase still looked a little sparse so I left a note for Billie telling her I'd be happy to come in any time she needed me. Being around the apartment was the last place I wanted to be.

I trudged through the snow to the bus stop and saw a group of students. Had I been alone waiting for the bus, I probably would have headed back to Julian's and called a cab. If nothing else, Bianca had succeeded in spooking me a little. Despite the fact that Zach no longer felt Bianca was a threat, I made sure I was always aware of my surroundings.

I read on the ride home to keep my mind occupied and luckily for me the bus stop was half a block from Zach's. As I scurried home, I cursed Bianca for what she was doing and myself for being scared. Each time she sent one of those ominous texts, she scraped away at my defenses.

"Hey, why didn't you call me? I would have picked you up," Zach said from his usual position in front of the television.

I hung up my coat and shrugged. "I wasn't sure how long I was staying."

I didn't stick around to make conversation. It was already past eight and I wanted to change, get my books together and go to sleep. I retreated to my room and organized. A knock at my door interrupted me and I let Zach in.

"So what's up? Why are you acting weird?"

"I'm not. I'm just tired. It was a long day today."

His brown eyes searched me, looking for cracks. "Are we going to school together tomorrow?"

"Yes. What time are we leaving?"

"My first class is at nine-thirty."

"So is mine."

Unsatisfied, he left. I finished putting together my school bag and changed into my pajamas. I pulled out a mystery novel and tried to escape my life.

MORE SILENCE IN THE car the next morning. I stared out the window, watching the snow-covered streets and boulevards whiz by. Sure, this was awkward. We used to chat the whole ten minutes about anything from politics to hockey, but I didn't feel like talking and didn't have much to say, anyway. The minute we parked the car I went one way and he went another. We'd agreed to meet at Drake Hall at two-thirty.

I sat through classes, barely taking notes. My mind wandered to all sorts of places, like were they already sleeping together? Probably. When did they start dating? Likely right after Christmas. I bet they even spent New Year's Eve together. Worst of all, when would he bring her back to the apartment for a sleepover? The thought of making breakfast for the three of us made my skin itch and burn.

I hiked across campus to Drake Hall, kicking at sticks peeking through the snow. I was mad at myself, but not mad enough to do something about it. And even if I did something, what would it be? Tell Zach to dump her and then do what? Tell him what?

I stopped short when I saw Zach with Heather at our usual meeting spot. Neither saw me as I stared at them. She couldn't stop smiling as he spoke about who knows what. Jealousy devoured me. I turned away from them and waited by the doors and when I glanced back just one time, they were locked in a kiss. It felt like someone was reaching into my chest, yanking out my heart and squeezing it as hard as they could. I faced the doors, this time not vowing to look back.

"Waiting long?" Zach asked a minute later. He was at my side, a satisfied smile on his face.

"Just got here," I lied.

"What are we having tonight?" he asked as we drove home.

"I have a killer headache. Could you order out?"

"Oh, okay."

He sounded dejected and I didn't care. The moment we were home I barricaded myself in my room and didn't come out.

CHAPTER TWENTY-SIX

ZACH

I rummaged through the fridge and made myself a sandwich. Emma had been in her room for nearly three hours, not coming out for even a glass of water. Did I know what was wrong? Sure. I'd heard some rumors that Bianca had seen the photo from the paper. It seems everyone had seen it. Brett was still breaking my balls about it. But Bianca was seriously pissed off. I couldn't figure out why she even cared.

I'd cornered Brett that afternoon and asked him what he knew. At first he insisted that he didn't know anything, but by the way his eyes kept shifting, I knew he was full of shit.

"Tell me what you know."

He sighed. "Not much. I heard she had some temper tantrum or something. Started saying that she wasn't finished with Emma."

I pulled out my phone and searched through my contacts for Bianca's number.

"Hey, you're not calling her, are you?" Brett asked. "Don't stir it up again. I'm sure she's over it."

"Doesn't sound like it," I said, my jaw clenching in anger. Bianca had a real screw loose.

"If it helps, I even said a few things to one of Bianca's friends. I told her that Bianca was showing a little too much crazy."

I narrowed my eyes. "You actually did that?"

"Look, I don't know Emma, but this is getting stupid now. Bianca needs to knock it off."

"You hear anything else, I want to know."

"Fine."

I was pretty sure Brett had told me everything, and I was also pretty sure Bianca had contacted Emma somehow. Had she shown up at Julian's? Got that idiot Jake to send her a message? Whatever it was, Emma wasn't telling me about it.

I ate my sandwich and watched some Monday Night Football. Emma finally came out of isolation and walked past me without a word and into the kitchen. A few drawers opened, some clanging of pots and then the smell of chicken soup, her soup, the one she made tons of and froze whenever there was nothing else to eat. My mouth watered and I followed the aroma into the kitchen.

"Any for me?" I asked.

"Sure," she said, her face focused on the pot. She was so detached. I wondered if she was mad at me for something. For not texting her again over the holidays? About Heather?

"Are you sure you're okay?"

"Headache," she said, pointing to her head.

"Have you taken anything for it? I think I have some Advil."

"No, I'm good."

I got some bowls and she continued to stir, like I was a ghost in the room. Yes, something was bothering her and the only person I could think of who might be able to get it out of her was Genie.

She poured the soup into the bowls and we ate in relative silence other than a few sentences about school. She then got up, washed her bowl and went back to her room. Once I knew she was tucked away, I called Genie.

"So you want me to find out what's wrong? Did you ask her?"

"Of course I did."

"I'm going to point something out to you because I know you're a bit dense. When did your problems with Emma start?"

"After the kiss."

"But you talked to her after that by text? Everything seemed fine?"

"Yes."

"And what changed when she got back?"

"Nothing."

"Think harder, weenie."

I was at a loss. I had no idea what had changed and then it hit me. "Heather?"

"You're the biggest weenie I've ever met. What possessed you to get involved with her? I'm sure she's nice, but are your balls that blue? Emma is nervous, it's that simple. She's never had a boyfriend, she likes you but gets spooked by the kiss, and what do you do? You start dating some girl the second she gets back. You're an ass."

"But it's so casual."

"Ugh! Really! Are all boys this stupid? I bet her mood will lift once that girl is out of the picture, unless you like that girl."

"She's nice, but..."

Genie let out a pained groan. "Then dump her before she gets too attached." She paused for a long moment. "I'm going to ask you something, and don't even think about lying to me because I can see through your shit. Did you start dating this girl to piss off Emma? Get her to react? To prove to yourself that she likes you?"

"No." I said it so quickly I didn't believe myself.

"Are you twenty going on five? Emma isn't the kind of girl you do that to. In fact, you don't do that to any girl. What were you thinking?"

"I didn't intentionally do it!"

"Sure you did. You needed to validate that she likes you. I already told you that she does, so why push her buttons?"

"I wasn't doing that. I don't even know why I started dating Heather."

"Because you are a—"

I cut her off before she could finish. "Yeah, I get it."

"Like I told you before, give Emma a little space, and if you find yourself getting horny, get romantic with one of your hands."

With that she hung up.

I hated when Genie was right.

HEATHER MET ME O'CONNOR's, one of the lunch places on campus. I had an hour before meeting up with Emma to go home.

"Hello," she said, placing a kiss on my cheek and settling into the seat across from me. She set her overflowing school bag down and unwrapped the sandwich she'd grabbed. "How was your day?"

"Busy. Lots of assignments to do."

"I have half a textbook to read and two papers to finish by Monday. It's going to be a long weekend. Are you okay if we don't see each other?"

"About that, I thought we could talk. I'm getting swamped with school and I need to focus on my marks to get into law school. I think we might not get to see each other as much."

She was about to take a bite of her sandwich, but set it back on the plastic wrap. "I see," she said, her voice dropping off.

"I can't blow this chance. I have to stay committed."

"I understand. Look, it's not like we were serious or anything."

"You're a great girl. I hate doing this."

She looked off in the distance and when her gaze returned to me, she shrugged. "It's about your roommate, isn't it? I'm not going to freak out, I just want to know."

"It's not about Emma."

One eyebrow rose. "I haven't known you long, but I can tell that's a lie. Maybe you don't believe it yet, but this is all about her."

Heather really was a great girl. Not an ounce of bitterness was in her voice. It was all matter-of-fact, calm and understanding. Had it been a different time, if Emma had never come into my life, Heather was a girl I could fall for.

"You might be right, I don't know."

"You're a good guy, Zach Walker. Emma is lucky. I've had this feeling she's liked you for a long time. I see it when you meet up with her after classes. Tell her how you feel and she'll be putty in your hands."

I didn't know how to respond to that.

"I'm sorry this didn't work out," I said.

"Hey, it's only been a few weeks. I'll get over it."

She got up and so did I. I hugged her tightly and kissed her cheek. "Let's keep in touch, okay?"

"Sure."

She didn't say it convincingly.

"I mean it."

"Okay, Zach. See you around."

I sat again and thought about what she'd said. Emma, putty in my hands? Not a fucking chance. I may have cleared an obstacle, but I'm not sure it made a difference.

CHAPTER TWENTY-SEVEN

EMMA

Genie called and asked if I wanted to go out with her, Lucy, and Andrea on Friday. I accepted her offer immediately. Dancing the night away with a few vodka and sevens was definitely my idea of a good time. All week I looked forward to it and even went out shopping to pick up something new to wear.

Thursday after class Zach was waiting for me alone. No Heather. She'd been a fixture every day, saying goodbye with their long drawn out kisses. Yuck.

"I'm the driver tomorrow night," he said. "I'll drop you guys off and pick you up later."

"You have a hot date?"

"No, hanging out with the guys."

"What about Heather?"

"We stopped seeing each other. Nice girl but not right for me."

I stumbled and nearly hit the ground. Zach grabbed my arm to steady me. "You okay?"

"Tripped over my own feet." What I wanted to do was a happy dance. "Sorry to hear about Heather."

"No big deal. So what are we eating tonight?"

"It's nothing too exotic, just some Crockpot chili. I didn't have time for anything else."

"Homemade garlic bread?"

"Yup, but the bread is frozen. No time for fresh."

"Before you came along, dinner was either a sandwich or something I could nuke."

"Then you must be happy to have me around."

He smiled. "Yup, you're okay."

My body warmed and my skin tingled. "I was thinking of making roasted chicken tomorrow with lemon potatoes and a Greek salad."

"I love your lemon potatoes."

"I could use the rest of the lemons to make a meringue pie."

"I love lemon meringue pie."

I smiled. We were back to normal, just the way I liked it.

I LOVED DANCING. ANDREA, Lucy, Genie, and I danced at Diablo's, the latest and hottest club to open, and I didn't have a single care. With Heather out of the picture, the dark cloud that had been hanging over me for weeks had finally lifted. I was having fun again.

"Let's talk," Genie suggested. We were both glistening from sweat and in dire need of drink refills. We found a quiet part of the bar with a bunch of sofas and tables while Andrea and Lucy continued to dance.

"Thanks for inviting me," I said. "I'm having a great time."

"You're invited anytime. To be honest, this is first time I've been out since we got back to school."

"We've got to do it more often."

"Let's toast to more girls' nights out."

I sucked back half my drink, letting the alcohol roll down my throat. I could have done a toast to fake IDs, but that was for another time. Instead I scanned the crowd, a contented smile plastered on my face.

"How have you been? We really haven't talked much," Genie said, sipping her rum and Coke.

"I've been good. Work and school keep me busy."

"Any Bianca sightings?"

I stiffened a little. She, or one of her cohorts, had sent another text. "No, I don't see her."

"And everything is good with my brother? He hasn't driven you crazy yet?"

"No, we have a good time."

"You know, he cares about you."

"I'm care about him too. He's done so much for me and I don't know how I'll ever repay him."

Genie grinned devilishly. "That's not what I meant."

So many times things went straight over my head. For instance, my friendship with Jake was full of hints that I was a bother to him, but I'd missed them all. Or the time at summer camp when I was twelve—the only year I went to summer camp. I was hanging out with a couple of girls who I thought liked me up until I caught them in the showers telling other girls how creepy I was because I read a lot and didn't like to talk about boys or talk about much at all.

But this hint was hitting me straight in the face.

"I know what you're thinking, but I'm sure you're wrong."

"I've known Zach for twenty years. We shared a womb together so I've got a pretty good read on him. I know when he likes a girl, and he likes you a lot."

My mouth went dry. Coming from Genie, this was serious. Although I'd only known her a few short months, she wasn't the type of person to bullshit anyone. "I still think you're wrong."

"And how do you feel about him?"

"I don't know," I said, avoiding eye contact and stirring my drink over and over again. If I kept it up, I'd stir the fizz right out of it.

"Do you still like that Jake guy?"

"Not a chance."

"Then what's the problem?"

"We have a good relationship, so why complicate it?"

"Don't hate me for asking, but have you had a boyfriend before?"

"No, not really."

Genie chortled. "What kind of answer is that?"

"Well, a few months before my grandma died, I dated this guy at the tennis club. He was nice and I was curious. We went out a few times and had sex once. Looking back, I think I wanted to know what it was like even though I didn't really feel a connection with him. It's not something I regret."

Genie sucked back her drink and motioned to the bartender to get us refills. "You know, I have a lot of respect for that. You were curious, you got it out of the way. Was he cute at least?"

"I guess so. It was his first time too, so we were a bit of a mess. I didn't call him, he didn't call me, and I think we were both happy about that."

"The first time isn't memorable unless you really like the guy and he's super cute and has an amazingly beautiful sister."

I rolled my eyes and finished my drink. "Zach is great, but he scares me."

Had I said that aloud? Damn alcohol. And it wasn't like I was tipsy.

"Zach isn't scary. Why do you say that?"

"I don't want to go out with a guy for a few months. When I meet the right guy, it has to be long term. Zach isn't a long-term kind of guy."

"That's because he hasn't met the right girl. You're the right girl."

My cheeks flushed. "You don't know that."

"Remember, I shared a womb with him. I know what he's thinking before he does."

I fidgeted on the sofa. Did I tell her about the kiss? Maybe she already knew about it. My head was a whirlwind of jumbled thoughts, none helped by alcohol. "I'm not his type of girl."

Genie's eyes narrowed. "Oh yes, you most certainly are. And he knows it too, and that's why he's been very cautious with you. I think you should give him a chance."

The bartender came around with our drinks, and right after that, Andrea and Lucy collapsed onto the empty sofa facing ours. All discussion about Zach ended, and I wasn't sad about that.

SATURDAY NIGHT, AS I nursed the last of a mild hangover, Zach ordered pizzas. While I devoured a slice of pepperoni, mushroom, and black olive, he found a movie for us to watch.

"I'm starved," I said between bites. "This is good pizza."

"It's from Luigi's. Normally they don't deliver this far, but my family's a good customer."

I wolfed down three slices before sprawling out on the sofa. "I'm stuffed," I said. Zach got up to grab more beers, and I lifted my legs and tucked up my knees to make room for him.

"Stretch your legs, no big deal," he said, grasping on to them and laying them over his thighs. Sure, it was only an innocent touch, but it still got my blood pumping.

"What do you want to watch?" he asked, handing me a beer. "I've got it narrowed down to a few."

"Whatever you want."

"Action flick it is."

He settled on a shoot-'em-up movie. I watched disinterestedly, mostly from my carb coma, and didn't notice right away that both Zach's hands were on my lower legs, rubbing them ever so gently. I liked it, but it terrified me. My calves tensed and grew rigid. Damn! Why was I getting nervous? Deep down I trusted Zach, so why was I so scared?

I sucked back some beer and closed my eyes. I'd think some happy relaxing thoughts, like frolicking on a Hawaiian beach (even though I'd never set foot on one), or reading a book on a comfy lawn chair by the lake. At some point I drifted off to sleep and an hour or so later Zach was tickling my feet.

"Hey," I said, squirming.

"You missed the entire movie," he said.

I yawned and sat up. "Did I miss anything good?"

"It was all right. Want another beer? More pizza?"

"I'm good."

He got up and grabbed another beer and a slice of pizza. He munched away and I couldn't help but stare at his strong jaw line, his five o'clock shadow, and the muscles flexing in his arms. Feeling my eyes on him, he turned to look at me.

"Do I have pepperoni on my face?"

"No."

I wanted to kiss him so badly.

"Should we watch another movie or are you going to crash in five minutes?"

"We can watch a movie. I'll try to stay awake."

This time he chose an action movie with a hint of romance. A few minutes in and I was already envisioning wrapping my arms around him but I didn't dare move. I didn't know how to tell him what I wanted when I was scared of where it would lead. My conversation with Genie kept running through my head. What if she was wrong?

I leaned in closer to him, a completely involuntary action. He smelled so nice. What if he rejected me? But to have his arms around me, holding me close...I wanted that so much. But if he got mad? Asked me what I was doing? Made a big deal? I was a mess.

"What's up? Are you cold?" he asked, his hand resting on my thigh just above the knee. The heat radiating through my jeans and up my leg was like nothing I'd felt before.

I looked at him, wide-eyed and wanting. We stared at each other for what felt like forever. Reading my mind, he grasped my arms and pulled me close, and I closed my eyes with a contented sigh. His lips pressed gently against mine, testing the waters, waiting for me to respond. I kissed him back, feeling every inch of my body come alive. This was what connected felt like. He slid his arms around me, resting on the small of my back. Then he lifted me so that I was straddling him. The kiss intensified, his tongue meeting mine, still tasting of beer. My head was swimming with emotions and feelings so foreign to me.

Our breaths heavy, he pulled me closer, my chest pressed up against his. His lips left mine, passing over my earlobe sending the most marvelous chill through me.

"Come to my room," he said, his voice low and wanting.

My body went cold. His room meant sex. I leapt off him like someone had thrown a bucket of ice water on me. "No, I can't."

He looked puzzled, the euphoria of the last few minutes fading away. "Emma, we don't have to. Why are you so freaked out?"

Did I look freaked out? My hands were shaking but that could have been from our make-out session. "I'm not, I just can't move that fast."

"Fine, we can move slowly," he said, extending his hand to me. "I know it's your first time and I don't want to rush you."

"I'm not a virgin. I guess you just assumed that? Like no guy would want to have sex with me?" Why was I getting so defensive? I had to rein it in.

"Sorry, you just never mentioned a boyfriend."

"I had sex with a guy once. Now you know. I guess you don't get to bang a virgin."

What was wrong with me? Now I'd pissed him off too. I could see his face souring by the second.

"I'm beginning to think that your opinion of me is pretty low. Like I just screw around, have some fun then move on. I've known you for five months so if that's what I wanted to do, don't you think I would have tried it a long time ago? Emma, I like you... but you know what, never mind. Keep pining for Jake."

He got up, grabbed his keys, jacket, and left. I stood in the living room not knowing what to do or how to fix what I'd royally screwed up.

CHAPTER TWENTY-EIGHT

EMMA

I waited up for Zach, but he didn't come home until late. I wanted to talk to him but based on his expression the next morning, he was in no mood. He had his gym bag and passed by the living room and out the door without a word.

I slumped down on the sofa and wanted to cry. I thought if we talked it through, we could come to some kind of understanding, but I didn't even know what to say. I was getting worked up over so many things, too many to make any rational sense of. If we started dating and it got serious then what? First, I'd have to tell Dad; second, I'd have to be a girlfriend—and I had no idea what that entailed—and third, I'd have to let Zach into my personal space, and no one got that close to me. That was probably why I'd loved Jake so much. He was unattainable, just the way I liked it.

The hardest part of all would be talking to Zach. I didn't know how to have this conversation with him. What would I even say? For a brief moment I considered writing him a letter, like my old therapist told me to do after Grandma died. The letter was supposed to be to Grandma telling her how much I missed her, how angry I was that cancer had taken her away, and any other feelings I was having. I wrote the letter and it did make me feel better, but then what was I supposed to do with it? Mail it to heaven?

I made coffee and waited. He couldn't hide at the gym forever, and just after noon, he came through the door. I leapt from the sofa and caught him before he could retreat to his bedroom, change, and leave again.

"Can we talk for a minute?" I asked, blocking his path.

His expression couldn't look more disinterested. "About what?"

"Last night. Give me a chance to explain."

He set his gym bag down and grimaced. He was not happy, which made the butterflies in my chest flutter even more. "Fine."

"Let's sit," I suggested. He seemed less imposing that way.

He followed me to the sofa and we sat. He was staring straight ahead, tense and annoyed, while I faced him, a nervous wreck.

"I'm not the best communicator," I began.

"You can say that again," he muttered.

I let out a quick, halting breath. He wasn't going to make this easy. "Sometimes I just panic like I did last night. I wasn't ready to have sex with you. It doesn't mean I don't want to. It was just happening so fast."

He faced me, his eyes full of fire. "Answer one question: are you still in love with Jake?"

"No! Why do you keep asking that? I haven't talked to or seen him in months."

"I think you panic because if you're with me you can't be with him."

The longest moment passed, the two of us just staring at one another. I took one deep breath to calm myself and wished I had water to wet my dry mouth. "Jake's dead to me. He hurt me more than anyone ever could. He was my friend, or so I thought. Jake was supposed to be my soulmate, my forever, but that ended a long time ago. And you think I still want to be with him? I don't want to be in the same room with him."

"Then why haven't you told your dad the truth?"

So that was it? "I'm not protecting Jake, I'm protecting my dad. Dad always comes first."

More painful silence. I felt like I was teetering on the edge of a cliff and Zach had the power to give me that final push.

He crossed his arms over his chest, his face tight and grim. "What am I supposed to do? What do you want me to do?"

"I don't know because I don't know what you want from me."

"I don't know either. I just want to let things happen. I don't want to set out a plan or a schedule, that's not how it works. It has to be fluid."

"I can do that."

He rolled his eyes. "You don't even know what it is that you think you can do."

I let out a frustrated sigh. "Is this about sex?"

"No," he said, rising. "It's about you letting go, not being so introverted. I try to break your shell and you push me away. This is too much work. You're too much work. I'm going out with the guys so I won't be around tonight."

He went to his room and I sat there, dumbfounded and hurt. That was it, I was giving up.

HELEN WAS A NICE DIVERSION. We trained for the upcoming tournament and each time I hit a ball I imagined it was either Jake or Bianca. After about twenty minutes, Helen put up her hand and motioned me over to the net. She was huffing and puffing and I gave her a minute to catch her breath.

"Who pissed in your Corn Flakes this morning?" she asked.

"What?"

"I can't keep up with today. You've got no mercy for me. I know you want to whip me into shape, but you might kill me first."

"I'm sorry," I said. "I didn't mean it."

"You want to tell me what's wrong, or is it none of my business?"

"It's nothing. I'm fine."

"If you need to talk, this old broad can give you some sound advice. I've been around the block more than a few times."

"Thanks, I appreciate it."

I wasn't about to tell Helen my troubles with Zach. For a whole week he and I said little to each other. We went to and from school and most evenings he busied himself playing basketball, hockey, or studying at the library. Everything I didn't want to happen was exactly what was happening.

"Let's call it a night. We'll train again on Sunday?"

"Yes." Our qualifiers were coming up, not that I was worried. I'd seen a few other teams practicing, and they weren't going to be much of a challenge.

I went home and found Zach in his usual spot eating Chinese takeout. He didn't share and I didn't ask. Instead I made myself a salad and was eating alone at our dining room table when Genie stormed into the apartment, a few bags in hand.

"Steve and I are over," she announced.

Zach looked up from the sofa, chopsticks in midair, and I was still chewing my last bite. Genie threw down her bags and sat across from me.

"He's been screwing around behind my back. For months! That asshole!

Zach joined us and we watched and listened as she gave the play-by-play of Steve's latest shenanigans. A two-year relationship over, and Genie didn't seem exactly heartbroken. She was more furious than anything else.

"All those late nights working had nothing to do with work! The shit was sneaking around."

"You know I never liked the guy," Zach said.

"I know Mom and Dad are going to celebrate when they find out. I hate when they're right."

"I guess you're moving back here?" Zach asked.

"For now, yes."

"You can have your room back. I'd be happy to take the sofa," I volunteered.

"No, I'll take the sofa," Zach said, throwing me a look of disapproval. "Genie, you take my room until we figure something out."

"Sorry guys, I know you had a nice arrangement here. It's only for another six weeks."

"Zach cannot stay on the sofa for six weeks," I protested.

"Look, we'll figure something out. For tonight that's the arrangement," Zach said, exasperated. His fuse was short lately.

Zach helped Genie bring up the last of her things while I puttered in the kitchen putting together a last-minute dinner for her. We had lettuce, tofu, mushrooms and rice, so I put together some vegetarian lettuce wraps. A part of me was happy to have Genie around. She'd cut the tension in the apartment. A non-hostile face would be a nice change.

"This has to be homemade lemonade," Genie said while she ate. I had a lettuce wrap and so did Zach. We didn't want her eating alone.

"Pretty much everything around here is from scratch," Zach said.

"Emma, stop spoiling my brother. He doesn't deserve it."

"Sure he does," I said with a little laugh. Genie had already lifted the storm clouds hovering over the apartment.

He looked at me from across the table and gave me the smallest smile. My heart fluttered.

"And you just whipped up the ingredients for lettuce wraps? The seasoning is perfection."

"Sorry it's such a meager dinner. That's all we had. I was going to do groceries tomorrow."

"I could eat this every day. I'm so used to eating out. I think I'm going to look forward to the next month and a half."

We finished eating and Genie went to take a shower, to cleanse the dirt of Steve. Her words. Zach helped me with the dishes which was a pleasant surprise.

"I don't mind taking the sofa. I'm the interloper."

"Em, it's fine. It won't kill me."

He didn't sound annoyed anymore.

"I bet you're happy about Steve."

"Let's just say I don't mind sleeping on the sofa for six weeks if it means he's out of Genie's life for good."

"It's going to be fun with the three of us here."

He smirked. "Not exactly what I was thinking."

It made sense to give Genie back her old room. I took a few of my things and set up camp in Zach's room. In all the months I'd lived with him, I'd never been in there. He didn't have much in it other than the largest bed he could fit, a nightstand, a dresser, a mirror, and a three-shelf bookcase filled to the brim with all kinds of books from how-to to who-done-it with a modest selection of science fiction. On the nightstand was a simple lamp, an alarm clock, and the latest book he was reading on carpentry. The best part of the room was his fully equipped bathroom.

I set my stuff down and rejoined them in the living room debating what television show to watch.

"I'm not watching that," Zach said. "I suggest you watch television in your own room."

"Emma, how do you get him to change the station?"

"I usually don't mind watching sports, and when I get bored, I read a book."

She pursed her lips. "I guess I'll be watching in my room."

"Great idea. Glad I reminded you."

"I'm going to start unpacking. Emma, why don't you help? I was going to give away a bunch of clothes, but I wanted to offer them to you first."

I jumped at that chance. The thought of having some of Genie's designer hand-me-downs was a no-brainer. My wardrobe consisted of casual jeans, yoga pants, workout gear and knit sweaters. The runways of Paris, Milan, and New York had nothing to worry about.

I sat at the edge of my old bed as she went through her bags, piling clothes into the discard pile for me to look at. I took a couple of skirts, a blouse, a few dresses and all the sweaters, some with tags still attached.

"Thanks, Genie. Are you sure?"

"I'm sure! I have so many clothes that I don't have anywhere to put them. Next time you're at the house, we'll go through my closets there. I could probably give you enough stuff to have a different outfit for a month."

"I think you have an addiction."

"Yes, but I like it."

She put away the rest of her clothes, folding and arranging them neatly.

"So you and Steve are really over? You won't change your mind?"

"No, and it's been a long time coming. Lately all he was talking about was getting Dad to find him a job. I started getting the feeling he was using me. And then when I got the vibe he was cheating, it really went south. Once I had it confirmed, it was over. I don't forgive cheaters."

"I'm sorry that he hurt you."

She shrugged. "I'm over it. Like I said, it wasn't a surprise. How are things going with you and Zach?"

A flash of dread came over me. "Good."

"That's not what I mean."

It felt weird talking to her about Zach, but who else could I talk to? "I know. I think I frustrate him and I don't know how to change that. I'm not that fuzzy and cuddly kind of person and I think that's what he wants. And he's under the mistaken impression that I'm still holding out for Jake. I'm not. Not even a little."

Genie shut the door and sat beside me. "I'm getting that you're spooked and he probably is too. Zach's used to dating girls for a while, getting bored, and moving on. Emma, you're that it girl."

"It girl?"

"Yeah, the that's-it girl. And I can guarantee you that it freaks the hell out of him."

"I'm afraid too. I've never been a girlfriend and I know this isn't a casual dating situation. And I'm not planning any weddings, if that's what you're thinking."

Genie laughed. "I wasn't. Do you feel like he's pressuring you?"

"Yes and no. That's not much of an answer, is it?"

"I understand. If he cares about you the way I think he does, he'll wait for you to come around. Don't let Zach or any other guy push you into anything. Promise me that."

"I promise."

It was getting late and I could see by Genie's drooping eyes that she was exhausted. I wished her a good night and returned to the living room. Zach was now watching a late-night hockey game.

"I was going to go to sleep. Do you need anything?"

"Yeah, I should probably get a few things." He leapt up from the sofa and went to his room, returning with a few clothes and a pillow. I'd already taken a spare set of sheets and blankets from the small linen closet and set them down on the sofa.

"Do you want me to help with anything?"

"Nah, I'll be fine."

I felt horrible making him sleep on the sofa. I opened my mouth to offer one last time, but he cut me off before I got a word out.

"It's fine. I've passed out on this sofa enough times. It's comfortable."

Resigned, I went to his room, changed, got into bed and stared at the ceiling. Sleep had no intention of coming. A million thoughts streamed in and out of my head. I could have offered to sleep with

Genie so that Zach could have his bed back. I'd do that in the morning. It seemed reasonable. Or...no, I couldn't even go there, or could I? I closed my eyes, envisioning Zach in bed with me, platonic of course, or maybe...I opened my eyes. So many times I wanted to touch him, just like all the times I wanted to touch Jake, but this was different. Tangible. How many times had I longed to have Zach put his strong arms around me? And those kisses? His kisses lit a fire in me.

I sat up trying to shake my thoughts. Sex with Andy had been so mechanical, something between two curious sixteen-year-olds. Neither of us wanted anything more, or at least I didn't. I wanted to have sex, know what it felt like, and move on. But the thought of having sex with Zach was something different. I yearned for him, his touch, his kiss, his breath on my neck. I wanted to wake up next to him, wrapped up in his arms. I wanted him to hold my hand, hug me, and more than anything, I wanted the intimacy you shared with someone you cared for.

I slid out of bed and padded into the bathroom. I switched on the light and it temporarily blinded me until I focused on my surroundings. His cologne was there and I grasped onto it. I loved the way he smelled, fresh and crisp, like a woodsy winter morning. I set it down next to my toiletry bag. It seemed natural, the two of them together.

I ran some cold water and splashed my face. Probably the wrong thing to do when suffering from insomnia, but sleep was the not on the horizon. The hamster in my head was running at full speed on her wheel and until I got thoughts of Zach out of my head, I'd never sleep.

I massaged my temples as my heart raced. I felt like my brain wanted to shut down and sleep, boot that hamster off the wheel, while the rest of me had other ideas. An epic battle was going on and my brain lost.

I tiptoed to the door, opening it slowly so I wouldn't make any noise. The TV was off and no other sounds came from the apartment. I crept down the hallway not knowing what kind of sleeper Genie was. Once in the living room I listened for Zach's breathing and it was deep and even. Did I let him sleep? Did I chicken out and let my brain back into the match?

I made my way to the sofa and knelt down next to him. With the limited light coming from the window I could barely make out his serene face. I still had time to turn back and forget all about this stupid, spontaneous plan.

"Zach," I whispered.

He didn't stir. I grasped onto his arm and called out his name again and his eyes flickered open, adjusting themselves to the dim light.

"What's wrong?" he asked, his voice groggy.

"Uh, nothing."

"Why'd you wake me up then?"

This was already going so terribly wrong. "Um, I ..." My stomach was full of knots and my brain was telling me to go back to bed and let him sleep.

"Em, what's going on?" he asked, propping himself up on his elbows.

I wanted to kiss him, but I was such a coward. I slunk back, sitting on my heels and staring at him. Why did I start things I could never finish? "I thought ..."

He tilted his head even more perplexed. "Yes?"

Abort, abort! my brain screamed. I shook my head, my inner struggle unknown to him. I was not about to let my brain win this war.

"Come to bed with me." My voice was so quiet I wasn't sure he'd even heard me. His expression didn't change, and it felt like forever before he even blinked.

"Emma—"

"Just come," I said, taking hold of his hand. I threw back the comforter and pulled on his arm. I couldn't stop staring at his toned, bare chest. "Let's go," I said.

He got up and followed me into the bedroom. I closed the door gently and turned to face him. Blood raced through my veins as we stood facing each other.

"Kiss me, already," I said.

"Gladly."

He scooped me into his arms, effortlessly lifting me to his height. I wrapped my legs around his waist and he kissed me, a hungry kiss I happily returned. He brought me to the bed and set me down. He took a moment to stare at me in my t-shirt and pajama shorts. Was he reconsidering? I waited and then he smiled and stretched out onto the bed next to me. At first his kisses brushed against my lips as one hand caressed my back, but then they grew more and more intense, and I let out a small sigh of pleasure. His lips explored my neck before returning to my lips, his tongue passing over mine. I inched closer to him, touching, desperate to feel his entire body against mine. My body tingled now, every part of me wanting him.

His hand moved under my shirt to my breasts and he caressed each of them, pinching and tugging ever so slightly. It felt amazing. I arched my back, pressing my chest into him, feeling his erection against my leg. I wanted to touch it, but I didn't dare do anything wrong.

He helped me out of my top and threw it down on the ground before paying full attention to my breasts, his mouth playing, sucking, and biting down on each nipple. I groaned as his lips found my mouth again, hard and wanting.

His hand resumed its exploration and moved down my back, grabbing hold of a butt cheek. He squeezed—not too hard but enough to get me to lean into him. He broke the kiss and stared at me, not saying a word. His hand slid around over my stomach and under my shorts and down between my legs. His eyes never left mine as his fingers began to massage me. His touch made me shudder. Everything he did made me feel alive. Connected.

"Emma, you're so wet," he said, his voice low.

Just those few words had an impact. I moaned pushing myself into his hand. He slid two fingers inside me and I gasped as they moved, slowly at first before picking up speed. I came without much effort, a blinding ecstasy I'd never felt before and only read about in trashy novels. Zach kissed me to muffle out my cries.

"Are you okay?" he asked, our noses touching.

"Yes," I said, catching my breath.

He slipped off my shorts and underwear before taking off his pajama pants. I sat up, staring at his erection. It was going inside of me and I could hardly wait. He reached over to the nightstand, pulled out a condom and started to unwrap it.

"Wait," I said. "I want to touch you."

He stretched back out onto the bed and I took him into my hand, gently rubbing. He clasped onto my hand, moving it back and forth, showing me the way he liked it. He let go and let me continue, closing his eyes and leaning his head back, letting out a low groan of pleasure.

"You have to stop," he said, "or I'll come."

I did and he took a second before putting on the condom. I watched, taking in every second. He was then on top of me, kissing me, touching me, his fingers inside of me again.

"Em, you have to relax," he said.

"Okay," I murmured. I was anticipating it, him, what it would feel like and I could feel my body constrict. I took a few deep breaths, shutting my eyes and willing myself to calm down.

"Look at me," he said.

I opened my eyes and stared into his. I felt a release, my body opening for him.

"And stop clenching the sheets. Just chill," he said, his lips brushing mine.

I had no idea that both my hands were balled into fists. I opened them and wrapped my arms around Zach.

He moved between my legs, and I wanted to close my eyes, expecting the invasion, but I kept them fixed on his. He guided himself into me, just a little at first but as he sank into me, I felt a little pinch of pain. It had been three years and my only sexual experience had lasted less than thirty seconds.

He did nothing at first, just letting my body get acquainted with him, but as he slowly moved in and out, my body trembled with desire. It felt so good, him inside me, linked to me. He stopped and started, teasing me. I moved against him, thrusting into him.

"Em, I don't know how much longer I can go. You're so tight," he said breathlessly.

"Then come."

With a few frantic thrusts he came and I let out a quiet cry. We stayed that way awhile, his body pressed up against mine, him still inside me, kissing me as my body gently bucked against him.

"I've got to clean up. I'll be right back."

With his warmth gone, I pulled a blanket over top my naked, pulsating body. I tried to cement every moment in my mind. When he slid back into bed next to me, I wrapped my arm around him and nestled my head against his chest, not waiting for an invitation. It was like the spot was made just for me. He caressed my arm and I let out a contented sigh before closing my eyes and drifting to sleep.

CHAPTER TWENTY-NINE

ZACH

Normally the first time with a new girl could be awkward, but with Emma it was so intense and natural. She literally had me by the balls. Thinking about the previous night got my blood flowing. I badly wanted to wake her up with a little morning sex, but thought against it. This was new and I didn't want to push the limits.

I watched her sleep, her body curled up in a ball, the blanket wrapped tightly around her. She'd hogged it a few times during the night, but I didn't care. I rarely let girls stay the night, finding crafty ways to gently kick them out. Letting them sleep over gave them ideas, but Emma could share my bed for as long as she wanted.

Her eyes fluttered open. She looked at me and smiled shyly. Those big hazel eyes killed me every time.

"Good morning," she said, stretching out her body. I glimpsed her breasts and wanted my hands all over them. I expected her to quickly cover up, like most girls, but she didn't. She scooted closer and kissed me.

"Good morning to you, too." I put my hand on her waist, then her ass. She had the tightest body with the most perfect little breasts. Everything on her was just right.

"How'd you sleep?" A nervous smile crept up on her perfect, rosy lips.

"Very good. And you?"

"Well, thank you."

She reached out and let a finger trace the muscles on my chest. I stiffened and wondered if she could feel it. I would have done anything to have her again.

"Are you my boyfriend now?"

There was something so innocent about her, those big eyes looking at me, waiting for an answer. She seemed worried what I'd say.

"Do you want me to be?"

She ran a finger over my Adam's apple. "Yes."

"Then I guess I'm your boyfriend."

She grinned. "I was worried you were going to get mad at me last night."

"Why?"

"I don't know. I didn't want you to think I was leading you on or anything. I know I frustrated you and—" I stopped her with a kiss. The last thing I wanted to do was talk about any of that shit again. We were starting fresh, no crap from the past.

"I like kissing you," she said as if she shouldn't.

"I like kissing you," I said, giving her any reassurance she needed.

She bit her lip and giggled. "I really like having sex with you. I thought you should know."

"I really like having sex with you, too. That could be a problem."

"Why?"

"Because all I'll think about is this amazing hot body of yours and then I'm going to want to have sex with you again and again and again."

"Well, if you want..." I didn't let her finish. I kissed her, pulling her closer. She grabbed hold of me and stroked, just like I'd shown her. I was so hard it hurt. "Em, from the nightstand, grab a condom," I said. She reached over and got one. I put it on and motioned for her to get on top.

"Really?" she asked, those eyes sucking me in.

I nodded and she straddled me, uncertain of herself. She eased onto me, only a little at first, sending the blood pumping through me. I grasped onto her breasts, gently pinching and massaging. She sank down lower, slowly grinding. I pushed deeper inside her and she resisted a little. She rested her hands on my shoulders, supporting herself as she began to move. I rubbed her clit which made her gasp and sink even deeper. I wanted to get her on her back, but I didn't know her limits yet and the last thing I ever wanted to do was hurt her.

"Oh my God, this feels so good," she said, almost seeming pained to say it.

"It's supposed to."

"I think I'm going to ..." I felt her release and, in that moment, I held onto her waist, pushing her down on me. I came too.

She collapsed on top of me, her arm wrapped around me, her cheek resting on my shoulder. She let out a few deep sighs. "We should probably get up," she said after a minute or two.

"We should."

We didn't move, other than me caressing her back. Finally she sat up, her hair disheveled in a sexy kind of way.

"Do you think Genie heard us?"

"I doubt it. She could sleep through an air siren."

She pondered that then shrugged. "I'm getting hungry."

"Me too. How about a shower first?"

She smiled devilishly. "That sounds like a great idea."

We showered and the girl who barely let me touch her before now explored every inch of my body. Her fingers passed over every inch of my face, and she brushed her cheek against my stubbly one before kissing me. She broke the kiss and stared at me, an intense gaze that made me want her right there again. This girl was going to destroy me.

I tore myself away from Emma and got changed. Genie was in the kitchen reading the newspaper, a knowing smile on her face.

"I didn't see you on the sofa this morning."

I pulled out the coffee canister and put on a pot while Genie sipped her tea. "I slept in my bed."

"With Emma? In Emma?"

"Funny and really not your business."

Genie's face turned serious. "Don't break her heart. I really, really like her."

"Noted."

"I guess you won't be sleeping on the sofa then?"

I faced Genie, leaned up against the counter and crossed my arms over my chest, listening to coffee drip. "No arrangements have been made."

"I told you she'd come around."

"How did I get so lucky to have a genius for a sister?"

"Like I said, don't screw it up. What about her mom? Did you tell her?"

"Meredith talked to you, not me."

Genie tapped her fingers on the table. "Do I tell her?"

I'd pushed the whole Meredith fiasco from my head, but now it found itself back on my life's agenda. "I don't know. Why did she have to talk to you anyway?"

"I wish she hadn't."

"What's your gut telling you?"

Genie covered her face with her hands. "It's telling me how much I hate being put in this position. It's not like she and I had a long conversation. It was all so casual."

It wasn't often that Genie wanted me to tell her what to do, but this was one of those moments. "I say forget about it. If she doesn't have the decency to contact Emma herself, don't let her use you. It's not right."

"I agree with you. This isn't my circus. I hope it doesn't bite us in the butt later."

I DIDN'T FEEL LIKE I needed to make an announcement to Mom and Dad about my new relationship, so I told them in passing when they called to find out about Steve and Genie's epic breakup. If I could have seen Mom through the phone, she'd be smiling and giving me the I-knew-it look. Dad was more reserved.

"Let's say I like her about as much as I hate Steve," he said.

A ringing endorsement if I'd ever heard one.

"Let's have her over for a proper dinner. I think we should get to know her better," Mom said.

"It's been less than twenty-four hours. Why don't we wait a bit before we subject her to family dinners."

"I knew she was a special girl," Mom said, ignoring me. "I was telling your father that the other day."

"That's nice. I should go. I'm meeting Brett for a workout."

"Let's get her over before your father goes to Washington."

"Yes, Mom."

I hung up and drove to the gym. Brett was running laps on the track, huffing and puffing and glad to see me. He jogged over, clutching his side and trying to catch his breath.

"You're late."

"I had a busy morning. I just got off the phone with my parents who wanted to grill me about Genie breaking up with her loser boyfriend. Also told them about Emma, but they wanted all the gossip about Steve. They are as happy as I am that he's out of her life."

I figured if I kept talking, he might miss the Emma part, but when he leaned back and crossed his arms over his chest, I knew it hadn't escaped him.

"What about Emma?"

"We're together now," I said, walking over to the weights.

"That took a lot longer than I thought it would. So you dated that blonde chick for a week and now you're banging the chick you wanted to bang all along. Congrats," he said, rolling his eyes.

"I wasn't going to mention it, but you're my best friend, so I thought you should know."

"You chased after that broad for months. I was beginning to think she only liked other chicks."

"She's definitely into guys."

"Good in the sack, then?"

"Are we working out, or what?"

Brett smirked. "Nice guys don't tell," he said in a mocking tone.

I grabbed some dumbbells. "That's right."

"How are you going to deal with the fallout from this?"

"What are you babbling about now?"

"Bianca. She's the only person who's going to care."

"I never hear any of this shit, but you do, so pass this along to Bianca. If she touches Emma, even breathes on her, I'll ruin her life."

Brett stared at me, blinking a few times. "You sound pissed off."

"This has to stop. Emma stays away from Bianca, why can't she leave Emma alone?"

"I'm not arguing with you. I think it's stupid."

"Then get the word out to her. She'll be sorry if she crosses me."

"This is about that video, isn't it?"

"What video?" I asked, playing dumb. The less Brett knew, the less he could blab all over town.

"I'd kill to see what's on it."

"If Bianca keeps up her harassment, you and many others will."

Brett nodded and his usual happy-go-lucky demeanor faded. "Remind me never to cross you."

I patted him on the shoulder. "I've always got your back, but if you screw me ..."

"You'll ruin my life?" he asked with an uneasy laugh.

"Precisely. Now let's finish this workout."

CHAPTER THIRTY

EMMA

While Zach was at the gym and Genie was out with Andrea for the day, I called Dad. He was at the shop and I took the chance he wouldn't be busy and be able to talk.

"Andrew's Antiques," Dad said in his most cheerful voice.

"Hey Dad, it's me."

"Hello, Kiddo. You're calling early."

"Did I catch you at a busy time?"

"No, it's pretty quiet right now. Just a few browsers. What's up?"

"I could call later."

"No, it's all right. If it gets busy, I'll let you know."

My mouth went dry. Telling Dad I had a boyfriend wasn't something I did every day...well, never. And he was a senator's son to boot. "So Dad, I wanted to let you know that Zach Walker and I started dating." No use drawing it out or prolonging my own agony.

Silence. The longer it went, the more my heart raced. Was Dad angry? I wondered if I should have waited until I'd seen him in person to drop the bombshell. His only kid had a boyfriend, a boyfriend he'd never met.

"I see," Dad finally said. "I figured it was inevitable. When am I going to meet this young man?"

Dad's tone wasn't thrilled, but he wasn't furious either. "I don't know. I have a tennis tournament next week, midterms after that, and then it's spring break. We could come to Pine Falls then."

More silence.

"He's a good kid, right? I'm not going to lie. I've been asking around and I googled him. I even got Wendy to look into him. He seems fine. Does he do drugs?"

"No!"

"What does Jake think of him?"

I wanted to let out a sarcastic laugh. "Jake thinks he's all right."

"Well, then spring break it is. I want to meet him."

We talked a few minutes more before Dad had to go. I was relieved. Dad didn't have a coronary.

THERE WAS NO HIDING that Zach and I were dating. We kissed and hugged before and after classes, not the drawn-out PDAs or anything, just quick pecks and off we went. I expected the backlash from Bianca because one way or another she was going to find out. By Friday I started receiving a steady stream of texts. Some I deleted without reading, others I subjected myself to. The worst came as I was waiting for Zach. He texted to tell me he'd be a few minutes late. Almost immediately after I got another one.

000:000:0000: I'm going to mess you up.

That was the first one indicating violence. I looked around to see if anyone was watching me for a reaction, but there was no one. I didn't care about any of these harassing texts but this one had me spooked.

Me: I'm going to call the cops.

000:000:0000: Go ahead BITCH.

Me: Who is this?

000:000:0000: Your worst fucking nightmare.

Me: Leave me alone.

000:000:0000: Can't. And I'll get you when you least expect it.

My hands shook and I stuffed my phone into my backpack. Did I tell Zach? I'd been keeping the texts quiet because they'd been nothing more than an annoyance. Bianca was harmless, that's what Zach had assured me, but these latest texts crossed the line. Suddenly I felt exposed, a wide-open target. I hated that I needed Zach around to feel protected, but Bianca was sounding crazy.

"Sorry I'm late," Zach said, kissing me on the cheek.

"Oh, hi."

"You look upset. What's wrong?"

I'd reached my breaking point. I pulled out my phone and brought up the texts. I showed them to Zach, and he scrolled through them. His face went from cheerful to furious.

"Why didn't you tell me about these?"

"Before today they were all harmless and stupid."

"Do not reply to any more of them. I'm going to download them and see if Dad can help."

"No, please don't make a big deal," I begged. "That just pisses her off."

"I thought this was over."

"She probably found out about us and is pissed. Can't we just forget about it?"

He put his arm around me and kissed my cheek. "At the very least let me download them so we have a copy. Then I want you to delete them. And any other ones you get, I want to see and download. Okay?"

"Yes, fine."

I felt relieved telling him, but I didn't trust him to let it go. Just like getting Bianca not to press charges, I had a feeling he was going to do something. Secretly if it kept her from bothering me, I didn't care.

We got home to the smell of butter chicken in my Crockpot. I put on a pot of water for rice and prepped a salad and a vegetarian paella for Genie. She and some friends were going on a weekend shopping trip and she'd already informed us she'd have a quick dinner with us before packing. They'd asked me to come along, but Helen and I had our big tennis tournament Saturday and Sunday. She'd been practicing on her own all week in preparation.

"I was going to invite Brett over tomorrow night," Zach said. "We were going to watch hockey. Why don't we make pizzas?"

His voice sounded weird, taking on a bit of a higher pitch. "I won't be home until about six. Why is this a big deal?"

"It's not...well, it kind of is. Brett's my best friend and I want him to get to know you."

I involuntarily frowned. "You can't make him like me."

"He doesn't know you."

"All right, I'll make pizzas and hang out for a bit, but I don't want to be a third wheel. And you'll need to do some prep work. I'll leave you a to-do list."

He smiled. "No problem."

Genie breezed through the door like a whirlwind. "It smells fantastic in here! Are we eating soon? I've got to pack and turn in early because we're on the road at six am. Outlet shopping, here I come!"

"We'll be eating in about twenty minutes."

"Perfect. Call me when it's ready."

And she was gone. Zach and I looked at each other and laughed.

"So I was thinking," I said, handing him tomatoes to slice. "Spring break is coming and I'm going back to Pine Falls for a bit. Do you want to come out for a couple of days and meet Dad and Grandpa?"

He popped a chunk of tomato in his mouth and gave me a thumbs up. "I'd like that."

"There will be rules. You'll have your own room and no sneaking around for sex. I'd be mortified if either one of them caught us."

"I can be on my best behavior for a little while," he said with a wink.

I plated the food and put out the naan I'd bought the night before. I wanted to learn how to make it, but I had no time for that right now. Zach called Genie, and we sat down for the meal.

"Who needs a man when I can get an orgasm from this food," Genie said, savoring her paella.

"Really?" Zach said. "Steve was that bad?"

"Come on, maybe you're used to it, but eating like this? You're so spoiled. My compliments to Emma."

"Thanks."

"Emma, why are you wasting your talents here? Go to culinary school."

"There's nothing around here. I don't want to be a plane ride away to go to school."

"What are you going to do instead? Toil in some shitty job you can't stand? Zach talk some sense into her. Besides, once Zach graduates, he's not sticking around here."

"He's not?" That news was a punch to the gut. Zach had one year left. Not once had he mentioned leaving for law school; I'd assumed he'd stay at Western.

"Dad won't let him get his undergraduate and his law degree from the same university. As we speak, he's probably trying to get him into Harvard."

I looked over at Zach. He was biting down on his lower lip, trying to keep his temper in check. I thought he was going to reach over and strangle Genie.

"Nothing is set in stone," he said, shooting Genie the death glare.

"Law school is set in stone. Wherever Zach ends up, there has to be a good culinary school nearby." Had Genie realized she'd upset both of us and was trying to find some kind of bright side?

"And maybe you could just shut up?" Zach suggested.

"Oh shit, Emma, did I shoot my mouth off? I'm sorry. I thought you knew." The fun and lively Genie was replaced by an apologetic one.

"No, I didn't."

"Why don't you take your dinner and bugger off so that I can talk to Emma," Zach said to his sister.

She dutifully picked up her plate and disappeared.

Zach grasped onto my hand. "Emma, it's more than a year away and so much can happen before then."

"Like what?" I asked, taking my hand away and pushing my half-empty plate to the side. I'd lost my appetite.

"Despite what Genie says, I may not go to law school. And even if I do, it would only be half a year that we'd be apart. Then you could come out to wherever I am, get a job, go to culinary school, whatever you want. If I get into Columbia, there are a million culinary schools you could go to. I've already checked it out."

Columbia? Where was this coming from? Why hadn't he mentioned it before? "Or we might not even be together in a year."

"That wasn't one of my considerations."

"Why didn't you tell me?"

"Because it's so far off. I don't look that far ahead."

"But everything is already mapped out for you. And I don't even know what I'm doing with my life."

"Then what's to stop you from coming with me? Transferring out to another school?"

"Nothing, I guess."

"I might even end up here. Who knows? But wherever I go, we'll figure it out. I promise."

"I know."

"We have so much time to make plans. I don't want you to worry about this."

"I won't."

Now that I was over the initial shock, there was an upside to the thought of leaving this school and all its horrible memories behind. And he was right. It was a long way off.

"SHOULD I STICK AROUND and watch?" Zach asked, dropping me off at the tennis club.

"It's only the preliminaries. Semi-finals and finals are next weekend. That's if we make it."

He kissed my cheek before I grabbed my duffel bag. "I'm sure you'll make the finals."

"We'll see."

I waved goodbye and went inside. Helen was in the locker room, pacing in our usual meeting place. She already had her tennis outfit on and was chewing vigorously on her nails.

"You're finally here! I was worried you wouldn't come."

Was I late? I took a quick glance at my watch. I was fifteen minutes early. "You seem a tad nervous."

Helen stopped. "I am. We have to win. I always meet up with Sally's team and she knocks me out of the tournament every time. She cannot beat me this year."

Helen was wound so tight I could have spun her like a top. "Don't worry. It'll be fine. We'll have a great time."

At least I hoped we would. We'd practiced three times a week together and then she came in the rest of the week and played with anyone she could get her hands on. Her obsession with Sally Carruthers was making her crazy.

"This is the first year there's been sixteen teams. Sixteen! What if we don't win any prize money? I'll feel bad that you worked so hard for nothing."

I smiled. "Helen, don't worry about it. I got to spend time with you and work on my tennis game. Who cares if we don't win anything?"

She frowned. "I like to win."

I got that impression.

I changed and we made our way out to the courts. The round of sixteen started in twenty minutes for the adult ladies' side, followed by the adult men. The women's teams were on the court getting in some last-minute practice. I scanned our competition. Helen had nothing to worry about, but I didn't tell her that.

"She's over there, first court, pink outfit," Helen said under her breath.

I took a look. Sally was a decent player, but not a huge challenge. "Helen, are you sure I'm cleared to play in this tournament?"

Helen grabbed the only open court and a few balls. "Yes. Trust me, I made sure this was all kosher."

We warmed up with a simple rally. We then moved on to our serves and that's when I knew something was wrong. I didn't notice at first, mostly because I was focusing on hitting my points, but almost all the other ladies, including the few assembled to watch, had stopped what they were doing to watch me. I was getting ready for another toss when Helen waved at me to stop, then motioned for me to look over at the other courts. Faces were staring, some in awe, jaws dropped, others mortified.

Helen jogged over, a wide smile all over her face. "They're all scared shitless. Let's paste them."

I nodded. I'd have to take something off the serve. My intent wasn't to hurt or humiliate anyone even though Helen was out for blood.

Our first opponents were Kelly and Bree, two lovely ladies in their mid-thirties. Neither was able to return a single one of my serves, and that's after I took some heat off. In the history of my tennis life, I'd never served a perfect game. This new accomplishment did not make me proud.

And, as predetermined in our many practice sessions, I took any ball that was in my reach. In fact, some of the few points Kelly and Bree made were from Helen overestimating my capabilities. We won the match in thirty-two minutes. Both Kelly and Bree were gracious, but I had a feeling not all our opponents would feel that way.

The umpire came up to us at the end of the match as we headed off court. "Emma Andrews?" she asked.

A moment of dread washed over me. She was going to find a way to disqualify us and ruin Helen's dream. "Yes," I said.

"I remember you. It's been a few years. I umped a few of your matches."

The boom was about to be laid. Helen's moment in the sun was about to be dimmed.

"I quit when I was sixteen."

"I heard. A lot of us were shocked. I'm happy to see you playing again, but aren't you selling yourself short in this tournament?"

I cringed. "I think so. I've never played in one of these, so I had no idea."

Mercifully Helen had wandered off. She didn't need to hear all this.

"I know you're going easy on these ladies, but you want to turn it down at least another two or three notches?"

"I will. I'm sorry."

She smiled. "Don't be sorry. Win the damn thing! It will be nice seeing someone other than Sally Carruthers hoisting that trophy. Good luck, dear. And think about coaching. You've got a great game and so much talent. Don't waste it."

With the umpire gone, Helen returned. "What was that about? She getting us in trouble?"

"No, not at all. She remembered me from my competitive days."

"Make sure you take it easy tonight. We have to be fresh tomorrow."

I muffled a laugh. I was pretty sure I could show up in a full body cast and still win the tournament.

"HOW'D IT GO?" ZACH asked when he picked me up. "That was pretty quick."

I started laughing, an uncontrollable fit of laughter that soon had me in tears. Zach watched in bewilderment as I tried to pull it together.

"I didn't realize the question was that funny."

I blotted my eyes and composed myself. "Zach, they are all pretty mediocre players. I'm not one to boast, but I could wipe the court with half of them. Honestly, I should be disqualified. It's not fair. One lady I watched could barely serve. She hit three quarters of her serves into the net. When we win—and we're going to win—I'm going to feel like I'm stealing their entry fees. It's not right."

"That bad?"

"I served a perfect game. My opponents didn't return a single one of my serves and that's after I took off half the heat."

Zach chuckled. "I can't wait to be your partner in our summer tournament fundraiser."

"Let me just say that I'm not proud of myself."

"I should have stuck around to see this ass-whipping. Instead my horrible girlfriend had me slicing mushrooms and grating various cheeses."

"She does sound horrible."

"She totally is, but she's great in the kitchen and in another room," he said with a wink.

"Get your mind out of the gutter, Walker."

"But it's so fun there."

"When is Brett coming?" I asked with a swift change of subject. I had to keep to my schedule, and he wasn't going to distract me with any fooling around.

"He said around six."

That gave me some study time before he arrived. With all my newfound physical activity, both with Zach and on the tennis court, I'd fallen behind in my history and English Lit classes. I had a history paper due Monday that was only half-finished, and I needed to start and finish a book for my Lit class. Mercifully I was up to date in everything else.

The moment we got home I started the dough and the tomato sauce. The dough had two hours to rise while the sauce had an hour to cook and an hour to cool. I'd start sautéing ground beef and chorizo around five-thirty. My plan was to eat around six-thirty, attempt to ingratiate myself with Brett for an hour then hit the books again.

"Want to screw around a bit?" Zach asked.

As much as I wanted to, instead I informed Zach of the evening's itinerary which included him checking on the sauce every half hour and giving it a good stir.

"That's not nearly as fun as my idea."

"Sorry, but I have to hit the books."

My plan went ahead and by the time five-thirty rolled around, I'd finished my history paper and read the first few chapters of my English Lit book. Food was a pleasant distraction. I put Zach to work chopping green and red peppers while I tackled the meat. When he was finished, his next task was onions.

"I hate chopping onions. They make me weepy."

I rolled my eyes and smacked him in the ass.

"Miss Andrews, are you getting fresh with me?"

"Mr. Walker, just get back to work. I'll get fresh with you later."

Zach buzzed Brett up just after six and went to greet him. I popped my head out the kitchen to wave, like people do when they're being polite. I had no opinion of Brett because I didn't really know him. Zach talked about him a lot, they played hockey and worked out together, but beyond that Brett was a face I barely remembered from the infamous cabin.

"Want a beer?" Zach asked him.

"Sure. Smells good in here."

"Pizzas from scratch, man."

They settled into the living room while I rolled out dough and put together two different pizzas. I slid them into the oven and grabbed a beer for myself.

I was about to join them in the living room but stopped. Would it be strange with me in there? What if they were discussing boy stuff? But where else was I going to go? Hide in the bedroom and be antisocial? I decided to go for broke. I flopped onto the recliner no one ever used and pretended that I hung out with them all the time. Six months ago I wouldn't have dreamt of doing something so bold. I listened to the conversation, trying to act natural. The subject was hockey.

"No way!" Zach was saying. "Mason is not a thirty-goal scorer. Maybe twenty, but that's only in a good year. He's not trade bait."

"Mason and add in that rookie Swede, and you can get a decent goalie," Brett retorted.

"What have you been smoking? Best bet they get rid of Halstrom and Mason and someone dangles a goalie."

"Trade deadline already? Time is flying by," I said.

Brett looked at me like I'd told him I had three boobs.

"She watches hockey," Zach added nonchalantly. "Football, too. Not a huge basketball fan."

Brett recovered from the shock and returned to the debate. "Giving up Halstrom and Mason is too much. You can't give up two core defensemen."

"But Halstrom is always hurt," I added. "Who'd want someone so fragile?"

Brett's head whipped around to face me again. His brain was computing something before he spoke. "Exactly. She's right," he said cautiously, like I might suddenly attack him with my talons.

Cue my exit to check on pizzas and set the table since Zach had conveniently forgotten to. As I was putting out the plates and cutlery, I saw Brett lean over to Zach and whisper something. Normally I would have been offended, but I decided not to worry or care what he had to say. Besides, if I asked Zach, he'd tell me later.

I pulled the pizzas out of the oven and let them rest a few minutes. I threw a frozen apple pie I'd made weeks before into the oven to bake. It wouldn't be ready for an hour, but I was sure they could wait.

I moved on to making a salad. While I didn't care if I won Brett over, I knew it mattered to Zach. Had I been too pushy with the hockey talk? I was only trying to make conversation. And if he didn't like me before, was there really anything I could do to make it worse?

I sliced up the pizza and called them. They jumped to their feet and Brett took a seat while Zach retrieved more beers. Brett took four pieces and piled them on his plate. He didn't touch the salad. He took a bite, then another.

"Shit, this is good pizza," he said.

"Told you," Zach said proudly.

"Any night you're making pizza, I'm free," Brett said, his blue eyes lighting up.

And then they went right back to hockey talk.

"You see that hit Pennington took? They say it's an upper body injury, but I heard it's his shoulder and he's out weeks," Brett said.

"Separation or his rotator cuff?" I asked.

"I hear it's a separation, but it's pretty bad."

"If it's a third-degree separation, he's torn something. He's out at least six to eight weeks. I separated my shoulder and was out nearly a month."

"Oh, yeah. You played hockey?"

"Competitive tennis. I separated my shoulder on an awkward fall and it hurt like hell. Thankfully I didn't tear anything."

"I didn't know you played tennis."

He seemed genuinely interested in what I had to say, like I was one of the boys. Kind of. "I quit a few years ago. I still play for fun, though."

"That's cool."

They went back to hockey talk and I didn't say much else. I threw in the odd comment here and there, but I'd said enough. I think I'd gained some of his respect. They offered to clean up and I went back to studying. Overall, I thought it went well.

CHAPTER THIRTY-ONE

EMMA

It came as no surprise that Helen and I made it to the finals. Our semi-final competition put up a valiant fight and even returned some of my serves after I'd toned them down to a manageable pace. For the finals on Sunday, the club had pulled out a set of five rows of bleachers and about twenty people had gathered to watch. Zach was sitting among them.

"I think we can beat her," Helen said, her body vibrating with anticipation.

Think? I'd seen Sally Carruthers play. She was good, probably the best out there, but she wasn't going to beat us. "It's good to be optimistic," I said. Bursting Helen's competitive bubble was not on my agenda. Instead, it consisted of beating Sally's team in less than an hour, a celebratory lunch with Zach and Helen, then getting back to the apartment for last-minute packing so we could be in Pine Falls by dinner.

"It's so nice your boyfriend came to watch us play. He's so handsome and polite. My lazy husband said he's sick of watching me lose."

Helen had met Zach when we arrived. He charmed her up by telling her how good he'd heard she was. She lapped up all the compliments like a school girl.

"When you bring home that trophy, he'll be sorry he missed this," I said.

We hit the court for some practice. Sally watched us from the far court, tapping her foot impatiently. She had on a pink designer tennis outfit and the latest shoes. Her long blonde hair was tied up in a neat pony tail. There wasn't a flaw about her. She called over the umpire for our match, a woman I hadn't seen before. They spoke a few minutes, the umpire nodding here and there. Their conversation ended, and the umpire made a beeline for me. I anxiously watched her approach. Was the guillotine about to drop? Had the loophole been found? The umpire, all five feet two of her, looked up at me.

"Ms. Andrews?"

"Yes."

"Please promise me you'll kick Sally Carruthers's ass!"

And off she went to her umpire chair. I let out a stunned giggle as Helen ran over to find out what was said.

"I think Sally tried to get me disqualified. The ump told me to kick her ass."

That's what we did in thirty-six minutes. Every serve Sally saw was to the best of my ability, save the one double fault. I showed mercy on her shell-shocked partner and when we won 6-0, 6-1, Helen cried. Tears were streaming down her face as she collapsed on the court like she'd won Wimbledon. I let her savor the moment, then helped her to her feet. She bear-hugged me, thanking me over and over again.

I let her hoist the trophy to the cheers from the assembled crowd. Sally stormed off, her partner trudging behind.

"You know Helen's getting wasted tonight," Zach said after our quick lunch with her. It was Helen who rushed it. She had pictures to post on Facebook.

"I'm glad I could help her out. The prize money doesn't hurt." Prize money I insisted we split.

We stopped back at the apartment and Zach packed up his truck while I put the last of my things together. Spring break in Pine Falls was exactly what I needed, yet I couldn't shake the nerves. What if Dad and Grandpa didn't like Zach? I'd never really dated a guy before, let alone brought one home. What would they do? Grill him relentlessly? Make him walk over hot coals? Tar and feather him? I was sure Zach could hold his own, but I hated not knowing how things would be.

"We ready?" Zach asked, standing in the doorway, an exasperated look on his face. I'd been a bit spastic since we'd gotten home, packing, repacking, and adding things to my already overstuffed backpack.

"I think so."

We called out a goodbye to Genie who was on her phone. She waved and we were off. Pine Falls wasn't exactly a metropolis, so I suggested Zach only come out for a day or two, but he said he'd keep his options open. Other than the hockey rink, rec center, Walmart, and our mini-shopping center with a grocery store attached, Pine Falls didn't offer much. Its close proximity to Minneapolis was its only selling point. There were lots of people who made the daily commute, preferring Pine Falls' small-town feel to the big city. Grandma used to drive me three or four times a week to practice with my coach. When she got sick both Grandpa and Dad had offered to drive me, but without Grandma it didn't feel the same. I did keep it up though, until the week she died. That was it for me. I gave up my amateur career.

"Your dad and grandfather argue a lot? You know, running the antique shop together."

"Not often. A lot of their business is online and Grandpa's the one who travels and scouts for new stock so they aren't in each other's faces all the time."

"It sounds kind of neat. I hope I get to see the shop."

"I'll take you there."

The drive seemed shorter than usual and before I knew it, I was giving Zach the final directions to the house. We pulled up into the driveway, behind Grandpa's rusting SUV. He refused to part with it, especially when he was hauling big items. Why potentially damage a new car?

Zach grabbed our bags, and I walked up the three steps to the front door. My head was floating, my stomach churning and my heart racing. What if they hated him? What if they compared him to Jake?

I put my key in the door and went inside. "Hey, I'm home," I called out.

Dad came from upstairs and Grandpa from the living room. Interesting. Normally, one of them was always at the shop on Saturday, which was our busiest day of the week.

"Dad, Grandpa, this is Zach Walker."

Zach was a couple inches taller than Dad, and he towered over Grandpa. Zach shook both their hands as Dad and Grandpa sized him up.

"It's a pleasure to finally meet you," Zach said. "Emma speaks highly of you both."

"It's nice to meet you too. Come on in, Zach. I was about to put on coffee," Dad said.

Dad flipped on the coffeemaker while Grandpa motioned for Zach to take a seat at the kitchen table where there was a tray of cookies! Store-bought, but on a tray nevertheless. I'd never seen Dad or Grandpa do anything remotely domestic, preferring to eat cookies from the bag or container they came in. Were there mints on Zach's bed?

"Tell us about yourself, Zach," Grandpa said. "What are you taking in school?"

"I'm doing a Poly Sci major with history minor. I graduate next spring and then hopefully I'll be off to law school."

Grandpa's blue eyes widened. "Law school? What are you thinking of practicing?"

"I'm not sure yet, but I'm leaning towards privacy law."

"Any political aspirations?"

"Not right now. I'm only twenty. I have lots of time."

Grandpa chuckled, the fake politician kind of way. "Of course, you're so young. Any law schools in mind?"

Dad put out the fancy creamer and sugar bowl, the ones we only used at Christmas. It was Grandma's set, the one she'd left me.

"I'm still thinking about it. I'm going to start prepping all my applications in the fall."

"You aren't thinking Western?" Dad asked, putting one of Grandma's Royal Albert teacups in front of Zach.

"No, my parents are adamant that my undergraduate and law degree are from two different universities. Apparently, it's a thing."

"I see," Grandpa said, shooting me a warning look. Did he think Zach was blind? He could see it too.

"I've already told Emma, so she knows. We'd only be doing the long-distance thing for a year."

"Provided you're still dating."

"Grandpa!"

"Just want you to be realistic. Not all relationships last forever."

Dad poured coffee in Zach's teacup then realized he hadn't pulled out any more. He disappeared and returned with three more teacups and poured coffee for the rest of us.

"Cookie?" Dad asked Zach, holding the platter up to his face.

"Yes, thank you," Zach said, taking a digestive.

Dad sat and stared at Zach like he was a work of art at the Louvre. I felt uncomfortable for him and felt a need to jump in.

"So Dad, Zach wants to see the shop."

Dad snapped out of it. "Oh yes, we could do that later this afternoon. I'd be happy to take you there."

"I'll come too," Grandpa said. "We can go now."

"Why not finish our coffee first? Dad went to all this trouble."

Fortunately for Grandpa, the teacups were small and within ten minutes we were at the door, getting ready to leave.

"Separate rooms, young lady," Grandpa whispered in my ear as they were hurrying Zach out the door.

"Got it."

I watched them pile into the car. I was sending Zach into the great unknown. Would Dad and Grandpa be kind? If they weren't, I'd find out about it later, but I had a feeling Zach would be just fine.

THEY WERE GONE UNTIL late in the afternoon and by the time they returned, I'd started on dinner. Dad texted to tell me Wendy was coming too. In all the euphoria of cookie trays and fancy teacups, he'd forgotten to mention it. I looked forward to seeing her. We kept in contact with emails, and now she'd finally meet Zach.

Dinner was a roasted chicken, pesto green beans, a salad and garlic potatoes. I'd texted Dad to grab a few bottles of wine on the way home.

The men returned, joking, laughing, and talking sports. They barely noticed me as Dad put the wine on the kitchen table and went straight for the fridge and grabbed a couple of beers.

"Should I pull out the fine china for dinner?" I asked, my tongue firmly in cheek.

He playfully punched me in the arm. "Look, Kiddo, I didn't know what to do. It's not every day my daughter brings home a young man," Dad said, well out of Zach's earshot. "And a senator's son, no less. He's probably used to the finer things in life."

"Zach's pretty easy going."

"I've noticed. And we like him," Dad whispered.

Off he went with the beers. Wendy arrived shortly after, carrying a pie she'd made. Zach got up from the sofa where he and Dad had been enjoying their beers. I introduced them and Dad called Zach back to enjoy the rest of the afternoon hockey game.

"What a handsome devil," Wendy said. "So tall and muscular."

"Do I need to throw some cold water on you?" I joked.

She laughed and gave me a big hug. "How are you, dear?"

"I'm good. Very happy."

"I'd be happy too! What can I do?" she asked, looking around the kitchen.

"Would you mind prepping the green beans?"

"Not at all."

With the chicken in the oven and everything else prepared, I finally got a chance to sit. Zach made a spot next to him and I sank into the sofa wanting to wrap my arms around him, but didn't think it was appropriate in front of everyone.

"Another beer?" Dad asked Zach.

"Only if you're having one."

"You bet."

Dad went to the fridge and came up empty. "Crap, we're out. I'm going to run out and get some." Zach protested, but Dad was determined to please. "I'll be back before you know it."

Wendy wandered off to see what puttering Grandpa was doing in the garage, leaving Zach and I alone.

"So what do you think of them?" I asked.

"You've got a really nice family. And man, your Dad looks so young." He paused. "You guys don't look very much alike. I see some resemblance, but not much."

"I got Meredith's hair and eye color, but my height and nose from Dad."

Zach winced. "You don't call her mom?"

"Why would I? She's never been a mom."

"Point taken. But your dad...I'm not into guys, but he's pretty hot."

I laughed. "He gets that a lot, but he doesn't date much."

"How am I going to keep my hands off you the next few days?"

"I don't know. A lot of cold showers?"

"You could sneak to my room."

"Dad's probably got the entire house booby-trapped. They might like you, but not that much."

"And you will tell them about us living together, right?"

"I will, but after you've left. I promise."

"And while you're at it, I think they also deserve to know about the Jake and Bianca thing."

"I'll get around to it."

"I hate secrets."

"I know."

Dad returned and he and Zach each had another beer. I left them to check on dinner. I decided we'd eat at the dining room table. We didn't eat there often, only for special occasions, but I thought this was pretty special. Zach and Dad set the table while Wendy helped me plate and dress the food. Grandpa, as usual, supervised. We all took our seats but Dad. He pulled out a tripod with his camera attached.

"Thought we'd take some pictures. Now everyone scoot in close while I set this up." he said, fiddling with buttons.

He'd brought the fancy camera home from the shop—the one he used to take high-resolution shots of items for the website. What was next? Was a wedding planner going to pop out from one of the closets?

Dad rushed over and joined us. "Smile!" he said, as the camera took a shot. He went back to review it before making us take three more. He then took shots of me and Zach, Grandpa and Zach, and then made me take a picture of him and Zach. For good measure I took a few of Wendy and Grandpa since Dad seemed to have forgotten all about her. Come to think of it, after my photoshoot with Zach, Dad had forgotten about me too. I didn't really care. Dad and I had loads of pictures together.

"I miss your cooking," Dad said, biting into his chicken.

"I'm spoiled. Emma cooks for me all the time," Zach said.

Dad and Grandpa stopped chewing and looked at Zach who didn't let on that he'd just screwed up. "I mean, she's always cooking and having me over."

That answer seemed to satisfy them.

We stuffed ourselves and when the last bite was taken, I stood and started clearing plates away. Zach wanted to help, but Grandpa patted his arm and told him to sit. Men. Wendy helped with me the dishes and Dad roused himself to make another pot of coffee.

"You're going to tell them you're living with Zach?" Wendy asked, keeping her voice low.

"After Zach leaves, just in case the news sends them into orbit."

"And about Jake and his horrible girlfriend?"

I let out a pained sigh. "Wendy, I don't know how to tell Dad. So many times I've acted it out in my head and in every scenario, Dad gets pissed and his friendship with Uncle Ron suffers."

"I think you underestimate your dad. I get the impression his friendship with Ron is strong, so your falling out with Jake shouldn't affect it."

I weighed telling Wendy about the texts, but they'd stopped. What was the point? "I know, but I was going to wait until the end of the school year and give Dad the whole summer to accept that I was going to be living with Zach in the fall."

"I think you shouldn't wait too long. Things have a way of getting out." She was referring to Zach's slip up.

"I know. I just happen to be the world's worst procrastinator."

DAD PULLED OUT PHOTO albums. He wanted to show Zach what a cute kid I was. Zach appeared to be interested looking through the albums, commenting that I looked a lot like Grandma. I didn't see the resemblance.

"And who's this?" Zach asked, pointing to one picture. I couldn't see it, but by the way Dad suddenly got uncomfortable, I had an idea who it was.

"That's Meredith, Emma's mom."

Grandpa cleared his throat and excused himself. He hated Meredith for abandoning me. When she sent me gifts, Grandpa wanted to throw them away, but Grandma was steadfast that one day Meredith would want to come back into my life. Nineteen years and she still hadn't stopped by. She moved away with her new family and never looked back.

"She's pretty just like her daughter," Wendy said, her tone subdued as if to respect everyone's disdain.

Zach looked at Dad, then me and finally Wendy, the only safe face in the room. "I apologize if that brings up bad memories."

"That's all right. I keep the picture of her for Emma."

"You don't need to," I said, my bitterness bubbling to the surface.

"One day you might think differently," Dad said, flipping the page.

After the horrible walk down memory lane, Wendy got up to leave. It was getting late and after my long day, I needed sleep. "I'll show Zach his room, then hit the sack," I said.

"Zach, if you're not tired, we can hang out some more," Dad said, his face brightening at the prospect.

"Sure, right after I get settled."

We went upstairs to the spare room, the one Dad had meticulously cleaned. It still smelled of Febreze. Alone, Zach pulled me close and kissed me.

"You look wiped," he said, brushing a stray hair from my cheek.

"I am."

"I didn't know it was your mom."

"You're a liar," I said, slapping his ass.

He laughed. "I figured it was her. She is very beautiful, just like you. That's all I'm going to say about her."

"Good." I kissed him one last time. "Don't stay up too late with Dad. I don't want either one of you blabbing any of my secrets."

ZACH STAYED ANOTHER two days before driving back home. He had hockey games to attend as well as a family fundraising dinner. He invited me, but I wanted to spend the week with my family.

Grandpa had a road trip planned to hit some auctions and estate sales, which gave me and Dad a few days alone. He planned a movie night Friday and while he supplied the movies, I made the caramel popcorn.

"Steve McQueen?" Dad asked. He knew I was a sucker for 70s movies.

"I love Steve McQueen."

"I got the box set while you were away at school. We've got *The Magnificent Seven*, *Le Mans*, *The Thomas Crown Affair*, or *The Great Escape*. Which one?"

"Surprise me."

He flipped through the DVDs and settled on *The Thomas Crown Affair*.

"Dad, before we start watching, there's something I wanted to tell you."

The smile on his face disappeared replaced with a look of worry. "Please tell me you aren't pregnant."

I laughed nervously. "No, not pregnant."

He sighed with relief. "Good. Then what is it?"

I took the caramel popcorn and sat on the sofa. Dad sat down, too. His expression looked serious, and I felt the nerves building. "You like Zach, right?"

"He's a nice young man. Why?"

"I don't know how to tell you this because I know you'll freak out, but I'm not going to beat around the bush." I had an image of the day Dad tried to explain sex to me. Twenty minutes later and I'd felt like I knew less about sex than I had before he sat me down. "Zach and I are living together."

Dad leaned back on the sofa and crossed his arms over his chest. He was biting down on his lower lip, pondering and possibly fuming. "I see. How long?"

"Awhile. We weren't always dating, but I moved in because...well, Jake wanted more time with Bianca and, well, Bianca doesn't like me. So I did them a favor and moved in with Zach and his sister." These lies were just piling up now. I needed graphs and charts to keep track of them.

"Zach's sister also lives with you?"

"Yes." That was the truth.

"And you moved out of the apartment with Jake? Why is this the first I've heard of it?"

"I figured you'd be disappointed and wouldn't want me living with Zach."

"But his sister does live with you?"

"Her name is Genie and she's great."

Dad took a minute to absorb it all. "You're my daughter so we can have these frank and open discussions, right?"

"Yes."

"Are you having sex with him?"

Oh, God. "Yes."

"Are you using protection?"

"Yes."

"I'm going to tell you something, and I'm not sure how it's going to come out, so hopefully I don't screw it up." He took a few breaths, struggling with what was coming. "You are a gift to me, don't ever forget that. When you were born, I was a mess and if it wasn't for

Grandma and Grandpa, I'd have been lost. And as much as I love you and can't imagine life without you, I do not want you to make the same mistakes I did. Don't let him talk you into doing anything you don't want to do and always keep yourself protected. And remember I love you more than anything in this world even though I might have just sounded like the biggest jackass on the face of this earth."

"I understand what you're saying."

"And if for any reason you find yourself in trouble, you come to me. I will always support you."

"I know."

"Enough said. Are we going to watch this movie, or not?"

That was the perfect opportunity to come clean about the real story with Jake, and I didn't. I was a coward.

CHAPTER THIRTY-TWO

EMMA

With only a little more than a month of classes to go, the first few weeks after spring break flew by. And now that Bianca had finally stopped harassing me, I felt a need to gain a bit of my independence back. I insisted on taking the bus home on Thursdays when Zach's classes ended a few hours before mine. Sometimes he'd wait for me by working out at the gym and other times he'd reluctantly let me go home alone.

Sure, the walk through campus spooked me a bit, but there were so many people around, nothing could possibly happen.

"What do you have on her anyway?" I asked one night as we were lying in bed. He'd just finished telling me that he'd seen her at the gym that day and she hadn't said hello.

"If I tell you, I'd have to kill you," he joked.

"Come on," I said, squeezing his arm.

In an instant he was on top of me, kissing and caressing.

"No, you don't get off that easy," I said between kisses.

"Why do you want to know anyway?"

"Because I'm curious."

He slipped his hand beneath my underwear and started his careful massage. "It's not important," he murmured.

"You're trying to distract me."

"Is it working?"

"Yes," I said, kissing him back.

In seconds we were naked, him inside me, pushing deeper and deeper. Sex with him was so natural, so right. Sometimes in class, my mind would wander off to us in bed, on the sofa, on the kitchen counter, or in the shower, and I'd tingle with anticipation. My body craved him all the time.

"Back to Bianca," I said, after he returned from disposing of the condom.

He groaned. "I hoped you'd forget."

"No," I said, welcoming him back into bed and finding my spot in his arms.

"This is all I'm going to tell you. I may have a video of her doing something that would be very embarrassing to both her and her family if it ever got distributed."

"A sex video? Is it with Jake?"

"I'm not saying what it is and Jake isn't in it. It's from before he came along."

"Is she doing drugs in it?"

"I'm not telling."

"How'd you get it?"

"I'm not telling."

I pondered this. "Have you had it for a while?"

"Yes, and she knows I have it. Why are we still talking about her anyway?"

He was right. Bianca wasn't worth my time. I ran a finger up and down his arm, sleep had no intention of coming. "I've wanted to ask you something for a really long time," I said.

"Oh, yeah? What's that?" he asked, kissing the top of my head.

"When did you know that you liked me?"

He chuckled. "When did you know that you liked me?"

"I asked first."

He caressed my back and didn't answer right away. I waited, growing a little nervous that he hadn't said anything yet. Was I not going to like his answer?"

"I'm not a hundred percent sure. Sometime between opening the door at Brett's cabin and sharing a piece of chocolate cake and a beer with you a few hours later."

I lifted my head and stared at his serene face. I was speechless. For once my mind wasn't analyzing and dissecting. "Really," I finally managed to say.

"Why do you think I kept coming around?"

"I thought you were being nice. Or worse, feeling sorry for me."

"Well, I am nice," he said and winked. "I also liked you a lot."

"Why didn't you—" I stopped myself. I knew the answer. Jake. "I didn't know right away mostly because I couldn't believe you'd like a girl like me. Sometimes I still don't believe it."

"Like a girl like you? Em, you're amazing. I'm a lucky guy to have you in my life."

I kissed him and wrapped my arms around him as tightly as I could. I never wanted to let him go.

HELEN AND I PLAYED our weekly Wednesday evening tennis match. She was getting better and even had me sweating for a while. I tried to keep the matches close because who'd play tennis with me if I beat them all the time?

In the locker room I could tell she had something to say. She couldn't stop fidgeting.

"So Marc came and talked to me before you got here," she said, playing with the laces of one of the tennis shoes she'd just taken off. "And we had a chat about you."

"Only good things, I hope," I said and laughed. Then it hit me. "Is he disqualifying us from our next tournament?"

"No, nothing like that. I know you're in school and don't live in the city, but he wants to ask you to be an instructor here, perhaps coach some kids he thinks have a little talent. He asked me to poke around for him. By far you're the best tennis player here."

I smiled at the compliment. "Really?"

"Come on, you can kick my butt in your sleep."

"I don't know if I have the time. Between school and my other job..."

She motioned for me to move closer, out of the earshot of other players. "Marc has some really affluent members here with kids, and they want those kids to learn tennis. They pay well, I'm sure much better than your coffee shop job...not that I'm disparaging it in any way, but wouldn't you love to play a little more tennis? Teach kids?"

"Not a bunch of rich kids."

"He has a summer program for low-income youth. You could teach that, too. Marc wants you all over this place. You're a pretty girl who happens to have a killer forehand and backhand that shames us all. And did I mention your serve? You're the perfect role model for everyone here. They all love you."

"I don't know. Can I think about it?"

"Of course you can. Can I tell Marc you might be interested?"

Her eyes were beaming, begging me to say yes. "Sure, but don't make any promises."

"One last thing. I have something for you," she said, handing me an envelope.

"What is it?" I asked.

"Take it. It's a gift for you. I wanted to thank you for being the best tournament partner a middle-aged woman could have."

I opened the envelope and pulled out the card. Helen had written a few kind words that nearly brought me to tears. "Thank you," I said, fighting the waterworks. "And what's this?" I asked, holding up a gift card that had also been inside the envelope.

"That's for you. Go buy yourself some nice things. You wouldn't accept my portion of the prize money, so I'm making you accept this gift card. You can't return gift cards. It's a rule."

I thought to argue with her, but realized I'd be wasting my time. "You're the best partner I've ever had, too."

I showered, dressed, and pulled out my phone to text Zach on my walk to the bus. It was an unseasonably warm March evening, and I tied my sweater around my waist, one of Genie's old/new sweaters.

Me: Marc wants me to coach at the club! Rich kids during the year and low-income youth in the summer. Helen asked me for him, and I think I might be interested. And she gave me a two-hundred-and-fifty-dollar gift card. How sweet was that?

I was about to slip my phone into my pocket when I heard a crack, like a bat hitting a baseball. My phone flew out of my hand and through the air while my body hit the pavement with a thud. Only then did the blinding pain set it.

"I warned you, bitch." The voice was filled with rage.

Instinct kicked in as I tried to regain my bearings. I tried pushing myself up to my knees, but arms were all over me, pulling at my clothes and hair, using them to drag me off the sidewalk and into the bushes nearby. I panicked. If they got me to a secluded spot, I was doomed. I flailed my arms and legs, screaming at the top of my lungs as a foot connected with my chest knocking the wind out of me. There had to be at least three of them, all girls by the sounds of their voices. One was on ground, trying to pound my head with her fists, connecting a few times as I tried to shield my face with my hands.

"Get her in the head," one screamed. It had to be Bianca. "Fuck her up!"

One peppered blows while another kicked me in the chest and thighs. The last one tried to hold my legs down. I could taste the blood, the metallic tang of it filling my mouth. I coughed a few times, trying to scream, but only muffled sobs came out.

"Hey! Hey! What the hell?"

A male voice I didn't know. My attackers bolted, leaving me lying in the grass, partially hidden by the bushes. I started choking from the blood in my mouth, where it came from, I didn't know. I spit it out, relieved there was no more. My chest hurt so much I could barely breathe. I tried to stand but my head spun so much I fell back down.

"Are you hurt?" the man asked.

I couldn't speak. I couldn't even find breath. My vision was blurred by tears and searing pain. The man knelt down next to me and pulled out his phone, then dialed three numbers.

"We need an ambulance. A young woman has been attacked." He gave our location and then sat with me.

"My phone," I stammered.

"Who do you want me to call?" he asked, reaching for where it lay on the ground nearby. He was such a nice man, late thirties, his green eyes filled with compassion. That's when I saw his bag and the tennis racket sticking out. I suddenly felt safe with him.

"Zach. Call Zach." I managed to scroll to Zach's number and then rested my cheek against the cool, coarse grass. My head felt like it was being hammered with pointy nails.

"Is this Zach? Hi, my name is Frank and I'm with ..." he turned to me.

"Emma," I mumbled.

"I'm with Emma and she was assaulted just outside the Taylor Tennis Club." He paused. Was Zach freaking out? A stabbing pain seared through my side. "Yes, I've already called an ambulance. They should be here shortly. Yes, you can talk to her."

Frank held the phone to my ear. I didn't think I had the energy to do it myself.

"Em, are you okay?" Yes, he was freaking out. His voice pitched and I could hear him restraining his rage.

"I think so. Don't get mad."

"I'm going to kill her!"

"No," I said as tears slipped down my cheeks.

"I'm leaving and I'll be there in a few minutes."

"Talk to Frank."

Frank took the phone back. "Zach, I hear the ambulance. You should just meet us at the hospital. I'll stay with her and let you know where they take her."

I closed my eyes and my mind drifted away.

CHAPTER THIRTY-THREE

ZACH

Never in my life had I been angrier. The entire drive to the hospital I could have killed anyone who crossed my path. I wanted to smash things, but my steering wheel took the brunt of my frustration.

I got to the hospital before Emma had even been admitted. It was time to make calls. The first was to Dad. Sure, it should have been to Emma's dad, but I had an agenda. I told him what happened and asked him to pull a few strings at the hospital. I wanted her to have her own room and I wanted full access to it. No questions asked.

The second call was the hardest. Mr. Andrews picked up on the second ring.

"Hello, Mr. Andrews," I said, trying to keep my voice calm. "It's Zach."

"Well, hello there, Zach, and I insist you call me Paul. I'm surprised to hear from you." His voice dropped off. "Something happen?"

I took a deep breath. "Paul, Emma was attacked today outside her tennis club. They brought her to the hospital and I'm waiting to hear how she is. I did talk to her, so she's conscious and everything."

"What? No! I'm on my way. Which hospital?"

I gave him the details and told him I'd call once I knew more. I went to the emergency station and clearly Dad had already spoken to someone. I only had to say her name and the nurse nodded. "Ms. Andrews was just admitted. Dr. Lewis is in with her now and I will have him come speak with you when he's finished his exam."

Yes, having a senator for a father had its privileges. I didn't usually like to call in favors using my dad's influence, but this was an exception. I left the crowded emergency room to pace a nearby hallway. I had to keep calm for Emma and think things through carefully. My first instinct was to go after Bianca, send out the video, but what would it accomplish? Enraging her further? And what if it was linked to me? I couldn't risk it.

I took out my phone and made a third call.

"What do you want?"

I hated Jake and his attitude didn't help. Had he been standing in front of me I would have crushed him into the wall. "I'd like to say this is a courtesy call, but it's not. It's a warning. Emma was attacked today and I can only assume it was Bianca, or that she got someone to do it. Emma's at University Hospital. I've called her dad and when he gets here, I'm telling him everything. Every last detail, you motherfucker."

I hung up before he could speak and then made my last call to Genie.

"Do you want me to come down?"

"No, not yet. Once I know more I'll call you back."

"I can come if you need me."

"I'll let you know. For now, put a few things together for Emma. I'm sure she'll want a change of clothes, especially if they keep her overnight." The nurse came to get me and motioned for me to follow her. "Genie, I've got to go. I'll call you back later." I stuffed my phone into a pocket. My heart was pounding. What if she wasn't all right? My stomach flipped. I loved her. Yeah, I could admit it. From that first night at Brett's cabin, I couldn't get her out of my head. I tried to protect her and when I let my guard down, I'd let her down. I'd failed her.

"She's in here," the nurse said, taking me into a private room. "Dr. Lewis will be in shortly."

I gasped when I saw her. Her face was swollen, one eye shut, her lip split and scratches all over her face. I quietly pulled up a chair, but she opened her eyes, or what she could of the left one.

"How are you feeling?" I asked, clasping onto her hand and squeezing.

"Better now. I got drugs," she said, her voice groggy.

"What did the doctor say?"

"Nothing broken, but I have two cracked ribs and a concussion."

"I called your dad and he's on his way."

"He's probably upset."

"He was. I'm going to call him right after the doctor comes in and tell him you'll be back to your usual self in no time."

"I'm sorry, Zach." A tear spilled down her face and I gently wiped it away.

"Why are you sorry? Why are you crying?" Seeing her this way killed me. I wanted to scoop her up and take her away.

"I let this happen."

I shook my head and kissed her hand. "You didn't do anything wrong."

"I should have just left her alone from the start."

"None of this would have happened if she'd behaved like a normal human being. So I don't want to hear you blaming yourself again."

Dr. Lewis came in, interrupting her rebuttal. He shook my hand and gave Emma a warm smile.

"And how are you feeling? The medication kicking in?"

"Yes," she said, every word causing her obvious pain.

"Headache?"

"Yes."

Dr. Lewis turned to me. "We're keeping her overnight as a precaution, but other than a few cracked ribs, a mild concussion, and some scrapes and bruises, she should be fine. Emma's a tough one.

I've explained this to her already, and because this was an assault, we've contacted the authorities. They will want to interview her."

"Okay."

"Next of kin? Have they been contacted?"

"Her father is on his way."

"All right. I'll check in again later."

Once he was gone, I turned back to Emma. "Em, you need to tell the police the truth."

She let out a halting, tortured breath. Agony was etched on her face. "The truth is that I didn't see anyone. I think it was three girls and one voice sounded like Bianca's. It was dark. I can't lie and say it was her."

"She's going to pay for this."

More tears sprang from her eyes. "No! Please, I want it over. Promise me that it's over!"

"Emma, she can't get away with it."

"But then what? Tit for tat forever?"

"For now it's over. I'm going to call your dad and I'll be right back."

The truth was that I didn't want to argue with her and upset her even more. I went outside and there was Emma's dad, talking to a nurse at the emergency desk. He'd made good time. He'd probably speed the whole way. I jogged over to him and he saw me coming, relief washing over him. I briefed him then told him I had something else to tell him before he went in to see her.

I persuaded him to join me in the mostly empty cafeteria. I bought us coffees and we took a seat in a quiet corner.

"Zach, you have me worried. What's going on? Do you know who did this to Emma?"

"I have an idea, but wouldn't be able to prove it. Mr. Andrews—Paul, there's something Emma has been keeping from you and you have a right to know."

And so I told him, from the beginning, without holding back. From the day at the cabin when she'd seen all of Bianca and Jake's texts, to Bianca's harassment and Emma breaking her nose. Then I dove into me getting her out of jail and her moving in with me after Jake had kicked her out, to the texts I thought I'd stopped. Paul listened, his mouth gaping open, taking it all in.

"She didn't want to tell you because she was worried how disappointed you'd be. That it would wreck your friendship with Jake's brother."

He shook his head, leaned back in his chair, and let out a deep breath. "I knew something wasn't right with her and Jake. I just assumed it had to do with you, I had no idea it was all about this girlfriend of Jake's. I have so many questions, and I don't know where to start."

"I didn't want to be the one to tell you, but I figured that if it came from me, it would be easier for her."

"And Jake just kicked her out?"

"Yes. He called me because he knew we'd formed a friendship. He told me to get her from jail, pick up her stuff, and basically get her out of his life."

"Ron couldn't possibly know."

"Jake pressured Emma to keep it a secret."

Paul's face hardened. "What a piece of shit. I've always been so good to that kid, trusted him, but some girl comes along and he does this to Emma?"

"I'm afraid so."

"Thank you, Zach. I'd like to go see Emma now."

We went back to her floor and that's when I spotted Jake, wandering the halls. I marched towards him and when he saw me, he was about to speak, but he must have seen something in my eyes. He took a few steps back and that's when something came over me, pure rage.

It clouded my judgment and when I picked up my pace, Paul came after me and got between us just as I was about to throw a punch.

"Hey, we don't need this," Paul said. "Zach, you'll get thrown out of here."

"You're not seeing her!" I yelled.

Jake's shoulders sank. "Do you think I wanted this to happen?"

"You didn't do anything to stop it," I seethed.

"Everyone relax and keep your voices down," Paul said, pushing me back a few steps.

"She said she didn't do it," Jake said.

I tried to get at him again, but Paul grabbed me, shaking me for second. "Zach, get it together. Do you need to go outside and cool off?"

I put up my arms. "I'm fine."

Paul turned to Jake. "I'm not sure why you came here. I learned today that you turned your back on my daughter months ago when she needed you most. She was all alone here, with no one, and you promised me you'd take care of her. What happened to you? I thought you were a good kid."

"Paul, it got a little out of hand. I didn't know what was going on. Bianca said she didn't do it, that she had nothing to do with it...I know she's lying." He started to cry. I wanted to laugh, but he was too pathetic. "I'm so sorry. If I'd known...I would have never let this happen to her."

"What you did was even worse," I said. "The way you treated her. She loved you! She would have done anything for you."

Jake's bloodshot blue eyes stared at me, defeated. "I guess now you've replaced me. You don't know how lucky you are. I'd do anything to fix this. I would!"

"No, you wouldn't!"

"I think the best thing you can do right now is leave. If she wants to see you, she'll let you know," Paul said. "In the meantime, you might want to tell Ron about this. Now get out of here before I sock you one myself."

"I'm so sorry," he said one last time before slithering down the hallway and into the elevator.

Paul turned to me. "I'm going in to see Emma. Let's not tell her about this until we know she's ready."

"Yes, of course."

He went in her room and I sat in the waiting area. It was then I saw Emma's text from earlier that night. So happy and full of excitement. I may have told Emma it was over, but Bianca would pay.

CHAPTER THIRTY-FOUR

EMMA

I cried when I saw Dad. He pulled up a chair and gave me a kiss on the cheek. His bottom lip was quivering a bit, but he managed to keep composed.

"How are you feeling?"

"Like I've been run over."

"The doctor says you'll be just fine. Do you want to come home? Have Grandpa and I take care of you?"

"I don't want to miss school, especially with exams coming."

He squeezed my hand. "I'm sure Zach will take good care of you."

"He always does, although we'll be eating takeout for the next few days."

Dad smiled but I could see that more was going on. "Kiddo, don't be mad, but Zach told me everything. About Jake and that girlfriend of his."

I felt my insides cave, yet a part of me was relieved. "I didn't know how to tell you."

"It doesn't matter. I know now. But you better promise to never keep something like that from me again."

"I didn't want to ruin your friendship with Uncle Ron."

"Ron and I are tight. This won't change a thing."

"Jake really hurt me, Dad. Bianca is nothing to me, but Jake let me down."

"I know," he said, rubbing my hand. "Jake was here, but we sent him home. He seemed pretty sorry. Now when you go home, if you want to talk to him, that's your business, but I wanted you to know."

Jake was the last person I wanted to talk to. I didn't care about him.

"Zach offered me a place to stay tonight, so we're going to go. It's getting late and you need your rest. We'll be back in the morning with some breakfast. You cannot eat hospital food."

"Thanks, Dad. I love you."

"Sweetie, I love you too."

THE POLICE INTERVIEWED me the next morning for less than five minutes. I told them I didn't know who attacked me because, technically, that was true. I didn't see Bianca or the other two people, and I couldn't identify her by voice. And even if I did know it was Bianca, I wanted this over. She got her eye for an eye.

Genie, Dad, Zach, Grandpa, and Wendy piled into my room the next morning with breakfast from a fast-food place. I didn't care since it was better than the slop they served at the hospital. Genie brought a change of clothes and Grandpa and Wendy gave me a box of chocolates. Dr. Lewis assured me that I'd be sprung by lunch so we all waited around chatting.

Genie got me alone when everyone else had gone for coffee.

"Probably inappropriate, but your dad is hot."

I laughed, then groaned because it hurt. "Yeah, that's a bit gross."

"He's movie-star hot. When Zach brought him home last night, I couldn't stop drooling. I almost wet myself."

"Genie, we're talking about my dad," I said fighting back a giggle.

"Is he single?"

"Yes, but he doesn't date much."

"Does he date younger women?"

"Genie, totally gross now."

"I'm just curious. I wouldn't follow through or anything."

I was having a hard time believing that.

I had more visitors. First Helen, who'd found out from Frank. Turns out he was a member at the club and an acquaintance of Helen's. I asked her to thank him for me; I couldn't remember if I'd even spoken to him again after the ambulance came.

"You look like hell, partner," she said, giving me a gentle hug.

"Thanks, I think."

"I bet you fought like hell. Any idea who it was?"

"No."

"Did they steal anything?"

"No. Just some random attack."

"I'm glad you're fine. Make sure to take it easy. I need my partner back as soon as she's ready."

Next came Andrea and Lucy. Our visit was cut short when Uncle Ron called. I was nervous talking to him, knowing that he probably knew everything now. I was glad to be alone for the call. The last thing I needed was an audience.

"Hi, Uncle Ron."

"Hey there, how you doing, Emma?" His always cheerful voice was tentative.

"I'm doing fine."

He cleared his throat. "Your dad called last night. Emma...I'm gutted. I wish I'd known."

"Really, it's okay," I said as my eyes welled up with tears. I couldn't stop the heaviness that had descended in my voice.

"She's never welcome in our home again. I told Jake that."

"Uncle Ron, I want it over. I don't want anyone to continue fighting. As long as she leaves me alone, I'll leave her alone."

"I can respect that. Paul mentioned that you'll be home next weekend. I'd like to come see you if that's all right. I want you to know we all love you."

I grabbed a crappy hospital tissue and dabbed my eyes. "I'd love to see you too."

"Ah, don't cry," he said. "I don't want to make you cry."

"It's happy tears," I said.

"So I'll see you soon. Tell your dad I'm bringing burgers and fries from Harriet's."

"I will."

We ended the call, and I composed myself before everyone came flooding back into my room. I was released an hour later and insisted on going straight to the apartment. It would be at least a week before my face was back to normal, and I didn't want to have people staring at me. Zach was going to visit my professors and tell them what happened. He made me go through taking pictures just in case they needed more evidence. He promised to delete them when it was all over.

"Are you sure you don't want us to stay?" Dad asked after dinner. The apartment was filled with people I loved and normally I would have reveled in it, but my throbbing head would have none of it.

"I'll be fine and if I need anything, I know who to call."

"And we'll see you this weekend?" Dad asked Zach.

"Absolutely."

"I'd love to come too," Genie offered.

I was going to have to warn Dad about her.

I walked them to the door, giving each one a big hug. Despite what Bianca had done to me, I had everyone I loved around me. She couldn't take that from me.

CHAPTER THIRTY-FIVE

ZACH

I waited for Bianca. According to Becca, she had a psych class today and Becca was kind enough to tell me where and when. If nothing else, I knew when to lay on the charm; Becca had been more than willing to give up what she knew.

I leaned up against the wall, my arms crossed over my chest, and tried not to flip out. If Bianca thought I was going to let this slide, she had another thing coming. My only concern was making sure it didn't get back to Emma.

I checked my watch. Her class would end any second. I tapped my foot as rage boiled up inside me. If Bianca had been a guy, I would have pummeled her into next week.

The door to her class opened and a few students filed out. Bianca soon followed, alone, just the way I wanted it. She didn't see me until I was walking alongside her.

She jumped when she saw me. "Oh, great, what do you want?" she muttered.

"We're going to talk."

"I have class." She sounded bored, like I was keeping her from doing her nails or something.

"I guess you'll have to miss it."

She stopped and faced me. I saw a scratch on her neck, mostly healed, but a reminder of what she'd done. She caught me looking at it and turned her head the other way.

"Look, I don't have to talk to you. I think you should leave me alone."

I stepped closer to her. If it intimidated her, I didn't give a shit. "We're talking." I motioned to an empty classroom, and she reluctantly went inside.

"You're not closing the door," she said. "You do that, and I bolt."

"Fine. We can talk with it open."

I stared at her and she stared back, her pale blue eyes refusing to give an inch. "If you don't get to the point, I'm out of here," she said.

I inhaled deeply. I hated her. "We had a deal."

"I didn't touch her."

My hands balled into fists. "Bianca, we're past lying."

"I don't know what happened to her, and I had nothing to do with it."

"Is that how this is going to go? You went too far, Bianca. I told you what the consequences would be. But if you want to play, I'm game. Just don't come crying to me later. You asked for it."

She chuckled. "I'm not scared of you."

Her confidence enraged me further. "You willing to risk it?" I asked, moving in closer. We were inches apart now, and she took a step back into one of the tables but caught herself before stumbling.

"You can cut the act. You'll never share that video. I know that and so do you."

So that was it all along? She thought I wouldn't make good on my threat? I smiled, which caught her off guard. The first crack in her foundation. "Yeah, I'm going to share it. And I'm going to do it right now. I'll even send you a copy if you want. And to your parents too. I'm sure they'd love to see it."

"You post that video and it hurts you just as much as it hurts me. And what about your precious girlfriend? You don't think she's going to know you're in it? That she won't recognize you?"

"Here's the thing. I'm the only one with a copy and I've edited it. Pretty simple these days. No one's going to know I was ever in it.

And if I remember correctly, you're the star. The main attraction. Enjoy the fallout, Bianca."

I turned to leave and she ran after me, grabbing my arm. Her cold expression was replaced by wide-eyed fear. Desperation was ugly on her. "You wouldn't."

"You broke our deal," I seethed. "The only reason I came here is to give you one last chance, Bianca. And you know why? Because Emma wants me to forget about it. Call it even. Move on. But I can't do that because I have no idea what else you have planned. If I had my way, I'd ruin your fucking life! And what have you done since the moment I got here? You challenged me? Are you serious?"

"People think you've changed. You haven't changed a bit," she spat. "You're the same asshole you've always been."

"I guess you bring out the worst in me."

She swallowed hard. "I know what you've been up to. You're telling people that I beat her up. My friends are turning their backs on me. Everyone is turning their backs on me. That's because of you!"

I shook my head. "What are you talking about? I haven't told anyone. Don't you think they assumed it? Who else would hurt her? I guess Jake finally dumped your sorry ass?"

She started hyperventilating. "She's ruining my life. You are ruining my life," she said, pointing her finger at me.

Bianca went from bravado to all-out panic in less than a minute. She made me sick. "No, you ruined your life. What was it about Emma that threatened you so much? You had Jake, you got her kicked out of her apartment, nearly cost her the job she loved, what more did you need from her? A pound of fucking flesh?" My voice was rising now. I took a few steps back to regroup.

"I wanted—" she stopped. Whatever she was going to say, she clammed up. "I'm done with her, I promise." Her voice drifted to a whisper. "Please, don't share the video."

"How do I know I can trust you? You're not exactly a woman of your word."

"I'm done with her, okay! I'm done," she shrieked. "Do you want it in blood?"

She seemed to be losing it, but with Bianca, I couldn't know for sure. She was an aspiring actress. What a joke. "Let me make sure you understand this. If you call, text, contact Emma in anyway, I post the video. I won't give it a second thought. And I certainly won't give you any warning. I'll make sure to send a copy to all your friends and family. Your dad wants to be a judge, don't forget that. This video will end any chance of that."

She slumped down in one of the chairs and nodded. "I hate you," she said, her voice having lost its fight.

"I feel the same way about you."

"What is it about her?" she asked as I was leaving. "What is so fucking special about a small-town freak?"

I looked back at her, catching her wipe a single tear from her face. I didn't feel an ounce of sympathy. "You really want to know? I'll tell you. She's nothing like you."

CHAPTER THIRTY-SIX

EMMA

One thing I knew for sure was that cracked ribs hurt more than a separated shoulder. At least with a shoulder you could get immediate relief, but cracked ribs gave me a constant reminder that it hurt to breathe. But a week after the attack, my face had healed nicely and I'd gone back to classes. I'd even started cooking again, because the thought of anymore takeout Chinese food, pizza, or burgers turned my stomach.

I was puttering around the kitchen Friday night making a stir-fry with double the amount of vegetables, a food group that had been sorely lacking in my recent diet, when the buzzer sounded. Zach popped his head into the kitchen.

"Asswipe is here. Do you want to talk to him?"

I stopped tossing the vegetables. Jake? He'd sent me flowers and a card, but why come around? "Uh, sure, I guess."

Zach frowned. "You don't have to."

"I know."

I gave Zach some quick instructions regarding our dinner-in-progress and told him not to come out of the kitchen. I didn't want a fight. Then I let Jake in. He stared at the last of the bruising on my face and bristled.

"Hey, Emma. I thought I'd see how you're doing."

"I'm doing better. Thanks for the flowers." My voice held no excitement like it once would have.

"It's the least I could do. I wanted to come by and apologize for what happened. I know it's just words, but I'm so sorry. I know I screwed up our friendship over a girl...we broke up. I broke up with her. When I found out what she did, I told her it was over. I figured so much time passed that she'd forgotten about it...don't hate me, Emma."

"I don't hate you," I said. Strangely, I didn't feel much. There wasn't any tugging at my heart strings or remorse at our lost friendship. Nothing.

"I hope one day we can be friends again."

His blue eyes were welling up with tears and still I felt no emotion. "Jake, I don't hate you, but we can't be friends. Too much happened."

He nodded. "I understand," he said, choking out the words. "I know you're pissed so hopefully after some time passes you could reconsider?"

I nodded. "Maybe." I was placating him now.

"Don't be a stranger, okay?"

"I'm sure I'll see you around Pine Falls."

He turned and walked out. I went back into the kitchen to monitor Zach's progress. He hadn't burned anything yet. I took a second to watch him thoughtfully follow all my instructions, careful not to make a mistake. Yes, this was where I wanted to be. A couple of days at some rich kid's family's cabin, a place I'd never wanted to go to in the first place, changed the course of my life. It brought me to this place, brought me to Zach. Sure, there had been an awful lot of bumps along the way, but they'd been worth it.

He caught me staring and motioned me over. He put his arm around my shoulder and kissed my cheek.

"How'd it go?"

"Fine. It was goodbye."

He nodded. I bet he had a lot of things he wanted to say about Jake, but he kept them to himself. "You know what?"

"What?" I asked.

"I've never said this to a girl before, but I love you."

My heart soared. Three little words made my day. "You know what?"

"What?"

"I love you too."

THE END

ACKNOWLEDGEMENTS

THIS WRITING JOURNEY has been a long one, and when I penned my first story in the fifth grade, I had no idea where I'd end up. There are two people who encouraged me to continue writing when I thought publishing a book would never happen. Thank you, Dana and Alpha, for all the times we met at table 11 at the greasy spoon we frequented. Without you two, this book and every book after would have never happened.

I can't forget Katherine and Shelley, my two amazing writer friends from England and New Zealand respectively. We met by chance and an amazing friendship was formed. Your constant encouragement and virtual shoulders to cry on always kept me going in even the darkest of times.

And my dear friend, Ratna, who was the first to volunteer to read early drafts. I couldn't ask for a better beta reader and friend.

I owe great thanks to Wattpad and its readers. This book would have never been possible if it hadn't been for all the great readers who found my work among the millions. Your feedback was invaluable, along with all your kind messages. I also must thank the staff at Wattpad for seeing something special in me. I'm forever grateful for all the opportunities you offered me.

To my family, including my sisters, Vivian and Marina, my brother, Joe, and my sister-in-law, Lisa. Your love and support will never be forgotten. And to my mom, Mary, who has always been so proud of me. I can't forget my dad. I know if he were here, he'd be so proud of me too.

Finally, my partner, Michael, who has happily come along with me on this journey. Your patience and care is unending.

TEASER
THIS MUCH IS TRUE
CHAPTER ONE

EMMA

"Your mother called."

Three words I never wanted or expected to hear. My mother, a woman I hadn't seen in nearly eight years. Who'd dumped me on my dad and never looked back. "She did?"

"She wanted to know how you've been. I know you're surprised. I was too."

I pushed my breakfast dish away. Thankfully Dad had waited until I'd finished my Eggs Benedict before giving me indigestion. "I find it a bit odd that she's asking about me all of the sudden. Don't you?"

I looked at Dad and fixed my gaze on his. He pursed his lips and shrugged. "I have my suspicions as to her timing."

"So, who told her about Zach?" I asked, rising and taking away our empty plates.

"I'm guessing one of her old friends from around here. They saw him around this summer, made inquiries and that was that. Meredith had a lot of questions. She seemed sincere."

"Why didn't she call me?"

Dad's face softened, like he was about to tell me the dog we'd never had just died. "Kiddo, she doesn't have your number."

Point taken. "She could have asked you for it then called me."

I'd moved onto washing dishes. Dad came over and put his arm around my shoulder. "I think she's scared to call you. Worried you might not talk to her."

I grunted. "She's right."

"I took her number if you do decide to call. She gave me her email address too, in case you're more comfortable communicating with her that way. And you might decide you never want to speak to her again. That's all up to you."

I looked at Dad. Meredith was his Achilles' heel. Why? I didn't know. The woman had left him with a baby to raise. No calls, no support, nothing. She graduated and moved on with her life. Eight years and not a call from her. No visits. Nada.

"Let me get this straight. She finds out I'm dating Zach Walker and suddenly she wants back in my life? I think I'll pass on giving her a call or shooting her an email."

"Okay, that's your decision. I don't want to sway you either way. I will leave the info for you. I'd hate to lose it."

Dad lose something? He kept everything from my first day in nursery school to my last day of high school. He may have been a kid himself, but Dad was meticulous about keeping what was important to him. "Sure, I'll hang on to it."

"One last thing because I know you want to get the hell out of here and to that boyfriend of yours. She asked me for your email address. She wants to send you something. I didn't give it to her because I told her I'd ask you first. So, I'm asking. Can she have it?"

I took a long time mulling it over, the two of us standing in silence in the kitchen. Did I want her to have it? Did I want to hear from her? Maybe I was curious, but this was the same woman who'd abandoned me. "Sure," I said. I didn't expect those words to leave my mouth, but I didn't take them back either.

Dad smiled. "Remember that you're in control. You can cut off communication at any time."

Who'd said anything about communication?

"HELLO, GORGEOUS," ZACH said, scooping me into his arms and planting a kiss on my lips.

"Hello to you too! You're happy to see me."

"It's been one long week. Can't a guy miss his girlfriend? The girlfriend he's celebrating his six-month anniversary with."

I grimaced. "Are we celebrating those kinds of anniversaries?"

"For me, six months is like six years."

"Six glorious years," I said, playfully pinching his arm.

"Where is your dad?" Zach asked, picking up my backpack and throwing it over his broad shoulder.

"At the shop. He'd like us to stop by before we go. He doesn't want to miss seeing you."

Zach beamed. "I like your dad. He's a cool cat."

We drove the short distance and I couldn't help but lament. Nearly a year ago I was going to this same cabin with Jake, my former best friend, where I would meet Zach for the first time. The only friendly face, he'd taken me under his wing, made an uncomfortable situation tolerable, and now I was going to this same cabin not only as his girlfriend, but without a care in the world.

"Zach!" Dad said, giving my boyfriend a man hug.

"It's nice to see you again, Paul."

"Where are the two of you off to exactly?" Dad asked, ignoring the lone couple in the shop

"My buddy Brett's cabin in the Lake Sylvia area."

"Ooh, Lake Sylvia. Very nice. I've done some deliveries there. You drove all this way to pick Emma up just to drive back that way?"

"Anything for Em," he said and winked at me.

"Well, you better get off then. Text me when you get there."

I kissed Dad on the cheek and in minutes we were on the road.

"Dad laid a bombshell on me this morning," I said, fishing though my bag for a bottle of water.

"What's that?"

"Meredith called. She wants to reach out to me."

"Your mom? That's kind of cool."

"No, not cool at all, and calling her my mom is a stretch."

Zach rolled his eyes only half way and stopped when I glared. "Could she have had an epiphany?"

"Yes, and it has to do with her long-forgotten daughter dating a certain senator's son."

Zach groaned. "Oh, I see now."

"Right. Does she think she can worm her way back into my life because she asks? And she's so transparent. Obviously, I know why she called."

"Could you be wrong?"

I pffted him. "Not a chance in hell."

"Forget about her and let's enjoy this weekend," he said, reaching over and patting my thigh. "It will be our last before school starts."

Yes, school. Zach's senior year of college. He already had all his law school applications ready to be sent which meant he'd be leaving me behind. Off he'd go to Columbia, Harvard or whatever Ivy League school his dad wanted him to go to. I dreaded the prospect so much that on occasion I'd have the odd panic attack. I didn't tell him about it and he didn't need to know. It would only be a year, not even a full year, and I could deal with it. I'd have to. I'd also have to deal with all his new friends and worse, the new girls he'd meet. Nora, my therapist after Grandma died, always told me to confront my bad thoughts by saying, SO WHAT. She also told me to lie down and do twenty minutes of meditation but there was no time for that now. I pushed away the anxiety for now and focused on deep breaths and other thoughts.

I decided to think about the cabin and my weekend there. I wouldn't know anyone except for Zach and his best friend Brett. They'd invited along some of their hockey buddies and their girlfriends. There was no possible way this weekend could go any worse than the previous year's. So much had changed and now I had a lot more confidence.

"Are these girls going to be Bianca types? Because if they are, I'm spending the weekend in the kitchen or the bedroom."

Zach's eyebrows arched. "That sounds so 1950s of you. And I really like the bedroom part."

"Okay, not what I meant!"

He laughed and playfully poked me in the side. "You'll have a good time. I'm going to take you fishing and maybe we can do a little late-night skinny dipping."

I shook my head. "Try again."

"Prude."

After an hour and a half in the car we reached Brett's family cabin. For a split second a wave of nausea came over me. The place didn't exactly hold warm and fuzzy memories but this time was so different. I had Zach with me, a man who loved me, who defended me and who watched out for me. Jake and Bianca were distant memories.

"You're late," Brett said when we walked through the door. "Tell me you brought beer and food."

"I got everything you asked for."

Brett looked at me, his blue eyes still a little apprehensive. We were still getting to know each other and after my performance at the cabin the previous year, he had good reason to keep me at arm's length. "Hey, Emma. I hear you'll be feeding us all weekend."

"If you'll let me."

"You're an awesome cook, so we're giving you full control of the kitchen. We're having a pizza night, right?"

"Of course."

"My same room?" Zach asked.

"You bet. Settle in and meet us at the dock. We're swimming and trying to fish."

"Give us a few minutes."

Brett left out the massive patio doors and Zach turned to me. "Want to meet my bed?"

As hard as I tried, I couldn't wipe the smile from my face. "Maybe later? I think if we don't make an appearance, they'll know what we're up to."

"Such a prude."

At Zach's insistence, I put my bathing suit on under my shorts and t-shirt. We grabbed a few towels and headed out to the dock. It was after lunch and everyone was sitting around soaking up the sun with a few beers. Zach did a quick introduction and other than Brett, I was happy to see no returnees from the previous year. I knew I'd have trouble remembering names but I made a concerted effort to memorize as many as I could: Kaitlyn, Julia and Avery. Like the girls last year, these three were perfect right down to their beach hair and makeup. I could only hope their attitudes were different.

"Why is no one in the water?" Zach asked. He peeled off his shirt to the enjoyment of the ladies. Even though I'd seen him shirtless a million times, my heart fluttered a bit. He was in fantastic shape with strong shoulders and chiseled abs. How could anyone with a pulse not notice? He threw down his shirt and did a cannonball into the lake.

All the guys joined in along with two of the girls. Julia stayed behind. She took a couple of beers from the cooler and handed one to me. I guess that meant we were going to hang out together. I took a seat in the lawn chair next to her and watched everyone splash around in the water. The ladies had taken residence on two floating plastic loungers and were sunning themselves.

"I'm Dylan's girlfriend," she said.

"Nice to meet you." I stared off at the boys swimming to a large floating platform. They were in deep discussion about something. Likely sports.

"How long have you and Zach been dating?"

"Six months."

"That's a record for Zach. What's your secret?"

"I'm not sure."

She laughed and took a gulp of her beer. "I heard about that whole Bianca thing."

I bristled at the sound of her name. "Oh, yeah? Water under the bridge."

"I'm not going to lie. Bianca and I know each other. We aren't super friends or anything. I don't want you to think I'm picking sides."

I presumed Julia was another rich kid and I decided to be cautious. "I have no hard feelings towards her, and I'm not going to say anything bad about her. As far as I'm concerned, it's over with."

"I heard what she did to you. Aren't you pissed off?"

I glanced over at Julia. I couldn't figure her out. Was she sincere or not? Her tone betrayed nothing. She didn't sound entitled or that she was on a fishing expedition. It was like she was making simple conversation but I couldn't be sure.

"No, I'm not pissed. I don't want to be that person who holds grudges or has to get my revenge. I hope she feels the same way."

"I think she does. I think she got caught up in what you're saying: revenge. And once she had time to look back, she realized how crazy she was. She lost her boyfriend over it, but I think they were on the outs anyway. And Zach's video is certainly a deterrent."

I looked at her now, my gaze intense enough for Julia's grey eyes to grow wide. "Zach's video?"

She shrank back a bit. "Yeah, didn't you know about it?"

What did I do now? Let on that I knew and see what I could get out of her? Of course I assumed it was a video of some kind, that had been clear before Julia confirmed it, but how many people knew about it? I had to tread carefully. "I know it's a video, but I haven't seen it. I thought a lot of people didn't know about it."

"I think a lot of people forgot about it since Zach's the only one with a copy."

"Have you seen it?"

"No, but Dylan was there that night. He told me about it. To be honest, I'm not surprised he hasn't shown you. It's not very flattering."

Either Julia was a masterful manipulator, or a straight shooter. Since I'd only known her a whole five minutes, I didn't know which . . . yet. "How so?"

She squirmed in her lawn chair. "Look, that was the old Zach. I hear he's changed and from what I can see, that's true. You can't judge him on his past."

I nodded. "And I don't. So how is it unflattering to him?"

"He's taking the video."

The words hit me like a baseball bat to the face, but it explained how he had the video. "Oh."

"I can see you didn't know that. I think I should shut up now. I think you should ask him about it."

"Where was the video taken?"

"I'm not sure. His old frat house? I think you should talk to him. I don't feel comfortable and I haven't even seen the video, and Dylan hasn't seen it either. He only heard rumors."

"But you know what's on it more or less."

"Look, only a few people know or remember it. I think for Bianca's sake, that's the way she wants it. Zach, for his own personal reasons, has kept the video. The point is, he should get rid of it."

I narrowed my eyes. "Is that what this is about? You want me to tell Zach to get rid of it?"

Julia's sank further into her chair. "No, I didn't mean it that way. I just–I don't get why he keeps it. I figure he thinks he needs to keep it to protect you or something . . . I don't know."

"What's on it that's so vile?"

She took a few deep breaths. "Emma, you seem like a nice person, and I don't want to start on the wrong foot with you. I probably shouldn't have brought the stupid thing up in the first place. If you want to know more about it, you have to ask your boyfriend. I don't want to say things that are on it and then you find out that they aren't. I don't want trouble."

My initial thought was to go on the attack, to tell her she'd done just that, but I thought better of it. I had another two days with her. "Okay, let's drop it."

I looked over to Zach who was preparing to dive off the floating platform. Now more than ever I wanted to know what he was hiding.

Did you love *The Senator's Son*? Then you should read *This Much is True* by Anna Albo!

Emma has everything she wants. Good friends, family who loves her and the boyfriend of her dreams. She's also finally rid nemesis Bianca Smythe from her life.

But life is full of twists and turns. The first is a phone call from her mother, the one who abandoned her twenty years ago. Suddenly she wants a relationship, to patch things up with the daughter she dumped. Will Emma let her in to her now happy life?

The second is a chance encounter with Bianca in the school library. Their conversation will plant seeds of doubt about the only man Emma's ever loved. Could Bianca be telling the truth? And if she is, will Emma ever be able to forgive Zach?

Read more at https://www.annaalbo.com/anna-albo-newsletter/.

About the Author

Anna Albo was born and raised in Winnipeg, Manitoba. She's a prairie girl who loves the city.

From new adult to chick lit and everything in between, Anna writes contemporary romance and women's fiction that makes people laugh and love.

She received an Advanced Degree in Political Studies from the University of Manitoba and the knowledge she gained there creeps up in her books along with the occasional historical reference. She is a history buff.

When Anna isn't writing her latest book, she's blogging about dogs, or healthy living, or enjoying a cup of tea while attempting to create a culinary masterpiece.

She lives in Winnipeg with her partner Mike, their dog Rocco as well as their cats Joseph and Summer.

To get updates and information on new releases, visit her website at www.annaalbo.com and sign up for my newletter

Made in the USA
Coppell, TX
30 November 2021

66751661R00164